APOCALYPTIC

Other Anthologies Edited by:

Patricia Bray & Joshua Palmatier

After Hours: Tales from the Ur-bar
The Modern Fae's Guide to Surviving Humanity
Temporally Out of Order
Alien Artifacts
Were-
All Hail Our Robot Conquerors!
Second Round: A Return to the Ur-bar

S.C. Butler & Joshua Palmatier

Submerged
Guilds & Glaives

Laura Anne Gilman & Kat Richardson

The Death of All Things

Troy Carrol Bucher & Joshua Palmatier

The Razor's Edge

Patricia Bray & S.C. Butler

Portals

David B. Coe & Joshua Palmatier

Temporally Deactivated
Galactic Stew

Steven H Silver & Joshua Palmatier

Alternate Peace

Crystal Sarakas & Joshua Palmatier

My Battery Is Low and It Is Getting Dark

APOCALYPTIC

Edited by

S.C. Butler
&
Joshua Palmatier

Zombies Need Brains LLC
www.zombiesneedbrains.com

Interior Design (ebook): ZNB Design
Interior Design (print): ZNB Design
Cover Design by ZNB Design
Cover Art "Apocalyptic" by Justin Adams

Kickstarter Edition Printing, June 2020
First Printing, July 2020

Print ISBN-13: 978-1940709338

Ebook ISBN-13: 978-1940709345

Printed in the U.S.A.

COPYRIGHTS

Table of Contents

SIGNATURE PAGE

S.C. Butler, editor:

_____

Joshua Palmatier, editor:

_____

Seanan McGuire:

_____

Aimee Picchi:

_____

Tanya Huff:

_____

Nancy Holzner:

_____

Stephen Blackmoore:

_____

Zakariah Johnson:

_____

Violette Malan:

_____

Eleftherios Keramidas:

_____

James Enge:

_____

Leah Ning:

_____

Thomas Vaughn:

_____

Marjorie King:

_____

Jason Palmatier:

_____

Blake Jessop:

_____

Justin Adams, artist:

_____

Coafield's Catalog of Available Apocalypse Events
Seanan McGuire

Hello and welcome to our humble store!

So you've decided to end the human race and possibly the world. That's no small undertaking and we're happy to assist you in your endeavors. Please select your favorite apocalypse from the following list and allow our team of trained individuals to assist you.

A is for ANTIBIOTIC RESISTANCE.

Largely touted as the magic bullet of medicine, the discovery of antibiotics changed everything. Surgery became commonplace, dental work became infinitely safer, and the rates of death from childbed fever plummeted virtually overnight. Antibiotics created a safer, more stable world in which humanity could thrive. It's fitting, then, that abuse of those same antibiotics led to increasing resistance to their effects, until many became useless, and we faced a future devoid of any functional treatments for bacterial illness or infection.

With this apocalypse, you receive bonus pus, and the possibility of melting eyeballs as your vulnerable population begins to succumb to ailments unseen in over a hundred years. Easy, predictable, and once entirely avoidable, we file this option under "inevitable."

B is for BOTANICAL.

Most people don't think of plants as dangerous, but any botanist can tell you that the slowest of the biological kingdoms is by no means the weakest. Kudzu, poison, invasive species, the possibilities are nigh-endless. What's more, careless management of monocultures means that this apocalypse can easily be slotted into almost any scenario, kicking off a wide variety of secondary calamities as food chains are disrupted and populations are poisoned, subjected to violent allergic attack, or otherwise destroyed.

C is for CHEMICAL.

A single spill and a mutagen in the water supply wipes out a major metropolitan area. If their drains lead to the ocean, this single event can also be used to decimate fisheries, pollute coastlines, and expand the reach of that initial event beyond all logical barriers. Chemical warfare respects no geologic or political boundaries.

Everything is chemicals and this apocalypse can be tailored to take many forms, allowing you to be a true captain of humanity's fate.

D is for DINOSAURS.

Genetic engineering is a great tool of scientific advancement and, like all other tools of scientific advancement, is in the hands of human scientists, which means the question of it being used irresponsibly is not "if" but rather "when." The time between an extinct animal first being successfully cloned and herds of dinosaurs thundering across North America is likely to be shorter than the gestation period of an African elephant. When this inevitable misuse of scientific power occurs, the only question will be whether you're in front of the T. Rex, or behind it.

E is for EARTHQUAKE.

What better way to begin the end of days than by having the very ground reject humanity in all its forms and flavors? With a series of massive seismic events following all known faults—and a few unknown faults—we can bury mankind in the rubble of their own creations. Comes with the environmental benefit of not causing lasting damage to the water table or air (important if you want to retain mammalian life after eliminating the human race).

Associated risks include the compromising of nuclear waste storage facilities.

F is for FIRE.

We consider this option to be reasonably self-explanatory.

G is for GENETIC.

Oh, those wacky scientists. All it takes is one of them deciding to make some genetic "solution" airborne and the entire population wakes up with eight extra eyes, or starts belching spiders, or better! Mad science is a convenient, entertaining way to end the world and we are happy to supply a variety of mechanisms through which to make it happen.

H is for HURRICANE.

It's difficult to use hurricanes to destroy all mankind, given their difficulty forming under many conditions, but we believe in you. If we didn't, you wouldn't be here.

I is for ICE.

Once everything burns, it's time for everything to freeze. Superstorms and changing weather conditions could easily kick off another ice age, changing the face of the planet forever and making your dreams of an eternal snow day come true! Added benefit: you'll be able to keep your drinks cold even without a refrigerator.

J is for JET STREAM FAILURE.

There's no reason the jet stream *can't* abruptly fail, disrupting atmospheric patterns worldwide and making modern transportation impossible. This is difficult, but far from impossible, to engineer for the world-destroyer with a flexible budget.

K is for KRILL.

It may seem counterintuitive, but taking out the base of the oceanic food chain would quickly result in the death of most sea life, damaging the ability of the seas to continue scrubbing carbon from the atmosphere and accelerating the speed of climate change. This one isn't flashy and will require

some patience on the part of the would-be evil overlord or apocalyptic engineer.

L is for LOCUSTS.

A bit biblical, yes, but with sufficient numbers, they could disrupt the food chain to a high enough degree to kill people in prodigious numbers. Issue: may not be able to kill the people living in sufficiently cold climates.

M is for METEOR.

With the sky increasingly compromised by careless satellite placement and no viable global defense net, it's only a matter of time before a sufficiently large rock punches its way through the atmosphere and shatters the Earth's crust. A comet was good enough for the dinosaurs; it'll be good enough for us, too.

N is for NUCLEAR WAR.

Quick, easy, awful, over.

O is for OCCULT.

Would you like demons to crawl out of the electric sockets before ripping off the faces of your enemies? How about ghosts everywhere? No, we mean *everywhere*. Even there. Hell can walk the earth anew with this apocalyptic ending.

P is for PANDEMIC.

The nature of the disease doesn't matter, only that it spreads quickly and completely, leaving bodies in its wake. Can easily incorporate a variety of other apocalypse options, especially those which begin with the misuse of science.

This is the Swiss Army Knife of world-enders—efficient, impersonal, and everywhere.

Q is for QUANTUM.

Look, some letters are easier than others. And if you want an apocalypse that makes no sense under any other system of measure, just wave your hands and say "it's *quantum*" before your unspeakable slime monsters start biting heads off. It'll work.

Trust us.

R is for ROBOTS.

More misapplied science, yes, but this time it's misapplied engineering, which is a fun change. Also fun: lasers and massive property damage. You'll enjoy it! The rest of the population will not.

S is for SLIME.

The Blob is available to the aspiring destroyer of mankind, for a very reasonable down payment. All organic life will be consumed. All of it. Even the dogs. Know that before you let it out.

T is for TIME.

Destroy the fourth dimension and the first three will follow in…well, in no time at all.

U is for UNKNOWN.

Want something specific not offered by our list? Propose your own apocalypse and we'll help you with individualized pricing plans, based on the complexity of what you're hoping to achieve, the investment required on our part, and the amount of the planet estimated to still be useable after the apocalypse has run its course. End the world *your* way. Off-the-rack isn't for everyone and we're happy to help you with a bespoke plan that suits both your needs *and* your desires.

V is for VENGEANCE.

Let's be honest, we assume this is why you're here. But if you add the "vengeance" package to your apocalypse of choice, you'll have the opportunity to gloat after your plans have been put into motion and at a point where no recovery is possible! Kill them all *and* get your evil laugh on.

W is for WATER.

The classics are classic for a reason. Ending the world in water has a certain beautiful poetry to it. Very damp, waterlogged poetry.

X is for XENOLOGICAL.

Let's all face it: if the aliens put in the effort to come this far, they're not doing it because they want to be friends. Any visitors from space will be colonists at best, conquerors at worst (assuming there's any difference between the two). The end of humanity as we know it will be swift and conclusive, and as a bonus, you may get to see space when the invaders take you onto their ships.

Y is for YERSINIA PESTIS.

The bubonic plague has had its turn to kill people, and some would argue that this apocalypse is identical to antibiotic resistance, but in this case, we're not asking for every possible infection, just the ones which arise from a horrifying new strain of Y. pestis. Some things become old standbys because they're very good at their jobs and you can put your faith in the bacterial infection which wiped out half of Europe's population from 1347 onward. Global panic is surely to accompany this option, which may or may not be the desired outcome.

Z is for ZOMBIES.

Difficult. Messy. Scientifically implausible. But oh, so much fun, which makes this one of our favorite offerings. When the dead rise, we all get down.

Thank you for considering us for your apocalypse needs. We look forward to helping you destroy all the many and varied works of man.

Solo Cooking
for the Recently Revived

Aimee Picchi

I hide my right hand behind my back when Jamie steps into the rehab center's kitchen. Like all the rest of the reintegration counselors, he's a Survivor. And Survivors always stare at our scars.

"Let's start with our motto," Jamie says.

The class intones: "*Food is life.*"

My friend Myra hitches her thumbs on her belt, cinched to the smallest hole, and rolls her eyes.

"And?" Jamie prods.

"*To cook is human,*" we finish.

Every time I say it I imagine the motto will fix me, erase my scars and everything else that happened in the last year. Get me one step closer to Carter. I once confided my belief to Myra and she laughed. *That motto's not for our benefit, sweetie,* she had said. *It's so they can believe we're still just like them.*

Jamie gestures for me to join him at the front of the classroom, the home-ec lab inside a former middle school. About twenty of us are lined up at ovens and sinks and Formica countertops where students scratched blocky initials inside of hearts. I don't want to think about what probably happened to the kids.

"Edda's going to teach you a cake recipe."

I clear my throat. "It's called crazy cake because it doesn't include eggs or butter. I'm told there might not be much of either ingredient when we get back home."

Not that I ever baked this cake when I was a pastry chef—it's not sophisticated enough to sell at a bakery—but Jamie had said it didn't matter because the point is to help each other relearn basic life skills.

When I pass a photocopied recipe to Myra, she whispers, "What's crazy is to think this is going to make a difference. Look at us, Edda."

The kitchen is filled with a motley group of twisted limbs, faces calling out for reconstruction, missing feet and half-scalped heads. Myra's scar runs from her temple to her jaw. Even though our wounds are all different, we're all emaciated. Nothing more than bones covered with scar tissue.

"Broken things can be fixed," I say.

Myra dumps a cup of sugar into a bowl. "If you can actually enjoy eating this cake, I'll believe you."

We spend the next hour mixing and pouring, my unbalanced hands fumbling with the spatula as I scrape the batter from the bowl.

After we put the cakes in the oven, Jamie lectures about staying hydrated and well-nourished. As he wipes sweat from his forehead, it occurs to me he might be nervous, standing up here in front of two dozen of the Revived. He's avoided looking at Myra, who has a sly smile as she licks her lips every so often with the tip of her pink tongue.

Then the timers ding and the tension is broken as we gather near our ovens. "Smells great," Jamie calls from across the kitchen.

I avoid the flick of Myra's eyes. We can't smell anything.

We stab our forks into warm slices of cake.

Heat coats the inside of my mouth and a burst of hope expands inside me that maybe I'll taste something this time. My hope quickly fades as the cake cools on my tongue, leaving my mouth filled with a substance with the taste and texture of clay.

The cure flushed out the disease, but it also took away our appetites.

Around the kitchen, the other Revived struggle with the cake. After a half-hearted attempt to eat a few bites, Myra flips her plate into the garbage. She pivots to the fridge, cracking open the door and retrieving a can of En-Liven. She grins and places a finger up to her lips. We're not supposed to drink the energy drink unless it's an emergency, even though it's the only sustenance we can stomach. It has no taste, but the drink's mix of caffeine, sugar, and carnitine shoots a thrill through our bodies. She slams it down, then tosses the can in the trash before Jamie takes notice.

I shove another forkful of cake into my mouth and fight an impulse to toss my plate on top of Myra's. I'm annoyed that she was right, but unwilling to give up just yet.

Jamie strolls over with his tablet, taking notes.

"You've come a long way in three months." Then he says the words I've been hoping to hear since I woke up in the facility: "You're both ready to be reintegrated into society. What are you going to do after you're discharged?"

"I'm going to start fresh. Get a new job back in New York. Maybe in clean-up. You know, do my part in reconstructing the country," Myra says smoothly. But it's all a lie: she's told me she'll join the Revival, the traveling group of the Revived who subsist on En-Liven and shun Survivors.

Jamie nods, a relieved smile stretching across his damp face. "And you, Edda?"

"I'm going back home to Carter." Giddiness travels down my arms and to the ends of my fingers at the thought of going home. If they could, my fingertips would shoot out confetti and sparklers, like a parade on the Fourth of July. "We'd been planning our wedding. I put a deposit on a wedding dress and we'd picked a venue."

I push back the thought that the dress would be too large for me now, the hotel probably in ruins.

Jamie seems genuinely pleased as I rattle on. I've provided the correct answer; the government wants us to return to our former lives, even though the counselors have told us that the only jobs open to us will be in clean-up. Not many businesses from before the pandemic are still operating.

After he's out of earshot, Myra snorts. "They'll never see us as really human."

I press my lips together, then exhale quickly. "You might as well say, 'No use trying.'"

Myra turns away, hurt. The counselors have taught us to model our behavior on what we were like before the illness, and because I remember myself as a warm and kind person, I drape my right arm around Myra's shoulders in a shoulder-hug. She returns the embrace, but won't meet my eyes. It makes me want to throw the cake against the wall and admit that I often doubt whether I'm the same person. But I'm clinging to whatever hope I can find.

My arms tighten around her briefly. Then I toss the cake into the garbage.

* * *

A line has formed by the time I reach the only working phone in the center. Mobile phones are allowed, but very few of us have them. Lost in the weeks and months when we were sick, tossed under a bush or cracked underfoot as we ran in herds.

The others waiting to use the phone are adrift in their own thoughts. Me, I'm imagining Carter when I tell him the news. I can picture his slow smile, the one he wore when he proposed. The way his eyes squeeze at the outer corners when he's happy.

When I get to the front of the line, I dial Carter's mobile number and wait for him to pick up.

Carter doesn't pick up.

I hang up and keep my hand on the receiver. Maybe he needs a minute to reach the phone.

"Only two tries, Edda," Jamie warns. "Then it's Tim's turn."

"You ain't the only one getting out of here." Tim's a big man with most of his right calf missing. During the past few months, I've heard all about his husband and their small fishing boat in Portland, Maine. "Don't hog the line."

I punch each digit with deliberation. I imagine Carter running through our apartment, trying to find his mobile after missing my first try.

The phone rings.

Or maybe he's working late. Maybe he's on his bicycle and his phone is in his messenger bag and he can't reach it—

"Um, hello?"

"Carter!" My voice sounds too high. "I've got some good news."

A moment of silence. "Oh?"

"I'm getting discharged on Monday. I'll take a bus to Burlington and should be back at the apartment by dinner at the latest."

I hear the creak of his favorite chair. "Edda, whoa. What do you mean, discharged?"

I tell him about how we're learning how to stay hydrated and take care of ourselves. My right hand is slick with sweat and my thumb and two fingers are clutching the phone receiver so tightly their joints ache.

Softly, he interrupts me. "Are you sure you're ready? I thought the rehab process would take longer. I wouldn't want you to rush it."

"My counselor says I'm ready to leave."

Carter goes silent again. I can hear his breathing. I could listen to it all day. "It's a lot to take in, Edda."

"We've got a lot to do. Planning the wedding and all that."

Jamie is tapping his watch, signaling that I have to hang up.

"See you on Monday, okay?"

His voice is so faint that I almost can't hear it. "Okay."

I hang up and stare at the wall for a minute. It's hard for me to know where to begin, how to think about what he was saying. Or wasn't saying. I know it's going to be hard—I have no doubts about that—but I'm ready to get back to a normal life.

Tim swings forward on his crutches. He leans against the wall and gives me a quizzical look. "Everything good, hon?"

I hide my crippled hand behind my back and smile. "Everything's great, Tim. The phone's all yours."

* * *

On discharge day, Myra tosses a duffel bag onto her cot and starts throwing in socks, underwear, her two clean pairs of pants.

"Edda, promise me you'll come to the Revival if things don't work out for you."

"Plenty of the Revived go back home," I tell her. "Remember that documentary they showed us?"

Myra smooths her bedcover and screws up her face. "Mmm-hmmm," she said. "Propaganda."

"Cynic."

"They want us to believe we can integrate. If we can't, then the country's in deep shit. They need us to come back and start driving trucks and working road crews and cleaning up all the garbage that's left over."

"I have to try." I give her a quick hug and she stalks off in search of the bus heading to Woodstock, New York, where the Revival is camped out for the summer.

The other passengers on my bus are quiet, staring out the window. I try to strike up a conversation with my seatmate, but she pulls on headphones and closes her eyes.

Even though I've seen videos about the damage, I'm not prepared. Highway signs are riddled with bullets and buildings stand burned and desolate. Garbage, everywhere. Pieces of paper flying through the air; crumpled balls of clothing tossed in ditches.

I slump in my seat, pull my jacket around my ribs and avoid looking out the window for the rest of the trip.

By the time the bus reaches Burlington the sun is setting behind the Adirondacks, but there's still enough light to make out the shattered glass walls of the bus depot. The LED display lights are on the fritz, blinking random numbers and towns.

"Good luck," the bus driver says. The sincerity in his slurred voice causes me to turn around and take a closer look. Underneath his cap, his face is haunted by a missing eye and half a jaw. *One of us.* I give a brief nod and he closes the door and pulls out of the station.

Apocalyptic

The city looks like a scab: healing and bleeding, still itching and hurting. The streets are lined with broken-windowed homes and litter-covered lawns.

One of the few that has been cleaned up is the blue-turreted Victorian on the corner of my block. An older woman sits on a tattered lawn chair plunked in the center of its tidy front yard. Her white hair frizzles from her Red Sox baseball cap and her tie-died t-shirt features a blue heart bleeding into rings of green and yellow. Her legs are spread apart, feet akimbo, and she's looking up and down the street, taking note of everything in her field of vision.

Her eyes narrow as I pass by. I feel her studying my emaciated frame and missing fingers.

"We shoulda killed you all," she mutters.

I hurry to my apartment house, two doors down. My key slips from my shaking hands.

On my doorstep, the memory of the first days of the epidemic come flooding back. How Carter and I huddled in the apartment, arms wrapped around each other, as sirens screamed through our neighborhood. The silence that came afterwards was even worse.

But my memory is a blank from the day I grew feverish until I woke up in the facility.

My hands are shaking. I lean my head against the door and breathe deeply. *This is where you are now. Not lost. Not sick.* The crows call from the treetops. The smooth wood of the front door is reassuring, solid, an entrance that is still open to me. After a few seconds, my hands are steady enough to unlock the door.

I slip inside the apartment, calling Carter's name.

No answer.

The apartment hasn't changed. The Ikea bookshelves we bought in Montreal, the two paintings of red barns from the flea market. The hodgepodge brings back the excitement of decorating the apartment, our first together, and the plans we'd had for saving for a house after the wedding.

But the fridge shelves are almost empty, something that never happened before I got sick. All Carter's managed to stock is a head of lettuce, some tofu, hot sauce, a few peppers, and some beer.

I imagine Carter's surprise when he returns to the apartment, finding me there like nothing has changed. Dinner ready for him.

While I'm whisking the salad dressing and the stir-fry is steaming in the wok, a memory tugs at me: how Carter would avoid the apartment every time we got a visit from his brother, who struggled with addiction. Carter had harbored a grudge against him for what he put their parents through, but instead of just telling his brother how he felt when he visited, he'd vanish, making excuses about having to work or helping a friend.

The tug gives a yank and it's like a million tons of rock are falling on my chest.

I can't breathe. My legs feel as if they've lost muscle and bone.

Carter's not here because he doesn't want to be here.

How could I be so blind? I think back to our last conversation, how desperate I was not to hear his hesitation.

I find his note on the bedside table.

"Dear Edda," it says. "I'm sorry. I can't do this. I understand the Revived don't remember what happened before they were cured. I don't blame you, or anyone else. But the pandemic—it changed me. There were things I had to do, Edda. I printed out some of my journal entries from that time, to help you understand. Just believe me that I'll never stop feeling guilty."

I flip through the loose pages, my eyes glazing over the paragraphs. I pick out individual phrases and words: *Edda's sick, don't know what to do, locked her in the bathroom, oh god, we fought, knife, I sliced her hands, pushed her out the window. Can't believe she'd survive that fall, but she's gone.*

I glance at my missing fingers.

When the tofu stir-fry is ready, I force myself to eat. My mouth feels coated in sludge and my mind is running a loop of an old saying: "Tell me what you eat, and I'll tell you what you are."

I lift the fork to my mouth again and again, as if it will prove to myself that I'm no different than I was before.

A sudden rage sweeps over me, a red surge propelled by an arcane, unknowable force, and for a moment I'm able to push it away. I lean my head against the wall, feel its smooth coolness on my skin. Keep focused in the moment, as the reintegration counselors told us.

It works for a second.

Then the anger returns, even hotter.

I slam my fist into the wall.

Tears trickle down my cheeks and slip into my mouth. They're tasteless and bland, not at all like how I remember when I was a kid and big, fat tears rolled into my mouth with briny sadness. I'm not the person I was before. Home isn't the same, if I even have a home. I punch the wall again and again.

Life will never be normal again for any of us Revived.

* * *

On the bus to Woodstock, I keep my headphones on and stare at the seat in front of me.

My hand is throbbing and wrapped in gauze. No one on the bus is interested in talking and that suits me just fine.

The pulse of drums heralds the bus's approach into Woodstock. The Revived gather along the road to welcome us, pounding on animal-skinned bongos and tablas with triumphant rhythms.

The bus pulls up to a small park in the center of town, where the Revived mill about the green. A few wear tattered brown robes, their bony hands stretching from their cuffs like a scarecrow's twigs. En-Liven is everywhere: cans clutched in emaciated hands, empties thrown under bushes, in coolers resting under the trees.

Myra waves. Her eyes darken as she catches sight of my bandage.

"Reunion didn't go the way you planned, huh?" She gives me a quick hug.

I don't want to talk about Carter, so I shrug. "Looks like I found the Island of Misfit Toys." My breathing relaxes, as if a steel band around my chest has been released. For once, I feel at ease. I don't need to hide my missing fingers or skeletal frame.

The drums fade as we walk down a shady street. The homes are in better shape here, but everyone is as thin or thinner than me.

"Do any Survivors still live here?" I ask.

"If they do, they keep scarce."

She leads me to a big white event tent. It's the kind I had envisioned for our wedding. Glossy white on the top with peaks and valleys created by tent poles. Fluttering banners, fairy lights twinkling from the eaves.

"They won't let you have any En-Liven until you've gone through orientation with Father Harold." Myra shrugs. "It's not so bad. Find me when you're done and we'll crack open some cold ones to celebrate."

Worn oriental rugs line the tent's interior and a few people I recognize from the bus are already sitting around in a semi-circle in folding chairs. An older man is talking in a voice that, despite its rough edges, is muted—the tip of his nose has been shorn off and he's missing his ears.

They make space for me in the circle and I squeeze in. Harold is going through the basics of camp life: where to find En-Liven, the quiet hours, and what to do in case of a dispute with a neighbor.

"We operate on trust," Harold says. "Trust is sacred for the Revived. How many of you weren't trusted when you went home?"

A woman with short spiky dark hair and a missing arm leans forward. "They put me in the fucking garage. My own husband and kids. They said they needed to observe me before they'd let me out. Like I was some rabid dog."

"Mine's a doozy," says a man with a Florida State t-shirt. His arms are crisscrossed with scars. "I got home and found my girlfriend had changed the locks. Oh, and she was also dating my best friend. He claimed he had kept her safe when I was sick. Like it was my fault. They wouldn't even let me in the apartment to get my stuff."

Everyone's suddenly clamoring, talking over each other to tell their own stories, but I keep my mouth shut. It seems like a betrayal of Carter to complain about him, even though I'm tempted to chime in with my own grievances. I wrap my maimed hand in my sweater.

A hush comes over the circle as Harold speaks. He taps his knees with his index fingers with each word. "Each. Of. Us. Has. The. Same. Story." He jerks his head toward the outside of the tent. "No matter what color or religion, age or ability, we're not trusted out there."

I raise my hand. "At the reintegration center, they said to give it time. 'Wounds can't heal overnight,' they said."

"Some never heal." Harold gestures to his nose.

I nod and wrap my arms around my ribs.

He continues. "We were victimized, too. Which is why trust is so important at the Revival. Trust means relying on one another, always being there for one another, in health and sickness."

The Florida State guy is leaning forward, his eyes gleaming with hope at Harold's vision of a ready-made family, no conflicts or problems.

"Trust takes time to build." I venture. It seems like an even bigger jump of faith to trust a community of strangers.

Harold's veneer of benevolence doesn't crack. "It's facing up to the reality of a world that thinks we're beyond repair."

The woman with short hair is glaring at me, and the Florida State guy is staring at me with pitying look. Harold signals to assistants who have been waiting at the edges of the tent. They walk toward the circle, handing each of us a clipboard with a form.

The heading says "TRUST CONTRACT." Underneath, it outlines the rules of the camp: no contact with Survivors, even family and friends; half of any income we earn will go to the Revival, which will pay our taxes and provide us with unlimited En-Liven.

"Now, I don't expect you to sign this right now. Take it back to your tent and think it over. You'll have one week to decide," he says. But most of the people in the circle are already signing their names at the bottom, trying to prove they're happy campers. His eyes flick toward me. "Sometimes, it's hard for people to see the big picture."

That night, when Myra and I are inside her tiny two-person tent, I ask her about the contract.

She zips up her sleeping bag. "You signed it, right? It's kind of lame not to sign as soon as Father Harold gives it to you."

"Guess I'm a loser, then."

"Oh, Edda."

"Don't tell me you buy his garbage about creating a new family. It's Cult 101."

Myra's silent for a moment. She closes her eyes and the lines from her forehead are erased. "Weren't you the one who told me we have to believe in something?"

Soon her breathing slows. I listen to the hoots from a party somewhere in the encampment. A new family—maybe this is the only way to make sense of what happened.

The next few days pass in a swirl of En-Liven and camp work. I help Myra dig latrines on the camp's outskirts—the one time I can remember feeling thankful we have no sense of smell—and walk around Woodstock, picking up garbage. At night we slug En-Liven and tell stories about the rehab centers. I learn Myra and I were lucky—some of the centers were little more than holding pens.

On my seventh day at the camp, Myra and I join a crew driving to Poughkeepsie to buy a new shipment of En-Liven. In the parking lot, Father Harold holds the keys to the vehicles, three pick-up trucks and two minivans, and Myra and I call dibs on one of the suburban monsters, a tan Odyssey.

As I climb into the passenger seat, Father Harold sidles up to me.

"If you don't sign the contract today, you'll have to leave in the morning."

"Not contacting Survivors? Ever?"

His eyes harden. "Most of them want us dead. We're better off on our own."

Myra pulls away and we sit in silence until we pull up at the beverage warehouse.

Two beefy men and a woman in Carhartt pants stand quietly as we pull inside. Survivors. Their flesh is luxurious and sumptuous, their bodies the embodiment of three meals a day—veg, fruit, and meat. The Revived are like another race, thin flesh riding on our skeletons.

As soon as we pop the back hatch, the men start loading cases of En-Liven. They work with an economy of motion, moving the cases quickly and efficiently with muscular strength.

"Which one of you can come and sign off on the paperwork?" The woman waves a clipboard in the air. Myra shoves me forward and I follow the woman into her office.

Her computer monitor cycles through family photos. A man at a dock, an older couple on a boat. Everyone smiling and squinting into the sun.

As I sign the paperwork, she stares at the screen. "You're lucky, you know."

"How do you figure that?" I flip through the pages, looking for the places where a signature is needed.

"None of you remember what happened." Her hands tremble as I hand the clipboard back to her.

The photos are flipping to Christmas scenes: kids under the tree, a dog in the snow. I swallow.

"I'm sorry."

As I leave the office, she turns back to her computer, her hands motionless on her computer keyboard.

Throughout the day, the hardness I've felt toward Carter softens. I'm not sure the lady in the warehouse was right to call me lucky, but the Survivors certainly aren't either.

The next morning, before Myra wakes, I leave a note for her on the contract. *"If you decide to leave the Revival, you'll always have a home with me."* I jot down my home phone number, pack my bag, and head for the bus station.

* * *

The unfriendly neighbor is sitting outside her Victorian house, pulling on a cigarette. She's wearing a tie-dyed shirt with red stars on a field of orange waves.

"You lot didn't deserve to get cured," she mutters.

"If only I had gotten my hands on you before I was Revived—" I lick my lips.

Her mouth opens in surprise, then shuts again. She narrows her eyes. The rumble starts in her chest and expands into her belly, until she's leaning back in the chair, head tilted and stomach trembling in delight.

"Now you're fucking with me," she says, wiping her eyes. "I can respect that."

I hoist my backpack and keep walking.

"Hey, what's your name?" she calls after me.

"Edda," I say.

"I'm Barb. You're the first to come back to the block."

I turn around. She points her cigarette at my hand. "Got banged up in the fight, eh? Oh, I've seen worse. Hell, back when the virus was raging, I done worse to you lot."

A flush creeps over my skin, but she's just stating a fact. Not threatening me. "It must have been terrible."

She nods, taking a long drag on her cigarette. "Now, my Harold, that's who I'm waiting for. I sit out here from dawn to dusk, in case he comes back. He got out of a facility three months ago. You didn't happen to meet him, did you? Little man, with hair like a white Brillo pad, missing a nose and ears."

I open my mouth, but hesitate.

"Yeah? You seen him? He called me when he was discharged and said he was heading for the Revival. Haven't heard from him since. Makes me wish I had done him in when I had the chance." There's a hint of affection in her voice.

I shift my feet. "I wouldn't count on him coming back."

She exhales a long plume of smoke. "Asshole before the virus. Asshole after."

"My fiancé left when he heard I was getting out of the facility. He said he couldn't face me."

"Coming back takes balls." Barb opens up the cooler at her feet and hands me an En-Liven. "Been keeping these for Harold, but why waste them on him?"

I wrap my wounded hand around the can, two fingers and thumb, an uncertain grip. I pop the tab and take a long drink. It tastes like nothing. It tastes like everything.

When I'm done, I reach for another.

To Dust We Shall Return

Tanya Huff

"Where's Dr. Alison?" Nostril ridges clamped shut, Dirnir leaned out around Bogdan's bulk and squinted toward the barely visible sled.

"She wouldn't leave her lab." Bogdan shrugged, large enough the movement made visible ripples in the blowing dust. "I had a choice: pick her up and carry her, or assume that as an adult she could make her own decisions." He brushed his gloved hand over his filter, clearing away the layer of dirt. "Who knows, maybe she *can* find a way to stop the storms."

The winds dropped and, just for an instant, Dirnir thought she could see a patch of blue. The high, dry plateau where the three colonies had been dropped had been chosen because of the ore but it hadn't been a bad place to live. Not a great place perhaps, too few sizable trees for that, but not a bad place.

And then, 11.2 tendays in, the first storm had hit. It had lasted four days. Wind lifting dirt and pushing it into noses and machinery both.

Then the second hit.

Then the third.

The fourth storm had lasted two tendays. By the time it ended, they were nearly out of full-face filters—and they were mining colonies, they'd arrived with enough filters to keep the ore coming regardless of conditions underground. The constant abrasion had stripped gardens down to bare stalks. The local wildlife had disappeared.

When the fifth storm rolled in, Voice of the Company had finally admitted this was more than they could handle on their own and had sent a message back to headquarters.

Sixth.

Seventh.

The storms got longer and the time between them shorter.

Eighth.

"Dirnir?"

She started and shook her head, adjusting her grip on the cable they'd strung between the mine and the anchor so she could turn around. "Let's get inside."

"Any word from…"

"No."

* * *

"I can see you're broken up about the delay, Sarge." Private First Class Miri Opizzi grinned up at Torin. "I bet you've been looking forward to those eight weeks in Ventris, all spiffy in your Class Cs, minding your manners and learning how to do a job you're already doing."

Torin glanced down. The shorter woman wore a black t-shirt, ancient combat trousers, and a pair of boots with a gouge across the right toe—RECON default. Minus the age and the gouge, Torin wore the same. Sergeant or not, Class Cs could wait for Ventris.

"I mean, it must suck, knowing you're having to hang about with us poor grunts in RECON for one more…" Miri winked and fell silent as the briefing room door slid open.

Torin acknowledged Lieutenant Turrik, nodded at the four Marines already seated, pointed Opizzi toward a chair, and headed for her own. Lance Corporal Domini di'Naital and Corporal Bannon Lembede had, with Opizzi, been part of what she'd thought would be her final RECON outing. She should have remembered that plans rarely survived the reality of the Corps. PFC Phoela di'Kano and Wirekik were there to make up for the two lost off the previous team. Morrae had run out her contract and Servik… She touched her side where the cylinder of Servik's remains had rested, tucked into a pocket of her vest.

Servik had found a use for the demo charges he'd brought along.

As this particular team held no specialists, she had to assume the powers-that-be had no idea of what they'd be heading into. SOP for RECON at least eighty percent of the time.

She'd barely settled into her seat when the hatch opened again.

"Asses down," Captain di'Hirose snapped and continued as they sat. "We've got a three-anchor mining colony backed by the SSG consortium that's dropped out of contact. Didn't respond when the SSG checked in and then didn't respond when the Department of Colonial Affairs followed up. There's a signal from their satellite, but nothing from the ground."

"If the ground signal needed boosting, they could—"

"They didn't." The captain cut Bannon off, bronze hair flipping out to follow the arc of her hand. "Lieutenant."

Lieutenant Turrik touched the edge of the table. "Welcome to Hurasu."

"Is that the actual color?" Torin asked. The atmosphere of the planet rotating above the tabletop swirled with brown. Dark brown, light brown, pinkish in places—not colors the DCA looked for when placing colonies.

"It is now," the lieutenant replied, half-closed nostril ridges mirroring the annoyance in his voice. "It was never a green and pleasant place, but the air was a breathable compromise and the temperature cool enough outside the equatorial zone for Taykan without the rest of us freezing our asses off. Forests exist only at the edge of the polar circle, but temperate and equatorial zones have clumps of three to ten huge trees every three to five hundred hectares. Not a lot of global biodiversity so the DCA assumed a fairly recent extinction event."

As the planet rotated, Torin counted six—no seven—electrical storms large enough to have been seen from orbit. Looked more like an ongoing extinction event.

"Taykan and Krai make up thirty-eight percent of the colonial population. Humans, sixty-two."

"We're like cockroaches," Opizzi muttered gleefully.

No one argued.

"There's also seven statistically insignificant Dornagain at the kiddie table." Captain di'Hirose flipped the population breakdown into the air. "Voice of the Company—just what her name suggests—and two at each anchor on administrative duties. They weren't intending to stay once things got established."

No surprise. The Elder Races were settled, unwilling to risk the opening of new planets. The Younger Races—Humans, Taykan, and Krai—fought the war the Elders were too socially evolved to participate in and pushed at the edges of the Confederation.

"Families?"

"Human and Krai."

The Taykan would never send Qui to a new colony. They protected their breeding population and their children to the extent that even Taykan colony worlds had the rough edges blunted by the di'Taykan before family groups moved in.

Lieutenant Turrik spun the globe and focused in on a section of the northern hemisphere. "Anchor here, here, and here, two-hundred and fifty kilometers apart, shipping port to be built within the triangle, approximately eight hundred people per anchor, fifty/fifty mining professionals and support. Planet has an obscene amount of gold and the Confederation has an obscene need for conductive material."

"So it's a strip and skip?" Wirekik asked.

"An obscene amount of gold," Turrik repeated. "Initial reports said there's places you can sweep it up with a broom and a dustpan. Word is, they had another triangle nearly ready to go." He nodded at the storms. "Not so much now, I expect."

Torin frowned at the image and the fleck of light that represented the satellite. "Station?"

"Not yet."

"Space is big, Sergeant," Captain di'Hirose interjected before Torin could respond. "And there's a war on. The SSG will move a station into place as soon as there's enough product ready to make it worth the cost. And yes, a station would've helped figure out what's going on." She braced both hands on the table and leaned in, bronze eyes darkening as more light receptors opened. "The point is, this kind of an atmospheric change isn't natural. Not full planetary coverage, not in under two years."

"Enemy action," Torin stated flatly.

The captain nodded. "That's what the brass thinks. They pulled time on the susumi satellite to scan the system and found no other jump points, nothing to indicate ships in or ships out. Not that it matters, this didn't happen on its own and everyone's aware that a DCA satellite isn't military grade. If the Others have a planet killer..."

"Armageddon armament," Wirekik offered.

"Ecosystem explosive," Phoela countered.

Miri snorted, spread her arms, and declared, "Apocalypse bomb!"

Domini opened his mouth, visibly thought better of speaking, and closed it. The others froze in place as one by one they became aware of Torin's expression. After a long moment, she turned her attention back to the captain. "Is there a chance the Others were in-system when the SSG arrived? Odds are high they've got the same need for conductive materiel we do."

"It's possible," the captain allowed. "But when they arrived isn't the issue."

Bannon shook his head. "If they've been there for a while, they'll have dug in."

"It isn't an issue to the DCA," the captain amended. "They've got colonists who could be under attack, but, as a governing body, can't go in to check if there's a chance of enemy action in the area."

"*Could* be under attack, Cap?" Domini frowned, coral hair flicking back and forth. "*Chance* of enemy action?"

"If they were sure, they'd send the infantry."

"No one's happy about a potential apocalypse bomb," the lieutenant added.

Opizzi thrust a triumphant fist toward Phoela, who sighed and bumped it.

Captain di'Hirose slapped the table and the planet disappeared. "Since we don't know what the hell is going on, you lot are going in to secure the colonists."

"Green or black, Captain?" If they ran into the Others did they gather information, or kick ass?

"At your discretion, Sergeant Kerr."

* * *

"What if the surviors want to leave?" Miri waved her hand and nearly slammed it into the bulkhead. RECON travelled in a minimal Marine packet and the CFS Palmatier looked barely large enough to support her Susumi drive. "We sure as shit don't have room for them."

"Why wouldn't they want to leave?" Bannon asked, tossing Domini a pouch of coffee. "The entire planet's fukked."

"Twenty-nine distinct dust storms at last count." Wirekik set his pouch of *sah* on the table with his left foot and used his right to grab a bag of *korm* chips. "Though since they already volunteered to live on dirt…"

"On it, not in it," Phoela corrected.

"We pass the numbers on to the Navy." Torin looked up from the DCA information and glared Domini's boots off the table. "Navy tells the DCA and the DCA sends transport. Since they won't send transport until they know they aren't heading into a war zone, let's hope we find out what the Others are up to ASAP."

Domini's hair lifted. "I bet they have new cloaking tech!"

"Because that's just what we need," Bannon muttered.

"Hey, Sarge!" Miri swiveled to face her. "Why would the brass think the Others are stupid enough to stay on a planet after they trashed it?"

Torin shrugged. "Obscene amounts of conductive material."

"Why would the Others mess up the atmosphere then? If they can get in and out without being seen, they can do a strip and skip in another hemisphere. Or if they wanted to be shits, they could take out the colonies and use their gear to ghost the DCA. Or they could just monitor incoming traffic and take off before the DCA returns. Or monitor incoming traffic and call in reinforcements to take out the DCA. Which'd make it pretty definitively a war zone."

"Half of what the Others do makes no sense." Wirekik's nostril ridges closed at the sudden attention. "I mean, it probably makes sense to them but it's *serly chrika* to the rest of us."

Miri's brows rose. "I bet they were testing it and it got away from them."

"It?"

"The apocalypse bomb." She rolled her eyes. "They needed a test site with people right? They're not just testing the effectiveness of their new weapon but how adaptable we are once it's been set off. Hurasu is perfect. Twenty-four hundred people isn't enough to put them in danger of discovery before dustapolusa! They may not have even intended a full dustapolusa, but if the colonists leave because the Others have made the place unliveable, the Others can take advantage of the time it'll take the SSG to send in station-controlled drones and they can strip the place clean with giant mining robots!"

Torin held out a hand, stopping Opizzi on the way to the coffee pot. "How much caffeine have you had today?"

* * *

"With signals bouncing off the suspended gold dust, I can't scan for life signs any better down here than the Palmatier could in orbit. And speaking of the Palmatier..." Lieutenant Yerr paused to stroke the landing struts into the green with her foot. "...I can't reach the ship either. You need to talk to the ship, I'll have to go back up. Oh, and Sergeant, remember how there was only supposed to be one satellite on the roundabout? I'm 92.3 percent sure I pinged a second."

Torin paused, about to leave the cabin. "One of theirs?"

"Wouldn't that be nice. Just arrived and found the enemy already." She shook her head. "No, one of ours."

* * *

The air on Hurasu was breathable for certain semi-solid definitions of breathable. Torin considered stuffing the entire team into HE suits and compromised with gloves, hoods, and full face filters.

"I hate these things, Sarge." Domini scowled at the barely visible filter draped over his hand.

"We all hate them, di'Naital." Torin had lost an eyebrow removing one on Canifton. "Put it on anyway."

"Sarge..."

"Now."

Lieutenant Yerr had set the VTA down just to the east of the first settlement, close enough it almost felt like cheating. As they finished securing their gear, Torin pulled up the exterior view.

"Holy fuk," Opizzi breathed.

"*Ser le grine,*" Wirekik agreed.

The thing about dust storms, Torin realized, was that the *storms* emphasized the dust in the air and made it easy to forget about how much got left behind.

A break in the wind, showed a drift of gritty powder half way up the side of the two story anchor, gold specks flashing as the lights from the VTA swept over it. Most of the surrounding single-story houses had been buried and a few of the buildings had been crushed under the weight. The crushed buildings were all prefabs, snapped together immediately after the anchor had touched down. Given the number of houses built of the native stone, Torin hoped the prefabs had been empty when they collapsed.

"All dirtside communications are dead, Sergeant. Hope it's only the communications."

"Likewise, Lieutenant." Torin pressed the edges of the filter down behind her ears. "Opizzi, di'Naital, Lembede, check the mine. They might have dug in. Wirekik and di'Kano with me.

"The anchor?" Phoela asked, pulling her hood up over writhing hair.

"The anchor." The anchors were dropped from orbit containing the supplies new colonies needed to get started. They could handle vacuum, atmospheric entry, and impact—a little dust and wind wouldn't hurt them.

Halfway to the anchor, the wind picked up again.

Caught mid-stride, it hit Torin's raised leg with enough force to knock her off balance, two of the pieces of particulate large enough and hard enough for her combats to activate and absorb the impact. As she began to go down, Wirekik grabbed her hip, steadying her long enough to get both feet back on the ground.

She nodded her thanks and collapsed the formation, tucking Wirekik in tight behind her right shoulder, Phoela behind her left. Easier for the Others to take them out, harder for the storm to take them down and separate them.

Three steps further and the anchor disappeared behind a curtain of airborne particulate. Torin felt Wirekik and Phoela grip the straps of her pack. By step four, so much dust covered her filter she couldn't see. Nor could she ping the anchor. Bracing her KC against her hip in case she had to fire one-handed, Torin swiped her free hand over her filter and managed three fast steps, following her display's YBR before she had to do it again.

And again.

And again.

How many of the colonists had been literally lost?

When the proximately alert went off, she stretched out her arm, touched the anchor, followed the long wall around to the airlock entry, and had to actually touch the data port in her cuff to the lock.

And again to close it.

The inner door was open, drifts of dust up over the lower lip.

Scanner working again now it was out of the storm, Torin swept for life signs.

Nothing.

When Phoela opened her mouth, Torin raised a hand for silence and signaled a switch to night vision before sending the other two to search the second floor. When no one knew where the Others were, they could be anywhere. She headed for the power station, clearing each room she passed on the way. It looked as though the anchor had been powered down manually—there were no signs of a fight or of sabotage.

"The good news," she said, meeting Wirekik and Phoela back in the common room, "is that someone was alive to turn off the lights. The bad news, they didn't leave a note. Kitchen's been stripped of all edibles."

"Infirmary's empty too."

"But we found these." Children's clothing dangled from Phoela's hand. "All kids, but all different sizes."

Torin listened to dirt hiss against the windows. "Children's lungs fill faster."

"...geant Kerr! Can you hear me?"

The hiss had softened.

"Report Opizzi."

"No life in the...and no...of the Others, but there's something you...see."

The filter pressed against her eyelashes as Torin lifted a brow. "Something?"

"Looks like a grave. Hang on... Fuk it, only audio's getting through."

The hiss had dropped to a whisper.

"I'll be right there. Wirekik, di'Kano, start searching the buildings. East side, outer edge, work your way in. Move as quickly as you can. Don't split up. Lembede, di'Naital, same on the west."

"Copy, Sergeant."

The hazy outlines of buildings defined the road that led from the anchor to the mine. Torin took a ping off Opizzi's helmet, just in case, and began to run.

Two hundred and forty-two point seven meters out, the wind roared between the buildings, picked up a drift, and exposed the bodies of two emaciated animals, hides draped over skeletons, cracked tongues protruding. The lack of food in the anchor's kitchen and the presence of Krai in the colony, who could and did eat anything organic, suggested the animals had been buried before the colony had been abandoned.

Or had been wiped out.

* * *

Given its position by the entrance to the mine, odds were that the grave had been dug with mining equipment.

"There were two Dornagain, right?" Miri waved a hand at the area surrounded by the half-buried fence. "This could hold them."

Torin thought of the children's clothing. "And a few others. What's left inside?"

"Small digger and two haulers. All of them seized. Dust in the…"

Lightening danced along the top edge of the fence.

When her helmet visor depolarized, Miri shrugged. "Or that. Gold melts at just over a thousand degrees, lightening's closer to twenty-eight thousand, so it's possible the mechanicals got gilded to death."

* * *

The prefabs were empty. So were the houses.

If the Others had been here, if they'd finished the job the storms had started, the wind had scoured away all evidence.

* * *

"Found three dead *shonk*." Helmet in hand, Bannon pushed back his hood as they waited for the VTAs airlock to cycle. "Bodies were more desiccated than rotted. Lungs were full of dust."

"How did you…" Miri began then shook her head. "Never mind. Don't want to know. Dom! What happened to your hair?"

There was an oozing coral stub at Domini's temple. He sucked in air through his teeth. "Poked out, sanded off, Bannon sealed it. I'm fine."

"A quarter of the colonists were Taykan," Phoela said softly as the inner door finally opened.

* * *

"Can you keep her up in this?" Torin asked, peering through the windscreen at three-meter-high dust-devils. The plan had been to fly the VTA to the next anchor following roads built straight and wide enough for mining equipment, but VTAs weren't noted for their stability in atmosphere at the best of times and this wasn't that.

"I don't want to, but I can." Lieutenant Yerr flicked a weather map into the air above the control panel. "Terrestrial influences randomize the storms at ground level, but if I take her up twenty klicks the patterns are reasonably stable. My preference is up, over, and down." She sighed as Torin's brows drew in. "Or I can stay low and risk going belly up somewhere between anchors and your lot will have to walk the rest of the way."

At twenty kilometers they'd be a lot easier to spot should the Others be monitoring the results of their environmental destruction. *Pointless* destruction if they weren't monitoring it. Had it been up to Torin, they'd take the road but in the VTA Lieutenant Yerr was in charge.

"I'll get everyone strapped in."

* * *

The second site was essentially identical to the first. Buildings had collapsed, both mine and anchor were empty, there were children's clothes left in the anchor's infirmary. Instead of a grave they found a lake nearly empty of water, the shoreline scoured of plant life, and the bowl filled with dead fish.

"What killed them?" Bannon wondered, slipping a sample of the muddy liquid into his vest.

"Lack of water."

"Seriously?"

"They're fish," Torin reminded him, brushing the dust from her filter. The Others could have poisoned them, but most of the time the simple answer was the correct answer.

"They're destroying the entire planet," Wirekik growled, nostril ridges shut behind his filter. "Nothing's going to survive this."

* * *

The landing at the third site slammed Torin up into her harness. The VTA tipped sideways, then jerked back level as the struts compensated. Blood dribbled from the corner of Bannon's mouth, Domini cupped shaking fingers around the stump of his hair, and Miri muttered profanity under her breath— although the odds were high she wasn't actually hurt.

"Wind sheer," Lieutenant Yerr spat. *"You're going to want to wait a bit until things quiet down, Sergeant. You can see SFA out there right now."*

It took an hour and forty-three minutes before they could get a visual on the anchor.

There were lights on.

* * *

"What the fuk took you so long?" The Krai's nostril ridges were a pale, bloodless gray, and her clothing hung off her, a size too large.

The tall Human beside her shook his head. "They're not DCA, Dirnir, they're RECON."

"RECON?"

"Marines."

"I can see that." She ran her hand back over the short bristles on her scalp and showed teeth. "You deal with them then, I have things to do."

Torin watched her stomp off to where a small cluster of Krai children huddled against the wall of the large common room. The air was stale, the scrubbers running above capacity, and it smelled of too many people in too small a space. Had she not been a Marine, and a sergeant, she might have said it smelled of despair. A symphony of soft coughing suggested the colonists had given up on moving the dust out of their lungs and were concentrating on breathing instead—with limited success. A gesture sent her team out to do what they could to help, then Torin turned her attention back to the emaciated man in front of her.

"Bogdan Gozluv, Staff Sergeant with the seven/three engineers." He folded his arms and glared at her from under bushy brows. "I'd say you have to excuse Dirnir, Sergeant Kerr, but frankly, I don't give a rat's ass if you do. She's colony admin, she's got a lot on her mind."

She was in close conversation with a pair of di'Taykan now, and was, Torin realized, the only adult Krai in the room. "We were told the admin were Dornagain."

"Do you know what it takes to keep a Dornagain alive? How much food? How much water?"

Torin looked past him at the pallets and the people on them. Most of them coughing, all of them too thin. Where was the line when people were dying?

"We lost Live by Lists when a digger rolled on her, before we gathered here. The other six stopped eating," Bogdan continued, voice flat. "Stopped drinking. Wouldn't let any of us make it easier for them. Said they didn't want us to carry their lives for the rest of our own." He met Torin's gaze, eyes red-rimmed. "Stupid, hairy, giant assholes. It took them over a tenday to die. They're fukking heroes."

The Elder Races refused to fight. Sometimes they died anyway.

Less than four hundred colonists remained. Only thirty-seven of the two hundred and twelve children had survived—two hundred and twelve children who'd played outside while the early winds lifted fine particulate into their lungs.

"There were no signs of any of this in the initial assessments," Bogdan growled. "None. I'd figured the DCA screwed the pooch, but since you lot are here…" His gaze flicked out over Torin's team. "…I assume this isn't natural. Are the Others dirtside or did they do this…" He didn't wave his hand as much as move it in a jerky arc from the airlock though the common room. "…from further out?"

Torin watched children wander listlessly, listened to the coughing, remembered children's clothing, and packed it all away to deal with later so she could do her job. "If they know, they don't send RECON."

Bogdan's fists opened and closed, then he squared his shoulders and sighed. "Fair enough. How soon can you begin evacuation?"

"We don't have transport here, not for this many..." This few. "...but we can fit a dozen children on the VTA when Lieutenant Yerr returns to the Palmatier."

"Away from their parents?"

"Away from the dust, to a doctor and a full medical bay."

"We have a doctor, and three ex-corpsmen, and our kids don't go near the dust. We need food. And filters. And a ride out yesterday."

"Water?"

He shook his head. "Digger broke into an aquafer, that's why we gathered here. We've got plenty of water."

"Why didn't..."

"We move the whole colony to the mine? There's staph bacteria on the wet rock. Something our doc had never seen before. Lost four Human children, their parents, and a di'Taykan that way. Krai are immune so they're living in the upper chamber." His eyes narrowed. "Don't think you can suddenly come up with something we missed and save the day, Sergeant, all we want you to do is get us the fuk out of here."

Torin tapped her PCU. "Do you copy, Lieutenant Yerr?"

"I copy Sergeant. Your team's supplies and the two boxes of extra filters are on the ground. I'll inform Captain di'Merish of the situation and be back with everything the Palmatier can spare ASAP. Out."

With the anchor sealed, Torin couldn't have heard the VTA lift off although she thought she had. Or maybe it was the storm.

Bogdan raised a single brow. "Open com?"

"Easier than explaining."

"Easy way isn't always the right way, sergeant." His breath rattled deep in his throat. "We can leave Susumi space at the same time we entered it on the other side of the galaxy, but your lieutenant has to hand deliver her sit rep."

He sounded so weary, Torin found herself explaining. "The gold in the air..."

"Is scattering the signal from the ground. We *know*, Sergeant. But it's been a year and six tendays. Where was everyone?" He raised a hand. "Never mind. Space is big. There's a war on. The DCA bogs down in bureaucracy and the SSG got busy doing other things. I don't need to hear their fukking excuses."

"I wasn't going to give them."

His lip curled. "Good for you."

"Sergeant?" Dirnir rejoined them, nostril ridges half-closed.

Still angry then. Torin didn't blame her.

"When we combined the colony," Dirnir continued, "I sent Bogdan out to get Doc Alison, but she refused to leave her lab."

"Dr. Felicia Alison," Bogdan expanded. "She made a deal with the SSG to set up a small research station."

"Deal?"

"Transport, her own piece of dirt in return for a first look at her results. The DCA approved, and there were delusional words about the lab becoming the colony's first university. She's set up on the other side of the valley, same elevation, but about a hundred klicks north."

"A *hundred?*"

"Less than an hour," Dirnir snorted as Torin edited the profanity from her next question.

"What's she studying?"

"Planetary sciences," Bogdan began.

Dirnir cut him off. "Which we're disturbing. Thus, the distance. Before the storms started with this 27/10 nonsense, she'd come in once a week, teach a couple of science classes, have a meal, exaggerate her results." Nostril ridges relaxed and expanded with the memory. "Her whole response to the first tornado was a highly indignant, *That's not supposed to happen.*"

You were friends, Torin realized. "Why wouldn't she come in?"

Bogdan shrugged. "From what I could see of her lab, she was monitoring the storms. Not just locally; all the storms. I think she's trying to figure out a way to stop this."

"She doesn't need to die to stop it," Dirnir snapped. Her toes curled against the floor. "I haven't been able to send a ride since, they're too light and the winds are too high."

"She has…"

"The same ride. She can't get in; we can't get out."

There wasn't anything Torin could do here except hand over the filters. And she had to do more. "Do you have anything heavy that still runs?"

"Sure. There's a hauler that's in good nick." Bogdan reached out and put a hand on her forearm, as though he might need to stop her from immediately charging out the airlock. She wasn't positive he was wrong. "It doesn't matter, Sergeant. Visibility's a lie and we've already covered the impossibility of getting a signal through the dust."

"We don't need a signal. Not if you have the coordinates of the lab."

Nostril ridges closed again, Dirnir showed teeth. "Of course, we have the coordinates of the lab, but…"

This time, Bogdan cut her off. "Yellow brick road."

Torin nodded. "YBR is a standard RECON download. We shut down nearly every time out." She raised her voice. "Lembede! di'Naital! You're with me."

Bogdan folded his arms. "And if the Others attack while you're gone?"

Torin raised a brow. Had the man forgotten how to be a staff sergeant? "I'm leaving you three Marines."

His mouth twitched into what might have been a smile. "So you are."

* * *

The hauler's tracks rose up over Torin's shoulder, the floor of the cargo bed was a good half meter above her head, and the cabin a half meter above that. Gold dust had been ground into the rungs of the ladder.

"I emptied two packs to give you a full charge so transport better get its ass here before we run out of power." Germer, the Krai in charge of the vehicles, swung from a strut and dropped to the ground. "There's nothing between here and Doc Alison's place Beener can't get over or through. Keep her going in the right direction and you should have no trouble." He paused, tapped a front tooth with a grimy fingernail, and added, "Unless the Others have laid mines. There's no armor on her undercarriage."

"Why would you think…"

"This isn't natural." Germer flicked up a finger, not bothering to expand on what *this* was. It could only be one thing. "The Others have left us alone." A second finger. "So…" A third. "…they must be after the doc."

"Why?"

"No idea." He shrugged, no better at the Human gesture than most Krai. "They sent a peace delegation back in pieces. Why do they do anything?"

Half way up the ladder to the cabin, Torin paused and looked down. "You call the hauler Beemer?"

He laughed, nostril ridges fluttering. "No one says you have to. You sure you know how to drive one of these?"

Bannon snorted over the clang of his boot hitting the lowest rung of the ladder. "Please, she's a sergeant."

* * *

With the coordinates for the mine and the research center already in her helmet, Torin guided the big machine out of the vehicle bay, following the line on her visor. It handled enough like an APC she kept the lurching to a minimum. "ETA three hours, eleven minutes."

Bannon glanced over her shoulder. "I thought I heard Dirnir say it took an hour."

"Not at our top speed."

"Sarge, you're doing 31k."

"And that's our top speed."

"Hey Sarge…" Domini tossed his helmet on an empty seat and dragged his hood off, allowing his hair to spread out into a coral nebula around his head. "Do you think that mechanic was right? That the Others aren't after the gold, they're after the lab? Or the doc? Or both?"

"It's possible." It was all possible. Dr. Alison had been listed in the colony's personnel files as though she were part of the colony, not a separate, unique entity.

"So if we find the Others there? With the doc?"

"Then we know where they are."

Torin knew what do when faced with the enemy and none of that knowledge could be applied to the sick and starving. She almost hoped the Others were at the center. Making them pay for the dust and the deaths would give her something to do with the anger twisting under her skin.

* * *

They stopped ten meters out from the research center's coordinates after rocking over a large, unidentified object that compacted under the hauler's tracks.

Domini shut the engine down. "With any luck we just took out an enemy VTA."

Something slammed into the hauler, bounced off, and slammed in again.

"Debris carried by the wind," Torin said after a minute. Bannon and Domini nodded. The Others' weapons made a distinctive impact. "Let's move."

Visibility was nonexistent. She found the building by walking into it, the dust having taken out her proximity alarm. Leaning in close, her face little more than the filter's distance from the structure, she saw enough of the wall to recognize the distinctive outer layer.

An anchor.

Anchor's were dropped with colonies; they weren't research stations.

Dr. Alison must've gotten one hell of a grant.

The outer door was unlocked and the inner door was open. The airborne dust that had entered with them glittered in the ambient light from dozens of screens. Torin recognized the work bench along one wall, a couple of fabricators, and nothing else in the jumble of machinery. She sent Domini right, Bannon left, and moved carefully straight down the middle.

The screens were all tracking the storms. Three were locked on the mesosphere, although the data coming through looked spotty.

They found nothing to indicate the Others had ever been in the building.

They couldn't find Dr. Alison.

"Keep looking. If we can't find her, we need to find something that can tell us where she's gone."

The kitchen held eight dirty mugs and a floor-to-ceiling cupboard over half full of instant meals.

The large room at the narrow end of the anchor opposite the airlock took up the full two stories and had a retractable roof.

Torin scuffed through the dust to the almost familiar piece of equipment in the center of the room. "Lembede, could you send a satellite up with this?"

"Could send a lot of stuff up with this system." Bannon swung his KC across his back and crouched to look in under the main bulk of the machine. "Nothing big though. Needs to be under sixty kilos."

"That's admirably precise."

"Not really, Sarge." He tapped a finger against the curve of metal. "There's a warning label on the loader."

* * *

Dust feathered down the stairs leading to the roof. Off the top of her head, Torin could remember four instances of the Others landing on anchors. She signaled for silence and reached for the mechanism that opened the trap door.

It was jammed.

It took brute force and a fifteen centimeter serrated blade to get the door open. The metal screamed in protest when they finally forced it down.

By the time the accumulation had spilled into the stairwell, Torin stood ankle deep in dust. Half a dozen larger pieces of debris bounced past, the wind circled her, raising dust devils, and a thin arm wrapped in dust-colored clothing swung down from the roof.

Dr. Alison had died trying to get back into the anchor, the back of her head caved in by a triangular piece of metal about a centimeter thick. It looked as though she'd been buried before the storm managed to abrade more than just her top layer of clothing and when Torin turned her over, desiccated features glared out from behind her filter with an expression of extreme irritation.

"How long you figure she's been dead, Sarge?"

"I have no idea." Torin had seen a lot of corpses during her years in the Corps but they were usually... damper. "Wrap her in a couple of blankets and secure her to the cargo bed. When you're done, strip the kitchen and the infirmary. I'm going to try and figure out what she was doing up here."

"You think she might've been setting up some kind of gizmo to stop the storms?"

"Well, if she was, she forgot to turn it on."

* * *

Head ducked down to help keep her filter clear, Torin shuffled carefully around the roof, dropping to one knee during the heavy gusts to reduce her chance of going over. She found seven sensors still operating and three more reduced to jagged spikes, the broken metal polished smooth.

A gust out of the west took her by surprise. She stumbled, fell, and slid toward the edge, gloved hands cutting waves through the dust. She managed to stop herself just as her palm slid over a ridge in the seamless roofing material.

Her data cuff buzzed against her wrist.

The slate she lifted into the sepia light didn't look damaged. And it wasn't locked.

No reason for it to be. Dr. Alison had been working alone, a hundred klicks away from anyone who might read over her shoulder. Who might want to know what she was up to.

Crouched in the stairwell out of the wind, Torin flicked through files. Most had been corrupted and those she could get into were too far outside her skillsets for her to understand more than the basics. They looked like plans. Some were definitely schematics. She nearly missed the small text file. "Dear Diary," she muttered, scrolling back to it. "Saw the Others land yesterday. The coordinates are…"

In Torin's experience, scientists were seldom that helpful.

Most of this file had been corrupted as well but the Parliamentary seal at the top of the message remained recognizable. As did the smaller seal representing the Minister for Military Affairs.

Torin stared at it until she had to brush dust off the screen.

Dr. Alison *had* gotten one hell of a government grant.

From the Minister for Military Affairs.

Had the MMA heard about a new weapon about to be deployed by the Others and sent her here to figure out how to stop it?

Was it coincidence that the Others had used that weapon here, on Hurasu, miraculously providing the data Dr. Alison would need to counteract it?

Torin didn't believe in miracles.

Was it coincidence that the Others had used that weapon here, on Hurasu, after the colonists had settled in and the DCA had withdrawn?

As Opizzi had pointed out, *"They need a test site with people…"*

Hands sweating inside her gloves, Torin tapped a fingernail against the parliamentary seal. But who were *they*?

Back on the roof, she braced the slate against the lip around the trap door and brought her boot down on it. The Corps issued slates that were Marine resistant; a civilian slate didn't stand a chance. Gold had already begun to adhere to open circuits when she picked it up.

Prying the memory chip out of its protective casing with the point of her knife, she dropped it into the cupped palm of her left hand and used the hilt to grind it to dust.

Then she let the wind take it.

And heard Opizzi's voice in memory. *"Why would the Others mess up the atmosphere then? If they can get in and out without being seen, they can do a strip and skip in another hemisphere."*

"Sergeant Kerr?"

"On my way down."

Bannon met her at the bottom of the stairs. He gestured up at the open trap door. "We can't close that."

Torin raised a brow.

"I mean, there's a lot of expensive equipment in this place that's going to get ruined."

"Probably." She led the way back to the airlock.

"We're going to let that happen?"

"How do we stop it? If people object," she continued before he could answer, "it's on me. We did our job, we secured the colonists. We can't fight this kind of destruction."

No one could.

Maybe Dr. Alison had been working on a solution.

But most of the time, the simple answer was the correct answer.

Torin followed Bannon out into the storm, licked her lips, and tasted dust.

End of Eternity

Nancy Holzner

Another day, another sunrise. Beautiful, but unremarkable. Still, I love the light at this time of day. Standing by my penthouse window, I watch as the last pinks and oranges fade from the brightening sky over Boston Harbor. Behind me, some morning talk show is on. I enjoy the soft voices in the background, as though a congenial conversation is taking place in the next room. Suddenly a male voice announces loudly: "We interrupt this broadcast to bring you an important message from the President of the United States."

I pick up the remote. The vagaries of politics long ago ceased to interest me. Every channel shows the same image: a lectern bearing the presidential seal backed by a row of American flags. The president walks onstage, dressed in a dark suit and somber necktie. I'm about to click off the television when something about his gait makes me pause. As he adjusts his tie, I can see his hands shaking. He grips the sides of the lectern and opens his mouth to speak. No sound emerges. He clears his throat and makes another attempt. "My fellow Americans…" he quavers. I lower myself onto the edge of a chair and listen. This is the voice of a man gripped by terror.

"Today it is my sad duty to…" He tugs at his collar; sweat gleams on his forehead. "It is my sad duty to inform you of the inescapable tragedy we now face."

Ah. Another "inescapable tragedy." For a moment I'd almost been interested. The president drags his sleeve across his sweaty forehead, leaving his handkerchief tucked in its pocket. I keep watching.

Again he clears his throat. "Twelve years ago, astronomers at NASA spotted a rogue planet that appeared to be on a path toward Earth. Within months, its trajectory was confirmed." His voice is steadier now. "The United States joined with our allies in a secret mission to divert the planet, known as 2013SH56. That mission has failed."

There are gasps and cries in the studio and the picture tilts at a crazy angle. The President looks into the camera as his image slowly straightens. "I repeat: the mission has failed. Impact is inevitable. Our Earth will be destroyed—total annihilation of the planet and all life upon it. Scientists estimate that impact will occur in approximately two months, in the globe's northwestern hemisphere." A map of the United States appears on the screen, a large red X blotting out North Dakota.

"The apocalypse has arrived," he says. "Now is not the time to panic. Now is the time to look to the Creator and set your soul to rights. It is essential that everyone remain calm." His expression shows he recognizes the absurdity of his admonition. "For that reason, I am declaring martial law, along with a 72-hour curfew. Wherever you are, shelter in place for the next 72 hours. Thank you, and may God bless us all."

The television goes dark.

I sit back, staring at the empty screen.

I can still see the X over North Dakota. One phrase burns in my mind: *Total annihilation of the planet and all life upon it.*

I've never heard such beautiful words.

Perhaps my time has finally come. Perhaps, at long last, I'll be able to die.

* * *

I won eternity in a game of cards.

That is, I believe the game was a card game. Poker, most likely, although it could have been faro or piquet, pinochle or twenty-one. In truth it could have been any game where people throw money at the hope that some power in the universe favors them just a bit more than their opponents. When I try to recall, I imagine a game of poker, so that is how I shall tell the tale.

I had a good hand. Let's say it was a straight flush. The point is, I was fairly certain I'd won the game. So, apparently, was the player sitting across the table from me. The problem was he'd already bet all his chips, so when I raised him, he glanced around the table like a guilty man sizing up a jury.

"Well," I think I may have said, "are you in? Or has the game become too rich for you?"

"I'm in." Sweat bedazzled his forehead. "Will you take…will you take eternal life as my wager?"

Everyone around the table guffawed. We'd all had rather too much to drink and we laughed as though his words were the funniest thing we'd heard in a month.

"You're out," I said. "If you can't afford to stay in, admit it. Fold."

"I'm *in*," he insisted.

"What in blazes would I want—would any of us want—with your eternal soul? I'm not the devil come to tempt you."

"Not my soul," he said, his voice quiet and deadly serious. "Tell me: wouldn't you like to live forever? Never die? Stay eternally as you are in this moment? *That's* my wager."

We were, as I said, a little drunk and his offer seemed an excellent joke. "Live forever? Who wouldn't?" It was simply a game among friends. It didn't matter to me whether I took the pot or he did, but this was the best hand I'd ever been dealt, and I intended to play it for all it was worth.

"All right. I'll take your wager."

Grinning broadly, he laid out his cards one at a time: first the three of clubs, then the ace of that same suit. Ace of hearts. Ace of spades. Ace of diamonds.

"Four aces." He eyed the chips in the center of the table but didn't reach for them. His right index finger twitched as he held himself back.

"Well." I stared at him, my face blank, prolonging the moment. Enjoying it.

When I laid out the two of diamonds, one corner of his mouth quirked up. I followed it with the four of diamonds. My opponent watched, his expression unchanged.

Next the three of diamonds. I nudged over the four to make room for it in its proper place. Hope blinked out of his eyes as he started to realize the hand I was revealing.

With a flourish I slapped my last two cards down, in order. There it was—two, three, four, five, six. All diamonds. A straight flush.

My opponent stared at his four aces as though they'd betrayed him.

"Now what do you say?" I began, ready to tease him about how he planned to deliver my winnings of eternal life. He'd been my opponent during the game but now that it was over he was, of course, a friend, and his joke had amused me.

Before I could utter another word, he choked out a cry and fell over face first onto the table, dead. It took several minutes to determine the fact, but from the moment he collapsed, there was no hope. He was dead, a corpse, no more. Nothing.

Shaken, I returned home and told my wife what had happened. My friend's sudden death undermined the excellence of his jest—how could it not? Yet she smiled, a light in her eyes. I can no longer recall the precise color of her eyes. Some days I picture them as the pale blue of a sky just before sunset flames out; others as violet or amber or perhaps a deep gray. What I have not forgotten is that light.

"I have sometimes wondered," she said, her lips curved in an expression that could have been mirth or perplexity, "which of us would die first. It is a relief to know I shall never feel the pain of mourning you."

With that light still in her eyes, she put her arms around my neck. She pressed her lips against mine. And just like that the game—with its wins and its losses—was forgotten.

* * *

My wife was right. She never had to mourn me. At least, she never grieved my death. As the years passed, time softened her features; later, it sharpened them into lines and wrinkles. I did not change and that caused her a different kind of grief. My feelings for her never diminished—I swear it. Indeed, they grew through the experiences we shared, the life we built together. So many details of that life have fled my memory. I do not recall, now, where we lived or whether we had children. I do not know my profession or which language we spoke. It was all so long ago.

After so much time, I am not even sure of her name. I believe she had a garden that she loved, one filled with roses. And so I remember her as Rose.

But I am certain—*certain*—of one thing: she was the love of my life. Many times, I told her so.

But she, my Rose, did not believe me. When she regarded herself through what she imagined were my eyes, she saw a slender young woman grown plump—"gone to fat" was how she put it. Then the plumpness fell away. Her skin sagged. Her body stooped and shriveled. Her teeth darkened; one or two fell out. Her soft hands grew rough and crisscrossed with thick veins. She did not want me to look at her, and yet...

And yet none of that mattered while that light shone in her eyes.

She never understood this. She hid herself from me, my world growing dark as she turned her face away. And then one day she was dead, any hope of that light gone forever.

I wanted to be dead, too. I leaped off bridges. I blasted bullets through my head. I swallowed poison, gallons of the stuff.

None of it mattered. However I tried to destroy my body, nothing happened. Just...nothing. Slashing my throat caused no more harm than pricking a finger.

Whatever I tried, my body remained whole and hearty, exactly as it was on the day of that damned card game.

The card game!

It occurred to me that I could lose eternity in the same way I'd won it. I immersed myself in gambling, entering any game of chance I could find. I played recklessly, betting too much on hands that could never win. Still, I won more often than I would have wished. And when the cards went against me, putting me in a position to offer my burden of eternity as a wager, no one would take the bet.

And so I resigned myself to my fate. Until today. Today I have a journey to plan. I think of the president's map, with its big red X over North Dakota. In two months, that's where I will be, greeting the rogue planet that will destroy us all, welcoming total annihilation with open arms.

* * *

For the first hour after the president's announcement, things are quiet. I scan the sky over the harbor, wondering where 2013SH56 might be. Then, from the corner of my eye, I see what I think is a large bird but is in fact a neighbor, plummeting from his balcony. Other neighbors follow suit. A hailstorm of wealthy Bostonians falls from the sky. I hear shouts and bursts of gunfire. Smoke wafts across the water.

I decide to take a walk.

Outside my building, broken bodies litter the pavement. I step over and around them as I head northwest on Summer Street. I am not the only one to ignore the shelter-in-place order. The bars are overflowing. Liquor store windows are smashed, their shelves empty. People push shopping carts loaded with food. At South Station, tanks form a blockade, but no one is there. Military discipline can hold only so long, I suppose, before the soldiers take off for their ultimate R&R. Half a block further, a uniformed police officer lies face down in a pool of blood, still clutching the pistol he used to blow a hole in his head.

No one pays me any attention as I make my way to the Public Garden. I'm run off the sidewalk by two men carrying a giant television. Perhaps they'll get some use out of it before the power fails. I take a seat by the rose beds. The bushes are in full bloom, an explosion of pink and white and red and yellow. Their scent mingles with the smoke that billows from Beacon Hill.

I think of Rose. I've always felt close to her here. I try, as I always do, to picture her. And, as I always do, I fail. Her hair was dark, I think, and fell in soft waves past her shoulders. But just as I think, *Yes, that's Rose,* the image dissolves, replaced by another. Her hair a mass of curls, perhaps lighter. Was she tall or short? Curvy or slender? I don't know. I can't see her. The human brain is too puny to hold an eternity's worth of memories. My Rose has faded into the void.

In a few weeks, I'll finally join her there.

I close my eyes, basking in the warm afternoon light and the smell of rose-tinged smoke. I start to plan my final journey.

* * *

After days of riots, a new mood has taken hold. Apathy? Ennui? Perhaps it's simply acceptance. Isn't that the final stage of dying?

I wouldn't know.

I'm ready to set out. I have no need of food—I learned that centuries ago when I attempted to starve myself to death. My only requirement is gasoline, and I've stockpiled as much of that as I could get. I have a goal: McClusky, "the heart of North Dakota," population 380. The place where the two lines of that big red X crossed on the president's map, approximately 1800 miles from where I now stand.

The place that will be instantly vaporized on impact.

Rose, my darling, I'm coming. I'll meet you in the void.

* * *

I am barely twenty miles west of Boston when I see a pile-up of cars blocking the road ahead. I slow, looking for a way around. A bullet shatters the passenger-side window. I feel it strike my temple, but of course it has no effect. Another bullet whizzes past my nose and out the open window beside me. I cannot let the assailant destroy my vehicle, not so soon into my journey! I press the accelerator and swerve onto the median. My car bumps over grass until I reach the eastbound lanes. I speed westward, going a hundred miles an hour down the wrong side of the highway. There is no "wrong side." Not anymore. Not if it takes me to McClusky.

In Syracuse, someone pushes a concrete block from an overpass. It crashes through the windshield, bounces off my face, and lands in my lap. I push it aside and keep driving.

I won't let anyone stop me, Rose.

Outside of Toledo, I lose time when nails scattered across the road puncture a tire. I stop in the middle of the road and put on a spare. Astonishingly, no one shoots at me.

Each day, 2013SH56 grows larger in the sky. It's gone from the size of a pencil eraser to that of a dime. Astronomers have estimated it's speeding toward Earth at a rate of 25,000 miles an hour. I wish I could travel so fast.

East of Chicago, a massive pileup, hundreds of cars, blocks the highway. All of the drivers are dead, of course. That's the point: a high-speed game of chicken where no one blinks and more and more cars hurtle into the wreckage. Extra points for an explosion.

Not wishing to take part in that game, I make a detour through the city. I soon get lost and when I pull over to look at a map someone shoots at my car. There are no windows left to shatter. I peel away before they can hit my tires.

I decide to leave the interstate and travel on the back roads. Somewhere in Wisconsin I see a large camp set up beside a lake. Spray-painted signs on plywood face the road: SINNER, REPENT! MATTHEW 24:21! IT'S NOT TOO LATE!

I drive on. I siphon gas out of abandoned cars and farm machines. I sleep in my car, an hour here and another there. I awaken with Rose's name on my lips, searching my dreams for her. She is never there.

Now, I pass through flat farmland, fields stripped of whatever food they grew. Scattered bones are all that remain of what must have been a herd of dairy cows. The landscape is as empty as the sky. No, not the sky. Planet 2013SH56 looms there, larger now than the moon. "I'll meet you in McClusky, my friend," I say aloud.

I have not seen another person for days, so I am startled when a young woman walks out of a field into the middle of the road, waving at me with one arm. With the other, she holds something close to her body.

I start to drive around her. But I stop.

She comes to the driver's side window. She is perhaps twenty years old and wears a simple white dress.

"Do you need help?" I ask.

"Would you like something to eat?" She offers me a loaf of bread.

"No, I—" How can I explain I don't bother with food?

"Go on," she says, grinning. "It's good. See?" She bites into the loaf like it's a piece of fruit. Chewing, she passes it through the window.

There is something in the way she holds out the bread, a purity in her gesture. No guardedness, no fear. I take the loaf, tear off a small hunk, and return the rest to her. "Thank you." I drop the morsel on the floor.

"We have to be kind to each other in these last days." She takes another bite. "Reverend Ames said that."

"You are very kind. But I must go. Now, do you need help? Perhaps a lift somewhere?"

"What I need..." She smiles at me, a crumb sticking to her lower lip. "...is someone to go on a picnic with me. Come on. Please? I know a lovely spot." She gestures across the field. On the far side is a stand of trees.

McClusky awaits two hundred miles to the west. I still have five days to get there. This girl looks at me with an eager smile. Is she luring me into an ambush? I don't want to lose my car.

She waits, the smile never leaving her face.

I shake my head, but when I speak I'm surprised at the words that emerge. "Get in," I say. "We'll drive to your picnic spot."

She runs around to the passenger side. I smile as she carefully pulls the seatbelt across her lap and fastens it with a click. "That way," she says, pointing.

As we bump across the field, she looks out the window and hums to herself. I recognize the tune. *Amazing Grace.* Her humming is thin and sweet and goes straight through my chest.

I search for something to say. "Do you live around here?"

"I do now." She goes back to humming. After a few bars, she stops. "I came here with Reverend Ames and the others in our church."

I think of the camp in Wisconsin. "To repent before the end?"

"Something like that." Her laugh is as musical as her song.

We're almost to the trees. "Over there," she says, leaning forward. "Stop there."

There's no ambush. Just trees and a small stream. She gets out of the car and climbs onto a rock on the bank, holding her bread aloft like a trophy.

I go to the stream and let its cool water run over my hands. It feels good. I splash some on my face and neck and sit down next to the girl. She hands me the bread and I tear off another piece, a small one. I don't want to waste her food.

"What's your name?" I ask.

"Rose."

That single syllable hits me harder than any rogue planet ever could. In all my centuries, I'd never met another of that name. Unlikely, I know. But I believe it to be true.

Her eyes widen. "You don't like it?"

"No, it's a beautiful name. My favorite, as it happens. It's just that…a long time ago…I knew someone…"

"It's not my real name. Well, it is because I picked it myself. What I should say, I guess, is it's not my legal name. Although what's legal anymore, right? Not my *original* name. You know, the name on my birth certificate." Her words are like a cloud of butterflies. "You see, when you join the church, Revered Ames tells you to choose a new name. Something from nature. I like flowers, so I picked Rose." She holds out the bread again. "You want some more?"

I'm still holding the hunk I tore off earlier, clutching it so tightly it's compacted to a ball of dough in my hand. I shake my head.

Rose.

I try to explain. "My Rose…well, the Rose I knew. It's what I call her. Now, in my mind. But maybe it wasn't really her name. I try to remember, but so much gets lost."

"I know what you mean," she says. She has no idea what I mean.

She's nothing like my Rose, the way she chatters on, every other statement a question. Her hair, long and straight and parted in the middle, is a sandy brown. My own Rose's hair was wavy and much darker, I think. Wasn't it dark? And yet…I try to study this girl's eyes without looking like a threat or, even worse, a fool.

"Do you believe in reincarnation?"

She laughs. "Does it matter? Now, I mean?"

"I suppose not." No, she's not like my Rose. At least I don't think so. It's merely the coincidence of the name. "Why do people in your church choose their names from nature? To save the world?"

"No. The world is coming to an end. But it hasn't ended *yet*. Our names help us appreciate what we have now, before everything is lost."

"I'd like to meet this Reverend Ames. He sounds like a wise man."

"She was very wise. But you can't meet her. She's gone. They're all gone."

I bite my lip, reluctant to ask. "What happened?"

"Someone killed them. I was out scavenging, and when I came back, everyone was dead. Every single one of my friends. Whoever killed them didn't even take anything." She balances the bread in her lap and extends both hands toward me, palms up. "Why would anyone do that?"

I have no answer for her.

She looks straight into my eyes, tears brimming in hers, obscuring the color. Pale blue, perhaps, or gray. Pain clouds those eyes, as a sob catches in her throat. She reaches out to me, grabs my shirt, and I press her close against my chest. My chin rests on the top of her head. Her hair smells like grass and sweat.

When she pulls back and raises her face to mine, the clouds in her eyes dissolve, and light shines from them. It is a light I've seen before. A long, long time ago.

"I'll protect you," I say. My fingers lightly smooth her hair. Above us, 2013SH56 glows orange, twice the size of the moon. "Rose."

* * *

I no longer care about McClusky. I am where I need to be.

Rose takes me to her shelter, an abandoned farmhouse with broken windows and only half its roof intact. There's no front door. We step inside, into what was once a dining room, and I catch my breath at the sight of five corpses slumped around the table. A family, two parents and three nearly grown children, still in their chairs after their last meal of poison.

"They're my guardians," Rose says. "People see them and run away."

I'm not surprised. Even though anyone still walking the Earth has by now seen hundreds of corpses, the scene is unnerving. Scavengers would distrust the food in this house. A loaf of moldy bread sits on the table, gnawed on a corner. Inches away, two dead mice lay curled on their sides.

I glance at Rose, who has tucked her half-loaf of bread under her arm. "You didn't—?"

"Offer you poisoned bread?" She laughs. "You didn't eat it, did you? I saw." Her voice carries a lilt that's almost teasing.

"I was worried for you."

"Look at those poor field mice. They didn't even make it off the table." She turns to me. "If this bread were poisoned, I would've dropped dead back at the stream and floated away like Ophelia." She looks at her loaf. "I made this myself."

"How?" Baking bread, once such an ordinary endeavor, now seems like a miracle.

"Some stuff in the pantry is still good. There was an old packet of yeast pushed to the back of one of the shelves. I only had to pick a few worms out of the flour. I found a loaf pan, and down in the basement there was an old camping stove with half a bottle of propane…" She takes a bite. I watch the muscles working in her jaw as she chews. "I burned the bottom a little. Sure you don't want some?"

She gouges out a piece and offers it to me. This time I place the bread in my mouth and chew. Flavors I hadn't tasted in years flood my senses. Yeast and flour and salt. It tastes so good I want to weep.

"Thank you."

She puts her arms around my neck in a gesture that's achingly familiar. I almost can't look at her for the light in her eyes, and yet I cannot look away.

"Will you make love to me?" she asks.

I manage to swallow.

"The last thing we know in the world should be love, don't you think? When the moment comes, I want to have the biggest orgasm of my life. I want to climax as my body explodes into a million stars." Rose's eyes regard me from this strange-yet-familiar face.

I would do anything for her.

"We'd better practice, then." She's laughing at me as she says it, but I don't care.

Her body is warm and soft and smooth and pulsing with life. My own pulse—for how many years did I despise its wretched pounding?—meets hers, matches it. For so long I have wanted nothing more than to escape the confines of this body, to shed its wants and needs and pains and demands and simply cease to be.

No longer.

As we move together, I *remember*. I remember everything about my Rose. Somehow, she and this other Rose are one and the same. I can't explain it. All I can do is give myself to this moment and to all the moments of light and joy that have shined through my life.

I remember.

Afterwards, we lie on the floor, looking up through the space where the roof used to be at the fiery disk that has grown again in size. Surely it couldn't have gotten so much bigger in two hours?

"Are you afraid?" I ask.

"No," she says simply. "No, I'm not." She twists her head to look at me. "Are you?"

Before I can answer, she continues. "I thought I'd be afraid. Maybe I should be. But I think fear is just a different form of hope. When there's no hope left, fear disappears."

She turns on her side, her body fitting mine in a precise way I thought I'd never know again. Her breathing slows, deepens. Gentle snores tell me she's sleeping.

And suddenly I am deathly afraid.

* * *

Morning. Only two days left. We find some party hats—red and blue and yellow with *Happy Birthday* in block letters—and put one on each of the corpses. Rose uses the rest of the yeast to bake another loaf of bread. "The last bread on Earth!" she proclaims, and I surprise her with a dusty old bottle I found in the cellar. The wine tastes like vinegar—maybe it *was* vinegar—but who knew that sharp tang could offer so much pleasure?

"A jug of wine, a loaf of bread—and thou," I say.

She surprises me by continuing: "Beside me, singing in the wilderness…"

"O, wilderness were Paradise enow!" We finish the verse together.

"I like that," Rose says. "I came here expecting salvation, but when I saw what happened to the others…" She shuddered. "*This* is paradise. Here, now, with you. It's the only paradise we're going to get." She sips her wine and hides a grimace.

You'd think paradise would have better wine.

"A jug of wine, a loaf of bread…" she says softly. "But thou? I don't even know your name. You asked me mine. What's yours?"

All of the names I've used through all of the centuries whirl through my mind. I remember them all, but I can't pull one out of the maelstrom. "Perhaps I should choose a new one. Something from nature?"

She shakes her head. "I'll call you Omar. For quoting Omar Khayyam."

It doesn't matter what she calls me. She is Rose. I pull her to me.

* * *

It is the last day. It is *now*. I wake holding Rose, both of our bodies slick with sweat. The air is hot, unbearably so. The massive planet fills the sky—orange and fiery. No sky is left. The tree outside our window bursts into flames.

Rose reaches for me. I know what she wants. The room is on fire around us, our Paradise burning. Her arm slides from my grasp. Her hair catches fire. It's too hot, too bright. I can't see her eyes—

* * *

Darkness.

Rose?

No answer.

I do not know if I spoke her name aloud.

There is nothing here.

No light.

No sound.

No warmth or cold.

Nothing.

I cannot discern whether I have a body.

And yet I am here.

How can this be?

I do not know if I'm in the void, or if I am the void.

The distinction means nothing.

There is nothing here.

And yet I remember it all.

Winning the wager, my beloved Rose, our children, the many lives I lived, the riots, the suicides, my last journey, the deaths—so many deaths. My momentary paradise at the end of the world.

I remember all of it. It is all nothing.

Rose?

I am alone.

It is so dark here.

I long for light. For that special light that emanated from a pair of lovely eyes. The light I lost and then found again.

There is no light here.
There is nothing at all.
The darkness presses in on me.
Rose.
What happened to those lovely eyes?
What happened to the light in them?
The darkness is too much. I cannot bear it.
I cannot be without that light.
Let there be light.
Please.
Let there be light.

Little Armageddons

Stephen Blackmoore

"You've got to be kidding me."

Imani rolls her chair from her desk to Daniel's, squints at his monitor. "What's wrong?"

"The scenario end dates," he says. "They're all set for today."

"Those are supposed to be the start dates," Imani says.

"Yeah, no shit," Daniel says. "I told you we should have done another code review."

"We did five. And went over all our inputs three times. That should have been more than enough."

"Yeah, well, it wasn't."

Imani gets it. She's not happy about this, either. Five years of data collection, coding, test runs to get to this point. Five years of being stuck in this windowless closet of an office with too-bright fluorescent lights, air-conditioning that doesn't work, outdated computers, and Daniel.

No, Imani's not happy at all. But still.

"You know, we can always re-run the scenarios," Imani says.

"Not until we fix whatever caused this in the first place."

"Obviously," she says. "But maybe keep this in perspective."

Daniel closes his eyes, takes a deep breath, lets it out slowly. "I'm sorry," he says. "I just—I need a win. I need something to go right for a change."

Ah, Imani thinks. So that's what this is about. Daniel and his wife have been separated for the last six months. It's not really surprising. In fact, Imani wonders what took her so long. Or why she married him in the first place.

"I got served papers last night. Loretta wants a divorce."

It's a toss-up as to what drove her to finally cut the cord—how consumed Daniel's been with their project, or the fact that Daniel is, well, Daniel.

"It's not like I didn't know it was going to happen," Daniel says. "It just wasn't supposed to happen until Tuesday."

"Tuesday? How did you know it was going to happen Tuesday? How did you know it was going to happen at all? Did you—"

And this is where their work truly shines. Their algorithm processes and contextualizes a staggering amount of data at a ridiculous clip. Petabytes per second. Most of their work hasn't even been directly related to the algorithm, but simply gathering all the data. Everything they could get their hands on— scientific, religious, historical, cultural. Thousands of languages, customs, legends. Reams of climate reports, genealogy trees, fossil records, genomes of every species ever recorded.

They have taken all this data, fed it through their algorithm like a pig through a sausage press, and ended up with the most accurate simulation of the world ever built, the mother of all prediction models.

"It was just a test run," Daniel says. "Two, three years ago. I just, I don't know, kept running it. It got better as we got more data."

"You used the algorithm to see if Loretta was going to divorce you? Why didn't you tell me about this?" Imani says. This is a potential breakthrough.

"It felt weird. I didn't want you to think I was crying on your shoulder or something."

"Daniel, I give fuck-all about your imploding marriage. What were the results?" All of their test runs have been carefully controlled scenarios. Nothing too vague, too open-ended. They didn't think it was ready for that. Well, Imani didn't think it was ready for that. Daniel seems to have been doing just fine with it for years. "Will my spouse leave me?" might seem like a simple question, but the factors that go into it are mind-boggling. Who's spouse is it? What country do they live in? Is religion a factor? Finances? Social standing? Why are their finances the way they are? How did they reach that level of social standing? Why does that social hierarchy exist in the first place?

"It told me last year that she was going to start dating a guy named Phil Littlefield who lives on the other side of town who she'd meet at a co-worker's wedding."

"And?"

"Totally off base," Daniel says. "She met him at a co-worker's kid's Bar Mitzvah."

"Daniel." Imani pinches the bridge of her nose. "You have been looking for a specific answer to a specific question about an indeterminate future and the only thing our software got wrong is the specific event where she met her new boyfriend? And you didn't tell me about it?"

"He's not her boyfriend," Daniel says. "Oh, god. Do you think he's her boyfriend?"

"I'm going to murder you. Right now. I'm going to find the sharpest thing in this room and I am going to kill you with it."

"That's not right," Daniel says.

"Oh, I think it is the most right thing I will ever do," Imani says. Daniel reaches past her arm and taps her keyboard. Then again. And again. A rapid clicking of keys as he scans through the list on the screen.

Imani shoves his arm out of her personal space. "And for that I may murder you twice."

"Look at the end dates," he says. "I mean, not just the end dates. Scenario 8236: Observations of Asteroid 99942 Apophis in 2004 estimating a possible impact April 13th, 2029, are revised in 2016 when the asteroid's course shifts due to impact with a comet. The asteroid collides with Earth on April 17th, 2021 destroying all life on Earth within twelve hours."

"Ouch."

"Right? Scenario 13633: A mutation in Marburg Marburgvirus during an outbreak in Angola in 2004 spreads through aid workers to the Netherlands, France, Sweden, Australia, and the United States. The last human being dies on April 17th, 2021."

"Okay," Imani says, not sure what Daniel's getting at. "Doomsday scenarios are valid. We did eighty thousand runs. We're bound to get a few of them."

"A few," Daniel says, scrolling down the screen. "But every single one?"

"It can't be every single—holy shit, it is every single one."

"Are there even eighty thousand different ways to doom humanity?" Daniel says.

"Plague, plague, plague," Imani says, jumping down hundreds of entries at a time. "Plague, plague, nuclear war, plague, plague, bees, plague, plague—"

"Wait. Did you say bees?"

Imani pauses the data scrolling up her screen, adjusts her glasses. "Yes. Bees."

"Like massive colony collapse?" Daniel says.

"'Scenario 37482. March 3rd, 1984 to April 17th, 2021. Bees.' That's all it says. Tag that one for a look at the decision tree."

Imani reads off horror after horror, nightmare after nightmare. Plagues, wars, mass geological events, asteroids, nuclear disasters, nature lashing out at humanity, cluster tornados, tsunamis, technology gone horribly wrong, giant snakes, flying sharks, zombies, cannibal killers, mole men.

She stops. Takes off her glasses, leans in, leans back, cocks her head to the side. The data in front of her stubbornly refuses to make sense.

"Problem?" Daniel says.

"Bob Ross."

"Why do I know that name?"

"He's that painter on PBS."

"The 'Let's build a happy little cloud.' guy?" Daniel says.

"He destroys the world on April 17th, 2021."

"That can't be right." Daniel pulls up the logfile. "Didn't he die in the nineties?"

"July 4th, 1995."

"How do you know that?"

"I watch a lot of PBS," Imani says.

"Is it my imagination or are these getting stranger?"

"You mean besides flying sharks, zombies, and giant squid? You tell me. Scenario 67925. March 14th, 2008 to April 17th, 2021. The Baboon King."

"What the hell is the Baboon King?"

"No idea."

"Okay," Daniel says. "What's that one? April 17th, 2021 to April 17th, 2021. Inter-dime—"

The office phone rings, jarring both of them. Imani looks around the lab but, though she can hear it, she can't see the phone anywhere. She follows the sound and finds it buried beneath reports, white papers, notes, coffee cups, the detritus of science. "Don't answer it," Daniel says. "It might be Loretta."

"Why would she call you here? Does she even have this number?"

"You're right. It's probably Phil, that bastard. There's no way he's her boyfriend."

"Daniel, I—" She doesn't even bother to finish the sentence and instead picks up the receiver.

"This is Doctor Adebayo," she says. Daniel might be a little delusional about his wife's new boyfriend, but there's something about this call that doesn't seem right. It's that same dread one gets from 3am phone calls about dead relatives.

"Hello, Doctor Adebayo." A woman's voice Imani doesn't recognize. "This is the Director's office. She'd like to see you and Doctor Chun in half an hour if that would be convenient."

Imani hurriedly covers the receiver and says, "It's the Director. She wants to see us."

Imani has never seen Daniel's eyes bug out of his head before. She always thought it was just an expression but, no, they are actually bulging a little bit out from his face. A face which is beginning to turn bright red.

"We can't—we can't—the data. The scenarios—"

"We're just collating data from the first open-ended, multi-scenario run of our algorithm," Imani says into the phone. "Doctor Chun doesn't feel comfortable presenting our data just yet. Would sometime tomorrow work better?"

"She's all booked, I'm sorry to say. She was pretty insistent she wanted to see you this morning. In half an hour."

"We'll head right over."

"Excellent. I'll let her know." The other end of the line clicks with the finality of a courtroom gavel.

"Head right over?" Daniel says. "Are you out of your mind? We can't head right over." He waves his arm around to take in the entire office. "We don't have anything but a list of nonsense. We don't even know how we got these results. No. I won't do it."

"Fine. I'll go and tell her about Phil and the Bar Mitzvah, instead. That's, what—three?—four years of impressive results we can review?"

"I'll get my coat."

* * *

"If we take a shuttle it will take twenty minutes," Imani says as they walk out into a gorgeous day that they totally fail to appreciate or, in fact, notice.

"We're not taking a shuttle," Daniel says. They are both heads-down, typing furiously on their tablets, zipping data back and forth to review, analyze, collate.

"Obviously," Imani says. "But we can't stall too long. We were supposed to be there already." She steps to the side to avoid a bicyclist shooting down the path thumb-typing on two separate phones. She takes a quick look at some of Daniel's calculations and frowns.

"Why did you send me the bees?" Imani says. "You've got the Bees. I've got the Baboon King."

"Do I have Bob Ross?"

"Yes," Imani says, shooting his data back to him.

Halfway to the Director's office, Imani says, "How are you coming on the Bees?"

"They swarm and sting people."

"That's it?" Imani feels a little let down. She'd hoped there would be something more to the bees than just, well, bee things.

"Yes. But there are nine hundred trillion of them," Daniel says. "There are only two trillion in the world today. How's the Baboon King coming?"

"It isn't," she says. "Something happens in 1996 and the whole thing falls apart until 2002. It's like there's a Baboon King, then no Baboon King, and suddenly it's the Baboon King again."

"Maybe it's not really a baboon?"

"Then why call it the Baboon King?"

"I don't—oh. We're here."

Imani looks up from her tablet at the Administration building, an oppressive piece of Brutalist architecture, all hard angles, sharp turns. It's always made her think of a prison.

"Shit," she says, and pushes the doors open.

* * *

The Director frowns at her tablet, scrolls up, taps a piece of data, frowns some more. She's a tall woman who even sitting down gives the impression she's looking down on you. High cheekbones, indeterminate age, hair pulled back into a severe bun. The desk she sits behind is a well-organized wooden monstrosity that looks like it was made from the hull of a sunken whaling vessel. Imani's intimidated just looking at her, but she can't look away. The Director got this position through hard work, brilliance, and a ruthless stubbornness that didn't punch through the glass ceiling so much as burn a Director-shaped hole through it.

"Doctors, I understand you hit an important milestone last night, but in looking at these results I don't think you achieved what you'd intended. What exactly did you intend?"

"We're building an AI to predict global events," Daniel says a little shakily. "We feed it news, historical, cultural, and scientific data from across the globe. At this point it can parse data from four-thousand different languages. We use this to set the initial conditions of our simulation."

All in one breath. Imani is impressed.

"We're essentially simulating the world at a scale no one's ever done before," Imani says more slowly. "With each run the system changes a random number of events from the past and extrapolates what the future state of the simulation will be. Mostly we've been keeping our predictions simple using limited data sets." She glares at Daniel. "Mostly."

"Last night is the first time we ran the algorithm using the entire data set. We, uh…"

"We encountered some issues," Imani says.

"I see." The Director looks at her tablet. "Bees?"

"We decided to focus down on a few scenarios for analysis," Imani says. "For example, you can see one here about the asteroid Apoph—"

"Why are they all apocalyptic predictions?"

"That's part of what we're analyzing. We expected some, but we don't know why the system decided to focus on those. For example, asteroid Apophis—"

"What is the Baboon King?"

"Well, uh. We're not entirely—" Imani says.

"Bob Ross?" the Director says. "The painter?"

"I dug into that one a little further," Daniel says. He zips his analysis over to Imani's tablet. When she sees it her blood turns to ice. "We found—"

"That it was a mistake," Imani says quickly, but it's too late.

"It's not a mistake," Daniel says. "The math says—"

"We think it's a bug," Imani says, jumping in and hoping beyond hope that Daniel will take the hint and stop talking. He doesn't.

"It's not just Bob Ross," Daniel says.

"Daniel. This isn't—"

"It's a fifty-foot tall Bob Ross."

"Daniel."

"A cyborg."

"Daniel, please."

"With laser eyes."

Well, she tried. Imani closes her eyes and wishes the world would fall into the sun. She thinks that might be scenario number 14305. Or maybe 14304. She'll have to look it up.

"The world is going to be destroyed," the Director says, each word a carefully enunciated coffin nail, "by a fifty-foot tall. Cyborg. Bob Ross. The dead painter. With laser eyes."

Well, it was a nice career while she had it. Imani wonders if she could get a job washing test tubes at a remote biolab somewhere. Maybe become a hermit in a cave. Anywhere where she wouldn't have to be reminded of this embarrassment.

"Have either of you seen the budget sheet for your project?"

Imani smells a trap. She knows that any answer, even no answer at all, is the wrong answer. She says nothing, moves nothing, stares straight ahead.

Daniel on the other hand: "It's $15,783,453.18."

Of course he would know. Numbers stick in his head the way hair clogs a drain.

"That's very good, Doctor Chun," the Director says the way she might talk to a toddler. "That's per month. Every month. For the past five years. A total of $947,007,190.80. That's quite a bit of money. Now I know this is an ambitious project but I would have hoped you had come up with something, anything, worth over nine-hundred-million dollars. Instead, you bring me the Baboon King."

"We think he might not really be a baboon," Daniel says.

Imani hasn't had to update her resume in a long time. She wonders what font she should use. Something bold, sans serif. She's a scientist after all. Times Roman is for poets and college students. Arial, maybe even Calibri. Now those are fonts for a scientist.

"Thank you, Doctor Chun," the Director says. "Your contributions to a conversation are always a delight."

"Will someone from HR be coming to talk to us," Imani says, "or do we need to go to them?" Is there a severance package? She thinks there is. A couple of weeks, maybe. She's got enough money socked away to last her a while, but she'll need a job eventually. Maybe CERN is hiring.

"You're not being fired, Doctor Adebayo," the Director says. "You're being reassigned. Your work will be archived and, should I and the Board decide that revisiting your software is in the Institute's best interests, rest assured you'll be the first to know."

"Reassigned?" Daniel says. "Why would we be reassigned?"

"The Baboon King," Imani says. "I don't understand, ma'am, why aren't we being fired?" Not that she wants to be, but you don't blow nine-hundred million dollars and get a pat on the back.

"You're not incompetent," the Director says. She glances at Daniel who looks absolutely bewildered at what's going on. "More or less. This isn't a punishment, it's a matter of dollars. If you'd come to me with something more useful than…Weaponized Saxophone Music From That Shirtless Guy From The Lost Boys, or, let's see, Mole People Collapsing North America Into A Giant Sinkhole, or, and this is a good one, All of The Water In The Pacific Ocean Turns To Velveeta Processed Cheese, then I might have been able to justify continuing the funding. But this?"

"Thank you?" Imani says. "If we won't be on this project what will we be doing?"

* * *

"Analyzing quantum disturbances in the space-time continuum," Daniel says through clenched teeth. "How fucking pedestrian can you get?"

They're on their way back from the Director's office. Imani is still a little stunned. She doesn't know if she should be angry, sad, disappointed, insulted, or relieved. She should probably hate Daniel for bringing up Bob Ross.

Maybe if they'd shown the Director the data from Daniel's divorce. But would that even have done it? Sure, looked at one way it's an impressive example of their work. Looked at another way it's just sort of sad and creepy.

"How dare she," Daniel says. He's almost frothing at the mouth. "Doesn't she recognize just how important this work is?"

"Daniel, please stop."

"I mean, all of those scenarios are perfectly valid. If we'd had time to look at the log files, or rerun the sets with the correct data."

"Daniel, stop."

"Who knows what we could have—" Imani punches him in the face, dropping him like a bag of cement.

"This is your fault," she says. "I don't know how exactly, but it's your fault. Five years of ground-breaking research. Gone. State of the art technology, math that doesn't even have a name, yet. Gone. My career. Gone. Do you have any idea how hard it is for a woman to get into this field, much less position? And you pissed it away with a fifty-foot-tall cyborg Bob Ross."

"With laser eyes," Daniel says. Imani kicks him.

"This is not ending this way. I will not let my career end this way. Get your ass up off the ground right the hell now." Imani has never felt this furious before. Decades of pent-up anger stuck behind a dam of smiles, subservience, and forced laughter at jokes at her expense.

Daniel stands up. Imani punches him again.

"But you said—"

"Shut up. Come on. We're going to the lab."

"Are you going to punch me again?"

"Probably."

* * *

"Our code is still in the system but the data's already been archived and it's being overwritten," Daniel says, his voice thick and nasal. He's tapping at the keyboard and looking at the screen while trying to keep his head tilted back and Kleenex stuffed up his nose. Imani's pretty sure it stopped bleeding about twenty minutes ago.

"But most of it's there," she says. "Enough for us to do a few runs at least."

"The results might get a little weird," Daniel says. "We've lost an entire section on the migratory patterns of the Short-tailed Shearwater to a few thousand calculations of the Dirac Equation, and I think we're about to lose estivation triggering conditions of Achatina Achatina to some bullshit by Schrödinger."

"You were the one who was going on about how pedestrian analyzing quantum disturbances in the space-time continuum is," Imani says.

"Well, it is," he says. "What are you hoping to get out of this? I don't think the Director is going to change her mind just because we run a few thousand scenarios with the right start dates. Especially without all the data. Look, see? There go chlamydia infection rates of the Amish in Nappanee, Indiana from 1852-1857."

It's a good question. What is she hoping to get out of this? The Director's not going to change her mind. Maybe it's not about changing her mind. Maybe it's about something more important.

"Validation," she says. "We put all this work in and even with missing data—oh, hell, did we just lose Pre-Columbian tattoo styles of the Cañari in Ecuador? We put in a lot of work and goddammit I am not going to let my career be defined by the fucking Baboon King."

"If we're going to do this it needs to be now. We're losing too much data."

"Let's do it." Imani grabs her tablet and brings up the console. All their data is disappearing from the servers at an alarming rate. Her finger hovers over the icon that will kick off the simulations.

"What are you waiting for?" Daniel says. "Do it."

"You do it." Imani is suddenly filled with doubt. They're not doing anything wrong. They weren't forbidden from working on their algorithm. What's the harm? Still, it feels weirdly transgressive.

"I don't want to do it," Daniel says. "You do it."

"Goddammit, Daniel, just fucking do it, already." Something on the edge of her hearing catches her attention. Someone calling from the hallway? "Did you hear that?"

"Fine, I will." He grabs his tablet and stabs at the icon with his finger.

All the lights go out.

"What did you do?" The room is pitch black. Computer monitors are dark, emergency lights dead. The only light in the room is from their tablets.

"I did what you told me to do." Daniel's voice is a high-pitched shriek of panic that reminds Imani of a chicken.

Imani flips her tablet around, using it like a flashlight. The glow doesn't reach very far, but enough to show her that there is much more wrong than simply no power.

"I don't think it's a prank." The desks, filing cabinets, computers, monitors: everything is covered in clear plastic sheeting and a thick layer of dust.

Imani leans out the door. "Hello? Anyone?" There are thirty other labs along this hallway. There's always someone in at least ten of them at any one time. But no one answers. She picks up her tablet, heads down the hallway.

She's never seen it this dark before. She knows the layout well enough to find her way but she finds herself stepping past small piles of discarded computers, office chairs, and, for some reason, road signs.

The elevators are out so they head to the first floor via the stairs. They're five sub-basements below ground so it takes a while. By the time they reach the top they're both wheezing and out of breath. Neither one of them keeps up with their cardio.

The lobby is different only in that it's even more empty than everything else. Chairs, tables, wall monitors, inspirational posters—they're all gone. The only furniture remaining is the one long reception desk that's bolted to the floor.

Imani can see out through the grime-covered window that takes up the entire front wall. It's night, but there's enough illumination from a full moon that she can see weeds growing up through cracks in the pavement. In a daze, they push their way through the glass doors and marvel at the emptiness.

"What the hell happened here?" Imani says.

"Uh..." Daniel is looking up. Imani follows his gaze. She's having trouble registering what she's seeing. It looks like a massive, oblong asteroid, pockmarked with craters hanging in the sky. It's brighter than the full moon that she can see just to the side of it.

"How did that get there?" Daniel says. "Did nobody notice this? Did they just not bother to tell us?"

Imani gets a sinking feeling in her gut. She looks at her tablet. It tells her that Apophis 99942 is about to slam into the Earth and kill all life within twelve hours of impact.

She looks up at the sky. Apophis 99942 seems to be agreeing with her tablet that, yes, it is in fact about to slam into the Earth and kill all life within twelve hours of impact.

"This isn't possible," Daniel says when she shows him the tablet. "Our software just makes predictions. It doesn't make them come true."

"Is it getting larger?"

"Of course not," Daniel snaps. "Because it's not there. I refuse to believe there is a giant, planet-smashing asteroid filling the sky that's going to obliterate everything on Earth."

"It's getting bigger."

"No, it isn't. It's—oh, dear god, it is. How is this even happening?"

"Don't look at me," Imani says. "You're the one who pushed the button."

"You told me to."

"That," Imani says, pointing at the growing asteroid in the sky, "is not my fault."

"Well, it's not mine."

"I'm pretty sure everything is your fault." A red glow appears on the asteroid, growing brighter with every second. "I propose we table this discussion until we're not about to die."

"Agreed," Daniel says. "Still not my fault."

"Is too."

"Is not."

"Is—this isn't helping. Any ideas how we don't die?"

"We could try starting another scenario?" Daniel says.

"You think that'll work?"

"No, but it beats standing here and getting vaporized by a rock the size of New Jersey."

"Point." Imani hits the icon. The world goes white.

* * *

"I think we lost them," Imani says, listening to the sound of shrieking primates grow faint. "What were you thinking? We agreed we would *not* antagonize the Baboon King."

"He's an orangutan. The hell was I supposed to do? Accept bad taxonomy? How many is this now?"

Imani leans against the wall of the electrical room and slides down to the floor. Their travels read like a packing list of horrors:

- 374 Asteroids
- 282 Viral Plagues
- 247 Bacterial Plagues
- 118 Nanomachine Plagues
- 105 Global Nuclear Exchanges
- 93 Zombies
- 84 Death Cults
- 73 Dinosaurs
- 42 Vampires
- 37 Ape Revolutions
- 28 Giant Irradiated Slugs
- 17 Lobster People
- 1 Sentient World-Devouring Sponge Cake

"I lost count after the bees," Daniel says.

Ah, yes.

- 1 Bees

Imani's left hand is still swollen from the stings. She was lucky. Daniel not so much. Half of his face is a swollen mess. Maybe they'll find a universe with some Benadryl in it.

That's the working theory: new universes. Or old universes that the scenarios somehow match. From a many-worlds perspective it makes sense. At least as much as anything makes sense. It might explain how they're still connected to the servers, a link to their original universe that's powering the moving to or the creation of the scenarios.

Theories are good on paper, but they don't even have paper. Daniel has a chewed-on ballpoint and his forearm where he's been writing formulae. They don't dare use their tablets for anything but starting a new scenario. Neither of them wants to risk it.

They've been running scenario after scenario, jumping from one to another moments before calamity struck, or at least struck them. In most of the scenarios everyone was already dead. She's seen so many corpses she's not sure what living people look like anymore, and Daniel doesn't count.

They haven't had more than fifteen minutes in each one and most of that has been spent running for their lives.

"I think we might be creating and destroying new universes." She explains about the deletion of each scenario when they shift from one to another.

"That's troubling," Daniel says.

"I expected more of a reaction."

"I'm screaming on the inside if that helps. So, every time we shift scenarios the universe is remade. What about our original universe?"

"Either it still exists," Imani says, "or it was destroyed the second you hit the button."

"I didn't—"

"Fine. Whoever hit the button. My point is, what if we destroyed the world and replaced it with zombie dinosaurs?"

"I hated that one," Daniel says. "The dinosaurs didn't even have feathers. If we destroyed it why are we still connected to the servers?"

"I'm more concerned with why we still exist," Imani says. "Everything else has changed. Besides us, the server connection, and the tablets, nothing is consistent."

"Hang on," Daniel says, pulling out his ballpoint. He's run out of room on both forearms so he starts writing on his left leg. He talks to himself when he does this, usually in response to some unverbalized question. It's like watching a movie where every third scene has been cut out.

"Multiply that by Planck's Constant. Divide by—no. Carry the two. Uh huh. What about the llamas? Okay. The llamas align. Mass of a blue whale added to…huh. Oh. Oh, yes. That works."

"What works?"

"You're right. We've been destroying every universe and making a new one, including the one we came from."

"We destroyed our own universe?"

"Yep. Everyone's dead. We murdered them. Friends, family, they're all gone. Over and over again. Annihilated in a puff of particle physics. The Director. Loretta. This is fantastic."

Imani is appalled. "How is this fantastic? Everyone's dead. Your wife is dead."

"True," Daniel says. "But more importantly so is Bar Mitzvah Phil."

"There is something very, very wrong with you. Can we stop it?"

"We can't," he says. "At least I don't think we can. We'd have to prevent the scenario from happening in the first place."

"Stop Armageddon before it happens?"

"Except that all of these scenarios start years ago. Fifteen of the zombie plagues we've run into all start in a shopping mall in Monroeville, Pennsylvania, in 1978."

"But we keep landing on April 17th, 2021. We'd have to find one that starts today. Let's trace back. What happened when this started?"

"You pushed the button," Daniel says.

"I did not push the button. You pushed the button."

"I have perfect recall. You pushed the button."

"You can barely remember where the bathroom is," Imani says. "Anyway, that's not helping. We were losing data off the servers."

"And then you pushed the button."

"Do you want me to hit you again? We were losing data and it was being replaced with, what did you call it?"

"Schrödinger bullshit. Maybe that's what did it? A bunch of data about alternate universes and such, and our algorithm ran what was there. Poof. Alternate universe."

Imani is studying her tablet intently. "We still have a connection to the servers."

"Well, of course we do. Otherwise none of this would—how do we have a connection to the servers? I don't even have a wifi signal."

"If we have a connection to the servers then maybe we didn't destroy the universe. Maybe it's still there. We just need to find it."

"But all of the scenarios are apocalyptic," Daniel says. "So even if the universe we came from wasn't destroyed, something in it will happen that will end the world."

"So not necessarily destroyed, but humanity's doomed."

"The math says it was destroyed, but yes. We would have to stop whatever is going to happen from happening."

"Hang on." Imani pulls up the log files from the scenarios they'd run before this whole nightmare happened. She scrolls for a couple of minutes before she hits it.

"This one. April 17th, 2021 to April 17th, 2021. Inter-dimensional rift created by two idiot scientists—oh, come on."

"I'd hate to be those guys," Daniel says.

"That's us, Daniel. Our algorithm called us idiots."

"That ungrateful little shit."

"It's math," Imani says. "I don't think being ungrateful is a thing it can do."

"Oh, but the Baboon King can be an orangutan? What else does it say?"

"—sets off a cascade of alternate realities that culminate in the final destruction of the entire universe."

"Well, I wish it would get a move on, then," Daniel says. "I'm tired of outrunning zombies."

"We can fix this," Imani says.

"How? It's already happened."

"No, it hasn't. Everywhere we've been has been right before or right after the end. This is just another potential scenario. If we get there before you push the button—"

"You pushed the button. Ow. What are you hitting me for?"

"Say that again and I'll feed you to the Baboon King. If we can get there right before the button gets pushed, we might be able to keep them—keep *us*—from pushing that button at all."

"Preventing this from ever having happened. What if we get there after they pushed the button?"

"We're screwed. Which, let's be honest here, is no different from where we are now."

"Let's do it," Daniel says, "before the—" He freezes, looking over Imani's shoulder, his eyes filled with a terrified loathing. Imani turns, sees the Baboon King, long, red arms ready to grasp, toothy smile ready to bite. Daniel leaps to his feet and points a shaky finger at the ape.

"*J'accuse! Orangutan!*"

"Oh, for fuck sake," Imani says, and pushes the button.

* * *

People are walking on the grass, looking at their cell phones, tablets, and the occasional book. It's a beautiful day.

They are definitely on the Institute's grounds. But is it the right one?

It's taken them another 13871 scenarios to reach this point, a total of 72363 scenarios. Or maybe it's 72364? Five? She's not sure, and she's not sure it matters anyway. It took too long.

Daniel's lost at least a hundred-fifty pounds. He's just a walking skeleton at this point, his pants held up with a dried tentacle from some cosmic horror they managed to kill before triggering the next scenario. He's missing half his teeth, most of his hair, his left leg is barely functional.

Imani is no better off. She hasn't seen a mirror in at least three weeks and even then she looked awful. Her hair is falling out in clumps, she has boils all over her left arm, only one eye remaining.

"Is this it?" Daniel says. "Please tell me this is it. Please tell me we're home." His tablet shattered weeks ago when he used it to defend himself from tree climbing sharks. They've only kept Imani's powered by a hand cranked trickle charger they found in a sporting goods store.

Imani looks at her tablet and feels a weird combination of relief and dread. They are home.

"Yes, this is it," she says. "Let's go." She shambles down the bike path, everyone turning to look at them. She can only imagine what these people must be thinking. The awakened dead, shuffling gap-toothed across the grass.

She and Daniel have seen that one 18233 times. Amateurs.

"I can't keep up," Daniel says. In answer Imani knocks some guy off a Segway, who runs away in terror. She waits for Daniel to catch up and get on, joining her in a race neither one of them is physically or mentally prepared for.

Security tries to stop them at the building entrance but Daniel gives a Lemurian War Hiss that he learned a few months ago and they back off.

Down the elevator. Down the hall. There is serious work being done here. Everyone is heads-down on their own projects and no one looks out their door.

They hear the bickering three doors down.

"What are you waiting for?" Other Daniel says. "Do it."

"You do it." Other Imani says. They're so close. She can do this. She knows she can do this.

"I don't want to do it. You do it."

One more second. Just one more and they'll be there and they'll stop it. "Wait!" Imani yells, but it comes out as a coarse whisper. Daniel catches up to her, wheezing.

"Goddammit, Daniel, just fucking do it, already. Did you hear that?"

"Fine, I will."

They both collapse at the door of the lab as Daniel and her alternate pop out of existence. They were so close. So close. They hold onto each other. They're the only ones who know what's about to happen.

"I told you you pushed the button," Imani says.

And the universe ends.

Almost Like Snow

Zakariah Johnson

In the sweltering trailer, my drug-dulled mind stirs amidst the rising heat. The malodorous rag I curl beneath each night clings sodden and sticky to my skin as I tug and gather it to my collarbone. The stillness lulls me back to sleep, but then some deep, reptilian instinct jump-starts my impulse for survival and I snap awake at the realization of what the heat and silence mean:

"The solar panels!"

I fling off the grimy sheet and leap to my feet. Sucking in a blast of super-heated air that lathes my throat and doubles me over with coughing, I stagger to the trailer door, pressing the palm of my good arm against it for support until I regain my breath. A mylar curtain covers the door's little window and I draw it aside to peek out. Through the glass, the harsh light of the winter sun rebounds off the thick layer of white outside, assaulting my retinas like a blowtorch. Squinting into the blinding glare, my heart jubilates inside my chest as I gape openmouthed and childlike at the endless white that coats the barren hills of northern New Hampshire as far as the eye can see.

"Snow!" I cry, hearing my voice crack with hope. Then I remember: there's no such thing as snow anymore.

"Ash." The word rasps my throat. Something slides down my cheek, a tear or a bead of sweat, and I fight back the panic that comes with understanding: the new-fallen ash has covered my solar panels. In my opium-induced stupor, I'd slept witlessly as the ash fell, then the storage batteries ran down, the AC stalled, and the temperature inside the trailer crept slyly upward to bake me alive. I wince at the thought of climbing onto the roof with my bad arm, but find myself getting dressed without thinking.

* * *

In the first days after The Eruption, while everyone was scrambling for safe havens and saviors, I'd sheltered in place. Looters ransacked the big box store by the highway, but nobody thought to cart off the real prize: the store's massive AC unit, capable of cooling its 10,000-square-foot interior. The Earth grew cold those first couple months, so no one else wanted it. But I knew what was coming. The roving mobs withered away like the dying plants, the ash that blotted out the sun began falling from the sky, and then the ice began to melt. Fast. And not just on the local ponds: Earth's entire store of ice melted, all of it. The coastal cities are memories now, the high mountains the only places left cool enough to even try to hang on. With the January nights staying in the 90s for weeks, I've dared hope the Earth's climate might be stabilizing again, but by noon the broiling New Hampshire winter sun will still raise the temp outside to a baking 110° F. Without the AC and the solar panels that power it, the trailer will turn into a sauna.

"Get moving, Charlie," interrupts one of the voices in my head. It's the voice of the counter girl at the coffee shop, the teenager with the mole on her neck she was always scratching. "You got to clear them panels or you're dead."

"I know," I tell her. My injured shoulder twinges at the thought of climbing the ladder, but I've already slipped into three layers of robes to trap the cooling sweat against my skin. I glance through the window again to assess the danger. The initial ash that fell from the Yellowstone Caldera was dark gray, but this is white, more like wood ash.

"Was there a forest left somewhere to burn?" I wonder.

Not taking chances, I put on my ski goggles and particle mask to keep myself from breathing in the fine-silica glass that hides in volcanic ash like needles in an apple. I remember the hundreds of victims sitting wide-eyed on the ground or leaning against the walls of abandoned buildings, gasping ever-faster, ever-shallower as their shredded lungs betrayed them, their eyes beseeching me for aid I couldn't give. Walking past them, pulling wagon after wagon of canned goods, my head wrapped, my own breath coming loud and deep through a particle mask that wouldn't have done them any good by then if I'd given it to them, I reckoned from their perspective I must have looked like Death himself. And like Death, I was the last thing many ever saw.

* * *

I'd been the last licensed electrician in Coos County, right up on the Canadian border. I guess I still am, except for my apprentice. I was never a survivalist, but my profession serendipitously supplied me with everything I needed. Everything but pain killers.

Using my good arm, with difficulty I tie off the tablecloth round my head and then slowly open the door to avoid sucking ash inside. Stepping onto the first metal stair, my boot disappears into six inches of powder, raising a waist-high dust-devil. I shut the door behind me as I wait for it to subside. With my next step, I glance toward the storage shed where I keep the ladder. The double-doors are still held together with the big padlock, but they're lying in a triangular heap on the ground, pried off the shed by their hinges.

I've been burgled. *Help yourself* is the new watchword of the age and somebody had sure as hell helped themselves this morning.

"Flippin' hell," I mutter.

"Oh, Charlie," the counter girl sighs sadly in my mind. "I'm so sorry."

Me too, little girl. Me too.

* * *

By the early 2000s, we'd accepted that global warming would exterminate us by the end of the century. Not that we said as much, but inaction spoke louder than words. Fact was, dying via slow-motion suicide was easier than casting off the socio-economic system we'd fought five centuries of bloody wars to perfect—the system that fêted the most grasping among us and celebrated them for their gluttony. Through fanaticism or apathy, we agreed to defend the privileges of our masters to the death. Besides, we figured we had a few good decades left—enjoy the party and the hangover be damned, right?

But then an inscrutable synchronicity occurred, like a 10-point earthquake during a category-5 hurricane. Or maybe the planet itself figured out what we were up to and went for the sucker punch? Anyway, just as the methane ice at the bottom of the warming ocean was bubbling up, just as the thawing tundra was unlocking the whole Pleistocene's worth of carbon to superheat us into extinction, just as the last rain forest was being razed, just then, at that perfect moment when it would cause the maximum harm, the caldera underlying Yellowstone National Park reached its half-million-year reset point and blew the world to hell.

Everyone between Spokane and Cincinnati died the first day. We happy few farther east got to watch as the ash blotted out the sun for a summer, icing the harbors down to Savannah, then fell to earth, acid rain choking every waterway, killing the fish and the frogs, killing the remaining forests one after another. The gases, of course, stayed in the upper atmosphere, jacking up the mean temperature by 20° F as soon as the sky cleared and accelerating the feedback loop: more bubbling, melting, and burning, until nothing combustible remained. When September temperatures down in Massachusetts spiked at 125° F, the radio broadcasts explaining these things to me stopped altogether.

* * *

Approaching the ruptured shed, I find no footprints in the ash. Whoever broke in arrived before it fell. Inside the shed, it's worse than I feared. The useless ATV that hasn't had gas in forever is still there, but the little red wagon I've used to haul water since I injured my left arm falling off the trailer roof is gone, along with enough of my tools to fill it.

"The ladder!" I cry. Panicking at its absence, I kick at the ash, dragging my feet through it until I can't see through the rising clouds. My toes bump something hard and I stoop to grab it. Bellowing in triumph, with my one good arm I pull the ladder from the ash like Excalibur from the stone.

* * *

The ladder's yellow feet sink out of sight in the ash as I prop it against the trailer, shaking it to be sure it's steady. I climb up, broom held in the crook of my damaged arm, ascending the rungs with caution so as not to drop it. Once on the roof, I'm sweating and panting through the particle mask and pause to look around at the fire-denuded hills, the famous New England autumns now a thing of memory. I'd survived the fires by sheltering in a lake. For a moment, I close my eyes, remembering the coolness of the water as the trees around the rim bloomed into orange and yellow flame before toppling. I look down at my foot dangling at the edge of the roof. It might as well be the edge of the world.

"Focus, asshole," chides another voice in my head, my father this time. I tear my gaze from the endless hills of white and get to sweeping. I've cleared about half the panels when the AC kicks on with a whine and I realize the filters are clogged and it's going to burn itself out if I don't clear them immediately. I pause the sweeping long enough to take care of it.

By the time I get off the roof, the pain in my shoulder has grown from a snit to a tirade. I feel on the verge of heatstroke from the noonday sun, but without the ladder I'd be doomed, so I push through the pain, collapse the ladder, and drag it inside the trailer for safekeeping. Then I make three trips back and forth from the trailer to the shed, salvaging whatever's left.

It's deliciously cool when I stumble inside the trailer. I strip off the soaking robes and lie naked on the floor, shivering from the pain and the chills from the plunging temperature as the sweat cools on my skin. Once my core temperature lowers, I stagger to the bathroom where I store my water bottles and food stuffs. The pills I get from the Cave Woman still come in childproof bottles. I have to press the lid hard against the wall with one hand to twist it open. There are three tablets left. I take one and wash it down with half a gallon of the brown-tinged water from one of my three remaining jugs. I sit on the non-functional toilet and lean back as the pain starts to subside and the committee of voices in my head convenes to figure out what to do about the burglary.

I can't let a theft go unanswered or they'll be back. In times of trouble, ethics and empathy disappear like friends who owe you money, but fear and retribution are always good for a ride. The odds that a roving stranger robbed me are minimal. That leaves two suspects; realistically just one, but I need to visit them both anyway: one for my pain, the other for my thirst. Either possibly for retribution.

"Retribution?" Dad smirks. "You'll be dead of thirst in a week with the wagon gone. How you going to haul water when you only got one arm, smart guy?"

It finally comes to me: "A yoke! I'll use the broom as a yoke to carry fresh water back."

"But what have you got left to trade, Charlie?" the counter girl asks.

The committee discusses that as the temperature inside keeps dropping.

* * *

I head out an hour before sunset, dressed in dry robes and carrying the broom front-to-back over my good shoulder, twelve empty milk jugs and one full one balancing the weight. I've got my headlamp loaded with rechargeable batteries, but the moon shines bright enough over the star-white ash I don't need the lamp to find my way to the medicine-lady's cavern.

Even in the early days of the apocalypse, I never carried a gun. Against the armed mobs that roamed aimless and scared after the disaster, a gun would have been merely provocative. And the mobs are gone now. Moving through the dusty landscape, I note the location of each bump in the ash where the dried husks of the dead lie. Clasping each other eternally now in twos or tens, they mark my way like cairns wherever they murdered each other or died gasping for breath in each other's arms. The merry grins of the desiccated corpses I've passed so many times over the years, whose final moments I've reconstructed from supposition and experience, now lie beneath the white. There are no animals left to scavenge them, no vultures left to fly the empty air, so the positions and postures of these steadfast guides for my weekly visits to the cavern and the well never change. Walking through the empty hills, it saddens me to find their bodies and faces now covered and hidden, making me feel more alone.

On an ash-free outcrop, I find the young woman I was looking for and gently lift the child from her chest. The child was perhaps five, but his husk is featherlight. I take the umbrella from beside the counter girl, the mole on her neck indiscernible now in her jerkied flesh. I take her big flashlight from beneath her and fill it with freshly charged batteries. I click the button and, miraculously, the bulb still works. It should be worth something in trade. I reposition the child into her embrace.

"I really hope it was the Cave Woman," I confide to her. The counter girl doesn't answer, so I turn and descend the ridge, trudging through the ash that gives an illusion of cooling snow that I pretend to believe.

"You really care about him, don't you?" she finally asks. "Your apprentice?"

"I just hope it's the lady," I say again, not willing to share the pain of betrayal even with my private ghosts.

* * *

At the entrance to the drug woman's box canyon, I pause to watch and listen. I wait until the last of the talc-like sediment stirred up by my arrival resettles, then unwrap my headscarf and remove the breathing mask for a small swallow from my dwindling water. Nothing stirs above the canyon walls, so I rewrap and proceed until I'm outside her cavern's heavy steel door.

I knock hard and keep banging until she shouts from inside. "Who's there?"

"It's Charlie."

"You alone?"

"Of course."

I hear her fiddling with the metal latch and then the top half of her heavy Dutch door opens. She blinks, gaping at the brightness of the moonlit landscape.

"What?! Did it snow?!" she exclaims, her wrinkled face bursting into rapture at the thought. I give her a moment to savor the illusion before answering.

"It rained ash this morning."

"Ash?" she says, her voice cracking. "But it's white! Does the caldera make white ash, too?"

"I don't know. Maybe there was a forest somewhere left to burn? How are your solar panels doing? I brought some tools and my broom. I can go up and sweep them off, then check your system while I'm up there. And I need more pills." Years back, the old woman had raided the last pharmacy, able to do so because she'd worked there. Her supplies are dwindling now, most long-expired, but there's no place else to get them. Her cellar in the hillside stays cool enough she doesn't need AC, but she still enjoys the benefits of electricity my skills have been able to provide her.

"I wondered why my lights went out," she says, her face re-hardening. She shifts to lower her shotgun and adjusts the grip on the crutch under her other arm. The crutch is new. Is it real, or a trick to fool me?

"What happened to your leg?"

"Slipped," she says curtly. "You're welcome to sweep and tune my panels. But I can't give you much for that. What else you got?"

I sigh, wondering how best to get into her cellar, to look around the cave for my stolen possessions. With an injured leg she obviously hadn't traversed the rocky miles to my place, so if the goods are here I can't very well demand back what she took in honest trade. But I can ask who brought them.

"I'm hurting pretty bad," I tell her. "Let me clean your panels while I can, then I'll show you what I brought. I'll need to cool off before I go to the well."

I watch as she screws up her face and debates my offer and her safety.

"Get the panels working, then we'll parley," she says, shutting the door.

* * *

After a walk up and down her cliffside trail, I lean my bared neck against the delicious coolness of her cavern wall as she picks through the rows of pill-bottles arranged like dominoes over the rocky floor.

"These are expired," she says, scrutinizing a label. "They'll probably work though. It's all I can give you for what you brought." She doesn't apologize, even with her tone; one doesn't live past the end of times by making easy trades.

I hand over three cans of soup along with the big Maglite and the parasol; the latter will be useful in springtime. She hands me the bottle. There are only twenty pills in it. Rather than argue, I pluck one out and wash it down with the remnants of my jug. "Guess we'll see if they work."

"How you holding up?" she asks.

"My shoulder hurts all the time now. My panels are holding up, but if they shut down in the summer like this morning, well…" I turn out my palms in the universal gesture of resignation, then point to the pile of tools along the far wall. "Can I ask who brought the socket wrench set and what you paid for it?"

"You looking to buy?" she asks, chewing her lower lip as she looks away.

"Come on. You know it's mine. Who brought it?"

"You trying to get me in trouble?" she snaps. Then she goes on in a sing-song voice that sounds like a script she was trained to say on the phone years ago: "We don't give out customer information. Besides, I figured you were dead."

"Nope," I say, looking around the cave. "I don't see my wagon. They had it, though?"

She hesitates, then nods. "You should go now."

"All right." I press my good hand against the wall to stand, feeling temporarily strengthened as the opioid pill starts to pry out the talons of pain that grasp my injured shoulder a little tighter each day.

"How about this then," I suggest. "Who did you tell that I'm not healing?"

Apocalyptic
***

It seems farther to the Collective's compound than usual. About halfway there, I pick up new tracks—a set of footprints in the bone-white ash, like Neil Armstrong's on the moon (remember when we did that?) except these have two lines running beside them like the ruts of a toy wagon, my wagon, an indispensable toy now. Once I determine they're heading for the compound, I stop paying attention to the bone cairns and trudge head down following the tracks. As I walk, the empty water jugs balanced on the broom swing in rhythm with the added beat of a tiny maraca—the whisk-like jingle of the pills in the new vial in my pocket rattling with each step, reminding me they're there, taunting me to take another as my shoulder aches a little more with each step toward the adobe fortress.

I pause and look up to check the progress of the moon, figuring it's about midnight. When I look back down, I see a man sitting in a mud-brick tower pointing his rifle at me. I set down the broom and jugs and hold my hands out at my sides to show I'm unarmed.

"Hands over your head!" he shouts.

"I can't," I shout back, then hear him laugh.

"Oh. It's you, Charlie. We heard you were dead. Come on up."

***

The Collective invited me to join when they discovered my aptitude for keeping their lights running, not to mention for fixing the electric pump that runs their vital well. The cult had been set up with their mudbrick fort years before the extinction event. They hadn't necessarily been expecting the Yellowstone Caldera as the instrument of His wrath, but they'd believed something would inevitably happen, and now, who's to argue? Whatever their politics had been before the blast, their leader quickly settled into the role of an old-school village Big Man, a Gilgamesh-like figure who bogarts all property within the compound, including the women, and then doles it out as he sees fit, along with a capricious, self-serving justice. I could stomach a few hours each month fixing their electronics, but I knew I'd cross a line within a week if I lived among them. I'd become an electrician because I liked working alone, setting my own hours. Whatever else the end of the world might have changed, it hadn't changed me. Rather than risk pissing off the chieftain and ending up as another sunken-eyed, grinning corpse atop the hillock of bones outside the fort, I'd turned down the invitation. But I had consented to train one of the young men in my craft in exchange for water. I'd enjoyed working with him in the two years during which his beard had started growing in, but training him had proven foolish. Foolish, because for all the joy it gave me to preserve my skills through him, my success as a teacher had left me with less to trade. Foolish, because he'd known exactly what was in my shed and how to use it. The druggist hadn't robbed me. That left one suspect.

I think these things waiting outside for the fortress doors to open. When they do, two men with rifles beckon me inside and begin to frisk me.

* * *

"Thanks for the tea," I say, reclining against the six-foot-thick mud wall in a room that's even cooler than the healer's cave.

"Civilization must be cultivated to survive," says the big man on the cushion across from me, raising his China teacup with a grin. His black beard and hair are both braided with blue beads, a new look for him, but I don't inquire. A string of LEDs along the ceiling provides the light for the night's activity. At a table across the room, two young women and a much older one prepare cornbread for the solar oven in the courtyard. A brace of toddlers topples around the women's heels. At a bench along the adjacent wall, a young man with a bare wisp of a beard repairs a headlamp with a soldering iron, pointedly avoiding my eyes. As the big man pours out more tea, the youth and I finally lock eyes long enough for me to know he's guilty. Before I can say a word, one of the children, perhaps two years old, runs toward the young man, wailing.

The big man's eyes flash like furnaces. "Shut that kid up! Can't you see I have a guest?" One of the younger women breaks away from the others and rushes for the child, who's now pulling on my former apprentice's pantleg. The woman and the young man don't look at each other as she sweeps the child up in her arms and hurries away, but they also don't tense up in close proximity, and the young man doesn't shift away from the woman whom everyone knows the big man considers his personal property.

The chieftain glares at the woman's turned back, then at the man at the bench. I know he's also seen what I saw, but the youth has skills the Collective needs. I read the competing thoughts of murder and need roiling over the chief's face and realize I've saved the young man's life without ever meaning to. The chief rolls his bulk back in my direction, clapping his hands in false glee as a toothy smile breaks open in his beard. "Oh, my children!" he laughs, shaking his head mockingly. "Oh, my children, my children. More tea?"

"Yes, please."

"How's the shoulder?" he asks as he pours, cocking an eyebrow knowingly.

"Better, thanks," I lie. "It was just a fall."

"Mmm. That's all it takes these days."

He sips the fragrant tea—I have no idea what it is—and watches over the rim of the cup as the infants patter around the women's legs.

"Come to Papa!" he bellows, stretching an arm toward the one who'd been clinging to the young man. The same woman as before breaks off her work and presents the child to him. He takes it and it immediately starts wailing. "Woman!" he barks. The mother takes it back, the big man giving the infant's face a mock slap as he passes it to her. I catch the silent young man watching from the corner of his eye, never pausing in his work. He notices me and turns away.

"You listening to me?" the leader grunts from his cushion.

"Sorry, what?" I say, sipping tea to hide my lapse into thought.

"I said our well isn't producing as much this week," he repeats, then adds under his breath, "I think it's going dry. We may have to start rationing…or maybe cutting off some of our less-essential members."

"Are you sure it's not the pump? I could take a look."

He waves a dismissive hand. "The pump's fine. The boy there can fix it. The problem's with the water. The rains…." He breaks off to flick a quick glance at the women, then leans forward to speak in a conspiratorial voice with me. "When will the rains come?"

"Soon. The ocean isn't far. It has to rain sometime. I just need twelve jugs filled."

"Can't do it," he says, shaking his head as he leans away. "I can fill six of them for you. But you have to fix the wiring for the oven—and then you'll leave us your six other jugs. We need the storage. No discussion."

"I can't last a week on six gallons! You don't feel you've already stolen enough?" I snap, forgetting myself and where I am.

"What are you talking about?" he barks. I'm about to answer when I see my apprentice quivering at his table in the corner. I look back at the leader. He's angry, shouting now, perhaps merely bloviating to cover for my insult, or maybe…no, he's genuinely offended.

"What are you accusing me of?" he shouts again. "And you, a guest in my house!"

I've been looking for my possessions since I walked through the gates, but I haven't seen any. The druggist told me she'd mentioned my injury to one of the young women, no one else, but now I see that any of them could have robbed me in the night. I calculate the newly-bearded boy must be thirty years younger than me, and with two working shoulders. The big man's hand rests on the butt of his pistol.

"I'm sorry," I say. "It's just the pain talking."

"I thought you said you were better," he replies, mollified, smirking in victory. His voice begins morphing into my father's in my head.

"I'm fine. I just need water."

"You'll get what I offered, no more," he says, dumping the dregs of tea onto the tray between us.

"And next time?" I ask.

He shakes his head. "There'll be no more water for trade until it rains."

* * *

The rising sun is a raspberry smeared across the horizon when my property comes in view. In my drugged and injured state, I opted for the longer but flatter and safer route home. About halfway back, my particle mask finally clogged and I removed it, adjusting my headcloth to cover my mouth. I'm sure now this new ash isn't volcanic; it has a different smell and texture to it. Perhaps a forgotten forest burned, or even a city. Somehow the thought that there was something left to burn is uplifting, hopeful even. There may be something that remains.

Descending the final hill, the back of my neck starts to tingle. I turn and see clouds coming fast from the western sky.

"Rain?" I dare to hope, though it doesn't smell like it. I arrive at the trailer from the rear. Rounding the corner, I see the front door hangs open.

"Hello?" I call, my voice cracking.

I set down the broom bearing the too few jugs of rancid, yellow water, swallow hard, and call again. No one answers. The ash on the stairs has been knocked away. Despite the open door, when I enter the trailer, the interior smells of recent visitors, the stench of unwashed humans growing on us each day like our hair and nails. In the bathroom, I find my remaining tools gone, along with my canned goods.

"You have more food hidden behind the shed," the counter girl says, scratching at her mole. "You can survive this!" So far, so good, I'm thinking. She's right, the food is replaceable—then I find something that isn't: half the batteries I recharge daily to run the big AC through the night are gone. It will be useless now after sundown. I'll wake up covered in sweat every morning through the remaining winter, and by summer…

"You won't see the summer," she tells me. The edge in her voice conveys a bitterness tinged with victory; my final companion, turning on me at last. Was it the flashlight I took from her?

I step outside to retrieve the water jugs and notice something I'd missed before. In the ash are three pairs of footprints: two adults and a child. They show where they grouped together at the shed, then turned and headed north. The rolling tread of a single tire, probably a wheelbarrow, forms a line in the middle of one set of footprints. More tracks show someone pulling my stolen wagon, the smallest footprints sticking close enough they may have held hands as they fled. The prints remind me of something I saw on television once, of a set of footprints fossilized in the ash of an African volcano a million years ago when a family of unknown survivors walked away from their ruined lives toward the unknown. What were they called?

"Laetoli," says the boy, the man now, my last apprentice, though I know he's only talking in my head. "The Laetoli footprints."

"That's right," I answer. "Laetoli. I remember now."

Before I can say more, a roar rises behind me. I turn just as the gale of ash engulfs me with a gust that staggers me back. Gagging on a mouthful of ash, I grasp blindly for the broom with the water jugs, close my fingers around it, and rush up the stairs into the trailer. I barely have time to slam the door before the trailer moans and rolls off its moorings. Tumbling round in the bouncing trailer, I feel nothing as the wind rolls it over and over again until it catches on some unseen obstacle and halts as glass from a shattered window above me rains down. I lay on my back against the wall that's now the floor, the door blocked by the ground it rests on. Through the smashed window above, white ash pours in like water from a hydrant. I reach back to push myself up, but the bones of my injured shoulder grind and pop, my arm flops useless, and I fall back into the deepening layer of white.

With my good arm I reach for the pills in my pocket, press the bottle against the wall with one hand and twist it open. How many to take? One? Two? All of them? Blinded in the swirling haze, I hear my wheezing like the voice of someone far away as the ash coats my clothes, my face, and, with each gasping breath, the insides of my mouth and throat. The sediment pouring over me casts shadows which become black spots in my fading vision, three little spots that turn into the parade of a tiny family trudging north.

"Wish them luck," Dad says, reaching out an arm to lift me from the thickening mass of ash that covers me in a shroud almost like snow.

Shadows Behind

Violette Malan

"Boss wants you."

I pressed my eyes tight shut so no one would see them roll. Of course the Boss wanted. "It's someone else's turn." I'd only just come in from seven days on the road, tramping all over the ruins of an old shopping mall with Maklaren, his dog Spark, and the new guy, finding only one artefact that had probably been a toy in the first place. Even my eyelashes were tired.

"Get up." Usually there's a tone of *before I make you* in Maklaren's voice, but not this time.

"Is this it?" I kept my voice low. "Are we ready?" But when I saw the look on his face I knew that Mak wasn't here to put our plans into action. Even Spark looked upset, like he was ready to bite someone. Of course, he looked that way a lot of the time.

"What gives?"

"Client."

Okay, that made a total of *no* sense, which might explain why Mak was worried. In all my time with the Boss I'd met, what, maybe three clients? Yawning, I stood up as slowly as I could. Once I was on my feet Maklaren turned and went out without even looking back to see if I was following him, which of course I was. The ten-by-twelve room held nothing but three sets of bunk beds covered by three sets of grimy sheets, the windows closed over with scraps of junk wood that seemed to let in everything but fresh air. Where else was I going to go?

The front room was a little more comfortable with a sofa, two arm chairs, and a huge big sheet of cloudy plastic nailed down over where the window glass used to be. I'd heard they were making glass again, that someone had found the recipe in a pre-mage-era book, but even if it was true, I hadn't seen any. Nor was I likely to.

Everybody knows what happened. The Mages College had been in charge of things for as long as there had been things. Longer probably. Story was there came some disagreement at the College between two different and equally powerful mages. Some said it was more subtle than that. All I know is, once the shouting was over, the mages were all gone and civilization with them, though the sky was still blue, the grass still green, mostly, and birds still sang, in a way. Some smaller cities like this one survived. Other, bigger places are mostly piles of rubble where no one but scrappers went.

Scrappers like the Boss.

I straightened up and tried to look interested when I saw the client sitting to one side of the window space. He was older than I expected, so he was better than most, otherwise he'd have been caught and hanged long before he reached this age. Maklaren took up a spot by the doorway, Spark sitting next to him. The client was so nice and neat I wished I had another coverall to change into, or that this one was clean. Seemed the client agreed.

"*This* one? This is your best?" Looked me up and down, a line forming between eyebrows too black to be natural. Maklaren frowned at the guy's tone, and Spark curled his lip in a silent snarl.

Maybe I was a bit raggedy, and more than a bit unwashed, but I really was the best in the Boss's crew. Best at tracking down old magical artefacts, best at finding pockets of usable magic power, and best at storing it until it could be sold to the highest bidder. Best ever, was what Maklaren had told me once Spark had let him know I was okay to talk to.

"Don't let appearances fool you," the Boss said now. "She's small, but her capacity hasn't been reached yet."

Time was a bit of praise like that would have made me warm all over. I knew better now.

"If she's so good, why are you willing to sell her?"

Wait. What? I thought the Boss planned to lend me out on a job, like he had once before. Maklaren had gone with us—this was before he'd found Spark. No way the Boss would trust a client to bring me back—or me not to take off. He didn't trust anybody. Leave your harvesters running free and the next thing you know they've set up their own gang. Word said that's how the Boss got started.

"How do I know she's worth the price?"

I clamped my jaw so tight the muscles in the side of my face hurt. Stupid, stupid, stupid. Seems like I'd actually thought—after everything I'd seen—that the Boss would never sell me. Other people, sure, but not *me*. I was special. When I heard Maklaren shift behind me, that's when I really knew, beyond all doubt. All our plans to get away just shadows, just dreams after all.

"Examine her yourself if you don't believe me."

Clients don't usually touch us directly, that's what artefacts are for, and I was too numb to flinch when this one grabbed me by the chin, even though his fingers were icy cold and hard, like the bits of tile flooring left in the bathroom. I wasn't carrying power, though, so I didn't know what he expected to get out of "examining" me. Then I felt a sharp, pointed thrust into my brain, pure power spearing through, cold like a jagged chunk of ice. The sharpness felt like it stirred around in my brain, went down my throat and through my bowels. My legs collapsed under me, and I felt Maklaren's familiar grip on my upper arms holding me up.

Suddenly it was over and I was dry retching. Maklaren gave me the subtlest of shakes and I did my best to get hold of myself, but all I wanted to do was fall on the floor and vomit away the feeling of the power searching though me.

I knew it was possible to transfer power person to person, but most clients didn't want that—didn't want to be touched by the likes of me, someone like them but less lucky. They wanted power stored in an artefact they could take away with them. This guy had only used his power to check me over. What he didn't know—nor the Boss neither—is that doing what he'd done had shown me what *his* power was like. That he hadn't bothered to examine me more gently didn't bode well for my future.

"She'll do," the mage said, "but one hundred's too much. I'll give you thirty."

I stopped listening. I knew the boss would eventually stick the mage for as high as he could get, I'd heard him do this before. Too same-old to listen to, even if I was the one being sold.

I know what you're thinking, but you'd be wrong. It's not like I could have gone to security services for any help. People blamed mages for the fall of the world, and what we were doing, collecting magic and selling it on, was about as illegal as it could get. A death sentence in a lot of places, even if the mob kept their hands off you. It's definitely illegal to be a mage, which makes it illegal to have the kind of talent I have, sniffing out artefacts and pockets of power in the old places for sale to others as beyond the law as ourselves.

There's not so many of us who can sense all these leftover bits and pieces, spots where the power still exists, we're just the shadows the old mages left behind. Most of it's concentrated in the rubble of the old cities, that being where the old mages set up. Nowadays those with power are real careful— don't want to get stoned to death, which still happens in some of the more crowded spots. Or so they say.

Another thing they say is that back in the day people like me were sent to the Mages College to be trained, taught how to manage the power without burning out. Seeing the mess they'd made of the world, I was just as glad all that was too far back in the past to matter to me.

The bargaining looked to be coming to an end.

"If you won't pay more I might as well keep her." The Boss sounded bored. "Tell you what," he added, nodding slowly. "Give me seventy-five and I'll give you twenty per cent off on power. You can fill her right up."

The mage agreed to that, and the Boss set me up to absorb some power. The mage must have bought pretty much all the Boss had on hand, even the little bit in the toy I'd just brought in. I had to keep swallowing to keep it all down—not that it's in my stomach, that's just how I manage it, mentally. The Boss had already turned away to recount his cash, but Maklaren kept his eyes on me until the last minute. I'd never seen that expression before. At the very last second, my last sight of them, Spark got to his feet and he and Maklaren both looked sideways at the Boss. I *had* seen that expression.

The mage walked me out by the lead attached to my collar. Even if I'd wanted to ask for help, no one seeing the leash and collar would have paid any attention. Since the world ended, lots of people sell themselves, or their children, or their neighbors' children, just to make ends meet. I wouldn't have asked for help anyway. I figured anything had to be better than the Boss's place. Too bad I was wrong.

We walked about an hour before reaching a main road where the mage picked up a runner with a two-wheeler. She took a route I didn't know to just outside of the city, one of those areas where the houses all look alike. We got out on a corner and, after he'd paid her off, we walked another mile or so, turning corners and backtracking before we reached his house. He had his workshop fixed up in what would have been a two-car garage, if there was still enough magic around for the roads to work. I've never seen a car on the road, though I've siphoned off the power from one or two I've found buried in rubble. Some of those had dead people inside them.

We had to go through the house to reach the workshop; he'd welded shut the doors that would have rolled up out of the way of the cars. The first thing I saw was shelf after metal shelf covered with artefacts. I'd never seen so many in one place before. Full up as I was, I could tell some of them even had wisps of power remaining. Once he'd locked the house door behind us, he unhooked the leash and pointed to a stool against the wall shared with the house.

"Sit." My legs felt the magic in the order and I sat. I'd no idea there was anyone this skilled around—nor anyone with enough power to waste it this way. "Sleep here." He pointed at the pile of rugs and blankets under the worktable next to my stool. "Bucket," he said, nudging it with his toe.

"Food?" Two could play at this game. He blinked at me, just as if the stool I was sitting on had spoken.

"Later." He tapped a set of bowls—some crockery, some metal—with the index finger of his right hand. The Boss had a couple of these; they used to be self-heating he told me.

Starting the next day, after he had me empty the bucket, the mage fed me some absolutely flavorless mush for breakfast and started me powering artefacts, to figure out, if possible, what they actually did. I got interested despite myself.

Once he was working, it was like he couldn't stop talking, not like it was being recorded, but like he was talking to himself. He never really spoke directly to me unless to give me an order.

"Found this one myself," he said, picking up an artefact that looked like a small glass box, a shimmery blue color. "At the site of a Mage school in Carletin City where no one else would go. I hoped I'd get a lot more but Security took over that section before I could go back. Who knows what else there might have been?"

He put the thing into my hands. "Must be a neutral box, can't be anything else. Place your fingers here, thumbs there, concentrate." He went on lecturing me on it like I'd never seen neutral boxes before. People trying to be mages always paid high for them, figuring they stored important artefacts. Sometimes that was true.

All in all, it was sort of interesting. I wasn't tied up or anything. I don't think it occurred to him that once he'd told me to stay I wouldn't stay. But I was like Spark—Mak might tell him "Stay!" but he decided for himself whether to do it or not. So I had a good look around the place, though I was careful always to be sitting on my stool whenever I heard him coming. Couple of times at night I thought I heard snuffling outside, especially around the welded door. If I'd been kidnapped or something these would have been the perfect times to start screaming. But I figured it was probably a racoon. Plenty of them around.

One day maybe two weeks after he bought me he came in with a basket and set it down on the worktable to the right of my stool and my bed. It was one of those baskets with a handle in the middle and two lids that opened one from each side. He got as far as untying the cord holding down the lid nearest me when he heard the chime that warned him someone was coming up the front walk and he took off fast, though carefully locking the door behind him. I was amused to see the basket moving as if it had something alive inside it. It didn't worry me, I figured I could deal with whatever was small enough to fit inside.

They say people used to keep animals in their houses. Plenty of them got eaten in the chaos after the magic fell. Even if you loved your dog or cat or guinea pig too much to eat it, your neighbors might disagree. People with starving children have to do what they can.

Nowadays people like Maklaren train dogs for hunting, hauling, and so forth, now that most of the machinery has finally stopped working. I think people just like to have dogs around, but there's practically nobody rich enough to feed something that doesn't pull its own weight. Maklaren found Spark hurt in the ruins one time and nursed him back to health. Lucky for the dog, otherwise the Boss might have turned him into stew.

Cats got eaten, too, but they're better at staying out of sight, and less dependent on people. Plus, they help keep the rodent population down, which keeps other food safe, so people aren't so ready to kill them. And there have always been cat people, just like dog people.

So I wasn't really too surprised when a kitten pushed its head out of the top of the basket and plopped out onto the table. Kind of grayish with spots. Cute, fuzzy, big eyes, big ears, teeny little tail. The mage didn't have much experience with animals, that was certain, or he wouldn't have left the basket open.

The kitten got to the edge of the table and looked at the floor. I was afraid it would try jumping down and hurt itself. Maklaren told me once that all cats fall neatly on their feet all the time, even from heights as relatively high as this one, but kittens? I wasn't so sure. This little guy seemed to be having trouble getting her back feet coordinated with her front.

I jumped out of my chair and caught her just as she was about to tip over the edge. I rubbed my face against the soft fur, I don't know why, and the little beasty pushed her head against me. We were touching noses when I heard the front door close. I scooted over to my corner, tucked the kitten into a fold of my blankets, and climbed onto my stool. "Stay still," I whispered to it. Footsteps paused while the mage unlocked the door. My kitten moved around a bit, then settled down and started to purr. I'd never heard anything so loud come out of anything so small. Fortunately, just as the door was swinging open, she fell asleep. I didn't know they stopped purring while they slept, but I was sure glad.

The mage opened the basket, setting off some frantic mewing. He frowned for a second and then shrugged. Nice and quiet, I let out the breath I'd been holding. Maybe he wasn't sure how many kittens he was supposed to have.

"Not easy to get so many at once with no questions asked." He left the basket open and took a large glass bowl out of the equipment cupboard. "People used to keep fish in these bowls, back in the day." I couldn't see how you could grow fish large enough to bother with in that bowl, but what do I know. He set the bowl down on the table, not far from the basket of kittens, and turned back to me.

Up until then the mage hadn't used me for power himself, he'd just had me power up other things. This time it was different. I expected the cold, sharp power spike like last time, but now it was more like an icy hand reaching down my throat, the feel of phantom fingers enough to trigger my gag reflex. I tried to pull away before the hand could reach my guts.

"Hold still, damn it." He grabbed my hair and used it to hold my head back. I almost wished the hand was real so I could bite the bastard.

Finally, he finished and let go of my hair. I had to grab the stool I was so shaky.

What happened next was pretty awful, so you'll have to bear with me.

He went back to the basket and grabbed a kitten. It squirmed in his hand and tried to reach around with its tiny legs and maybe bite him with its tiny teeth, but he held it too firmly. He put it into the big glass bowl, taking care not to bang it against the side as he inserted his hand.

The kitten snagged his sleeve as he pulled his hand back and he had to reach in with the other hand to get it to let go. It was all I could do not to laugh. I didn't see how, but just as I thought he'd have to smash the bowl in order to get both his hands out he managed it. He put the back of his wrist to his mouth and sucked on it. The kitten must have snagged more than his sleeve.

He took the bowl over to the water barrel and opened the tap. I couldn't see at first, but when he had to shift his grip I saw that he was filling the bowl with water. The kitten was meowing and swimming okay, but he didn't stop until the bowl was about two-thirds full, too deep for the beastie to put its feet on the bottom. Then he brought it back to the table and fitted a lid on it. The lid had holes to let the kitten breathe, but that didn't help in the long run. I guess it didn't really take long for the little scrap of fur to exhaust itself and drown, but it felt like forever. I'd closed my eyes long before it was over. Not that it kept the tears in. My kitten woke up somewhere along the line, but somehow knew to stay still and quiet.

"Nothing," he said, shaking his head. His shoulders looked disappointed.

Luckily, he wasn't paying attention to me at that moment, because I'd finally figured out what he was doing and I know I made a bit of a choking noise. There are lots of stories about where magic comes from—not just the bits we find lying around, but where it comes from in the first place. So there was a theory that said killing something released magical energy. I knew he was going to test that by killing all the kittens. Maybe each one in a different way until he was sure, one way or the other. More tears leaked out of my eyes, but I couldn't stop. He was still absorbed in what he was doing, so he didn't see.

My kitten was thinking of coming out from under the blankets. "Oh, don't move, oh please don't move," I thought at it. I don't know whether it actually heard me, but it stopped moving. I must have made another noise because this time the mage turned around and focused on me.

"Stay," he said, pointing at me.

Later, I told myself there wasn't anything I could have done. If I'd tried to stop him I would only have ended up dead myself. As it was, I wouldn't be long for the world if he found out I could move.

I had to keep telling myself that.

When I held still he seemed satisfied and started closing down for the night. He could only stay so long in the workshop with lamps burning before someone would notice. He was very careful about that. He hesitated at the door, looking over his shoulder before coming back for the basket and carrying it away with him.

My kitten came out as soon as the mage was gone, climbed up my clothes into my arms and patted my face with her paw. Her toes were cold. After I'd finished sobbing, I wiped my face off on my sleeve, the kitten clinging to my shoulder the whole time. I don't know how much she understood of what was happening, but she didn't seem to want to let go of me, like she felt safer staying with me.

Safer than the one I'd let die, anyway. My tears weren't all for the dead animal. Some of them were tears of rage. At him, mostly, and at myself, for sure, for doing nothing.

I won't describe the next three days, I just can't do it. And all for nothing anyway. None of the deaths released any power, no matter what horrible thing he tried. Every night I checked the room all over—nine times, ten—looking for a way out, and for the ninth or tenth time I didn't find one. That didn't change the fact that I needed to escape, and I had to take my kitten with me. And I had to make sure he didn't come after us.

Which meant I had to kill him.

I realized then that up until the mage started killing animals I'd fallen into thinking like I had when I was with the Boss. I was warm, fed, had a place to sleep. All for not that much effort on my part. I'd fallen back into that lazy mindset where I thought I was too valuable for anything bad to happen to me.

As if sitting where I was sitting right now didn't put the lie to that idea.

And it would only get worse. *I* couldn't think of anything worse, but I knew *he* could. Maybe he'd try other animals, and then maybe people, like a street kid, someone no one would miss, or at least not for long. Someone like I'd been before the Boss found me. And once he'd used up the stored power, what would stop him from killing me?

My kitten stopped chasing something I couldn't see and raced over to tag me on the ankle. I never knew cats grew so fast. In just a couple of days she'd grown too big to climb up my pant leg comfortably. I scooped her into my arms and she bumped my chin and touched me nose-to-nose like she usually did—before suddenly jumping from my arms and taking a dive into my blankets. I was sitting nice and straight in my chair when the mage came in.

This time I must have moved something without putting it back exactly right because once he'd shut the door behind him, he stood with a fist on his hip looking around, frowning. His foot began to tap, and finally he froze and—

"Sit." He didn't point this time, he patted the air in front of me with both hands, and suddenly my legs wouldn't move. I could feel them, and the stool under them, and the pressure of the rung against the bottom of my feet, but I couldn't move them.

"Did you think I couldn't count?" he said to me. "It didn't matter to me that you kept a cat hidden, so long as it was here when I wanted it." He turned back to the door. "Did you know that dogs and cats are natural enemies? Will the animal release power if it's chased and frightened to death? What do you think?"

I wouldn't give him the satisfaction of an answer.

As soon as he was out the door I tried to move, really tried. Nothing. I couldn't feel anything at all. Beginning to panic, I tried sucking the magic out, but it didn't work. All I got was a numb right foot, so I stopped before it got any worse. All these nice weapons in the room, tools and knives and such, and I couldn't do anything about it. Why hadn't I hidden a hammer or something close to the stool when I had the chance?

Though there was still one person in the room who could move.

My kitten jumped back into my lap, hissing in the direction of the door, and then looked up at me. "That's right," I said. "He's a bad man. We have to kill him."

She blinked her eyes slowly, purred for just a couple of seconds, then looked straight at me and blinked again.

"You can understand me, can't you?"

Purr. Blink.

"I can't move. You'll have to do it. Can you?"

Arched her back, feinted left, batted me on the nose.

I took that for a yes.

I scratched between her ears. The kitten wasn't big enough to pick up the hammer herself—and even if she was, she still wouldn't have opposable thumbs—but I remembered the scratch on the mage's wrist. She had claws. Five on each foot. Twenty altogether. And if the claws were big enough, she wouldn't need a hammer.

We had to be ready for when he came back. I worried that the kitten would be easily distracted, being young and a bit fluffy-headed, but I worried for nothing. Whether she caught it from me, or whether she had reasons of her own, that cat was as focused on killing the mage as I was.

I rubbed my thumb between her eyes. "You need to grow," I said. She stood on my thighs and touched noses with me again, her paws on my shoulders. "But I don't know how to do—"

She patted me on the nose, rubbed her head against my chin, then touched her nose to mine. Gave me a look that I swear said "How slow are you?"

"Oh." I felt like laughing. How could I be this smart and this stupid at the same time? Until I started doing it on purpose, I hadn't realized that I must have been feeding the kitten little bits of power since I'd picked her up the first time. Nothing else explained how easy it was now. I used to wonder why animals—even Spark—did that nose-to-nose thing, especially moms and babies, and now I figured I knew why. They were sharing some kind of power.

I'd only managed to give her a bit more size when we heard him coming back. This time my kitten went no further than under the stool, where my feet obscured her. I'd been fairly sure he wouldn't notice her right away, because he rarely looked at me that closely, and I was right. He was looking over his own shoulder as he came through the door.

That's when I saw he had a dog on a lead. He was scraggly, wiry, short-haired, alert. At first I thought it was Spark, which was dumb. True, most dogs look pretty much the same, but this one was too dark, and then he growled at me and Spark would never do that.

Unleashed, the dog ran immediately toward me and the kitten took off, climbing up me fast enough to leave scratches as her claws hooked through my clothes. She launched herself from my shoulder, drawing the dog away from me, and he turned, following her with his eyes, like he was figuring out where she was going to land.

"Hmm it's bigger than I thought. That's no good." He made a complicated pass in the air with his right hand and the dog became bigger—larger mouth, with more teeth.

It took the wolf/dog a minute to get oriented to his new size, but he finally had my kitten cornered, and all she could do was dance and hop in a strange, straight-legged way, hissing and spitting, her fur all on end like she was trying to make herself as big as possible, which still wasn't very big, even after all I'd done.

I don't know what the dog had been told to do, but once he had her cornered he didn't advance at all, just dodged from side to side, like they were dancing. I knew it wouldn't take long for the kitten to tire, and then she'd be killed, maybe even eaten. I rubbed and pinched at my legs, but they didn't move any more than they had before. Desperate, nothing to lose, I raised my right hand, copied the gestures the mage had done, and flung power to the kitten.

This time I could feel the power leaving me and I remember thinking that no matter what else might happen, at least *he'd* never get it.

Where my kitten had been was the largest cat I'd ever seen, almost twice the size of the dog. Back legs longer than the front, thick fur a glossier gray with darker markings like spots, ears made pointy with longer hairs, though her tail remained stubby. Was I seeing what she'd look like when she was grown? The dog backed away, not cringing, but a deliberate, careful movement, designed, as I later figured out, to get himself out of the line of fire. She leapt through the space where the dog had been and landed on the mage's chest, knocking him over backward and sinking her fangs into his face.

The guy screamed, trying to get a grip on the scruff of her neck, but she had her huge front paws gripping his head with claws fully extended and her back legs began to tear at his belly. His hands were free but she was too close to him; if he aimed any magic at her he'd hit himself as well.

A week ago I would have looked away, too squeamish to watch, and maybe I'll feel that way again, but right now nothing gave me so much delight as watching my wild cat rip his stomach open.

Suddenly I was free, but I fell off the stool, my legs too numb to hold me. When the pins and needles began, I thought I'd die of cramp. I used the residue of my own power to help myself; didn't want to lose any limbs, not now. I relaxed as I felt it flow down into my legs.

The kitten lost its wildcat size and, calm as anything, sat down to wash herself, paying particular attention to the toes of her back feet. Meanwhile the dog—just a dog again now—barked and wagged its tail, coming over to me and nosing at my legs and feet and barking again. Had their fighting been just an act? When I didn't get up right away, he started licking my face and whining. This close I could smell the soot someone had used to make him look darker.

"Spark?"

He barked and bowed down onto his front legs, tail up and wagging. He trotted to the door and scratched at it, looking back at me and whining some more. Of course, the door only opened with the key. I would much rather not have had to search through the mage's pockets, considering what his opened bowels smelled like, but I didn't want to stay here any more than Spark did. My kitten came over to help me, but all she managed to do was get more blood on her paws—and on me when she climbed up onto my shoulder again. Finally, just when I thought I'd have to stop or puke, I found the key in a back pocket and staggered to the door.

Maklaren stood leaning his left shoulder on the wall, just outside. Spark jumped into his arms, something I'd never seen him do before. Mak jerked his head toward the garage space.

"He dead?"

"Yeah."

Mak smiled the biggest smile I'd ever seen on his face. "You know who should be next?"

"Yeah."

"Let's go then."

We were about a mile away when I thought to ask him. "How did you find me?"

"Followed the dog."

Author Note: The opportunity to have a character named after him was a Kickstarter perk purchased by Chris McLaren. You left the details up to me, Chris, so I've made you the only human in the story who has a name.

A Tale of Two Apocalypses
Flesh as a Roiling Wave, the Mind as a Dismal Oubliette

Eleftherios Keramidas

VIII

Yiannis' feet shuddered and he could feel them again. Then, his ankles. Then, his shins. When the shiver reached his lips, half-congealed blood oozed down his chin; no sound was uttered, his empty lungs hung limp in his ribcage. When the spasm reached his eyes, he opened them and looked around. Nothing had changed; it couldn't have been more than a few minutes since he fell.

He braced his elbows and pushed. Inch by inch, he slid his torso off the iron rods piercing it. The rough metal claimed tatters of fabric and flesh. His punctured innards made wet, sucking sounds as they came free.

He got up. He had to will his legs to stand straight, his fingers to relax from the curl of dying agony. In this new state of being, there was no natural stance, no reflex activity. And everything seemed to take too long. He felt the signals from his brain course along his nerves, flickering slowly like the fluorescence of a moribund lightbulb.

At least there was neither any pain nor the ravaging hunger he had expected. His thoughts were clear, transparent. His senses picked up everything, as before, and he processed even the slightest detail, with a mind uncluttered by sentiment and instinct. He was a being of pure intellect now; intellect that would never, ever dull.

His kin were shuffling down the street. Day and night, they would keep going, as fast as they could, until something worth their attention came up. He started dragging his feet towards them. He didn't bother with an attempt to call out. Even if his punctured lungs proved able to channel air for speech, he was sure the others wouldn't pay attention. Communication was beyond them. Not language itself; Yiannis understood the street signs. He just dismissed words. They were but noise; they carried no more meaning than the thump-thump of a dripping tap. With the distorting veil of emotions out of the way, gone also was the illusion that something may span the abyss between two human minds.

Yet, company was still valuable. With a totally numb body, Yiannis was in danger of becoming lost in thought and memory—of friends and family lost. Of her. Others like him served as a reminder of the passage of time, of the need to feed. Also, only with assistance could he hope to trap prey, slow and clumsy as he had become. As far as he knew, consuming living flesh was the only way to sustain his existence, and he was determined to sustain it. Dying had involved much more than physical suffering, an anguish he would rather not go through again.

There was also another reason for Yiannis to seek his own. A prisoner of his private world, stuck in the tiny cell of his mind, with no recourse to madness, he needed distractions, aid in his futile struggle against the ennui of forever.

THE END

* * *

FLESH AS A ROILING WAVE
by
Yiannis Nikolaou

ONE

"I'm hungry! Are we eating already?"

I hate the tone kids use when they insist on an impossible demand. The little girl's whining distracted me. I missed the iron lid and struck my hand instead, slashing the flesh from thumb to middle finger. I growled, dropped the flint shard, and tried to staunch the flow.

The kid kept pestering me, unfazed by the sight of blood. "Why is it taking so long to light the fire?"

"Shut up!" I exploded.

She scowled and huffed. A child's ire is a feeble and fickle thing, but her dislike for me was deep-seated. I could see it in her eyes, as blue as her late father's. And it hurt, because in everything else she was the spitting image of

Eleni, who approached us and hugged the kid protectively, without sparing me even a glance. Making her daughter loathe me wasn't exactly paving my way to her heart.

"It's getting dark," she said, coldly. "Without fire, we'll be defenseless against the mutants."

"Come here, darling." Kostas belatedly snapped up the chance to pretend that he cared about the child.

He was sitting on a fallen pylon, a dead cat on his lap. Even with no bullets left, he was still providing meat for all four of us, at least one meal per day. My job was setting up camp and it seemed I was no longer capable of even that, now that the lighter was out of fluid.

I sighed and picked up the iron lid and the flint shard again.

VII

Yiannis sat heavily on a pile of insulation boards. His soul felt hollow, like the walls of the unfinished building around him. He looked at her dead body, lying on the rough cement floor, and a sob shook him. The tears were a release, a relief. They washed some of the pain away. When they stopped flowing, he decided there was only one thing left to do: kill himself. If he could find no other way, he would just go out in the street and let them get him.

A rustle close by gave him goosebumps. One moment, he was set to commit suicide; the next, survival instinct took over. He wiped his eyes with his sleeve and scoured the room with his gaze.

He heard a shuffle.

He glanced at the floor and immediately wished he hadn't. It was her, she was stirring. Not dead anymore. Not alive either.

He sprung up and took a few steps backwards, stumbling on bricks and planks. Those things were weapons; he could use them. He imagined bashing her head in, impaling her on one of the iron rods that stuck out of the cement, pushing her out a window. The mental images appalled him more than the horrid reality before him did.

Slowly, she rose. She lifted her arms, finally offering him a hug. Her eyes were empty but, as she strained towards him, she opened her full lips, the lips he'd longed for years to taste. Her teeth were white and perfect, one more reason that he loved to make her smile. Now those teeth would gnaw his flesh, unless he acted.

He burst into tears again. How could he defend himself if that meant harming her? And yet, if he let that mindless thing consume him, his love would turn to hatred. There was only one way out of this.

He ran. He went straight for the balcony, which had no railing. He didn't stop at the edge. Off to the ground, to oblivion without staining his mental image of her. He closed his eyes.

TWO

"A dad, a mum, and a kid," Kostas said, as he searched through the ruins. "Me, Eleni, the girl. You're superfluous, Alex."

I hefted the wooden pole I had found. I could use it for the night's shelter. Or as a club. "You've had your chance."

He pretended he hadn't heard me.

"You could have married her after you got your doctorate," I insisted. "Instead, you dumped her. You'll dump her again, if you find someone younger where we're going. I know it, you know it, she knows it."

"Does she, now?"

I scoffed.

"How long do you think it will take her to figure out what you think of her kid, Kostas? It's just the two of us here, you can say it out loud; you don't give a shit. Women want stability. Women Eleni's age, with children, more so. Especially now that everything is in shambles."

I shut my mouth before any more crap could come out. I had spent my teenage years dreaming that Eleni would choose me over Kostas. Choose me for who I am, not for what I have to offer.

My rival had paid no attention to what I'd said. He was upturning broken cement slabs one after another, a task I could not accomplish without a lever.

Suddenly, he jumped back and swore. I thought he might have uncovered a snake or scorpion and I rushed in with my makeshift club. It was actually a mutant that had surprised him, a speckled rosy thing with countless hair-thin appendages that rippled like the tentacles of a sea anemone. It was tiny; before the plague turned it, it might have been a baby. Or an animal. We lived in constant fear that some strain of the virus would spread to pets, livestock, wildlife.

I struck the creature. Its blood oozed, too viscous to splash around. Gripping the pole with both hands, I lost count of how many times I hit the little monster. In the end there was nothing left, just a smudge that looked like a trampled orchid.

Kostas grabbed my arm and dragged me away. I thought he was trying to shake me back to reason. He squeezed my hand. Something stung me where the flint had sliced my skin open a couple of days before. I pulled free. Too late; a tiny black thorn was sticking out of the wound.

Kostas smiled conspiratorially. He showed me his own palm. It was riddled with quills. He'd gotten infected, and he'd made sure he'd infected me too. I looked at the ichor-splattered piece of wood I still clung to. I had to kill him, before he mutated and turned on Eleni and the girl. I had to kill myself, too.

But I was a coward and did nothing.

Footsteps broke the tense silence. Eleni. Kostas looked me in the eyes and licked his dry lips. I knew she wouldn't make it alone. She needed at least one of us along, if she and her daughter were to reach safety. Attacking Kostas there and then would probably result in both of us getting killed. I was armed, he was much stronger.

"What happened?" she demanded.

"Nothing important," I said.

From where she was standing, she couldn't make out our wounded palms. She scolded us for having yet another argument. And that was that.

VI

Yiannis couldn't stand still. Every now and then, he peeked out at the corpses that roamed the streets. They were opening doors; searching for victims, since Makis had escaped them in his way.

Their slow movements got on Yiannis' nerves. At least they stayed clear of the construction site. The half-finished building seemed to offer poor shelter, so they just skipped the trouble of going up all those flights of stairs, as he had hoped.

"Come, please," she called.

Her voice was hushed, but the invitation was enough to make his mouth go dry and his hands start shaking. He sat close to her on the cold floor, too timid to touch her. Unexpectedly, she laid her head on his shoulder. As she was taller, she had to slump. Her long hair fell on her face, spread on his chest. He barely kept from brushing it off her cheek, from caressing it. Was this the right moment? He hesitated, got angry with himself, hesitated again. He realized he was holding his breath, to savor the sound of hers.

As softly as he could, he moved even closer. She did not respond. Maybe she had fallen asleep. He put his arm around her shoulders. It felt like hugging one of the cement pillars of the construction site; there was no connection, no rapport.

"Listen…" she said.

It took him a moment to decipher the word, it was barely audible. Was she going to express remorse for all the times she had rejected him? Some other regret? He leaned slightly towards her, ready to shush her with a kiss.

His empty stomach rumbled, ruining the moment.

A sob wracked her. No, not a sob. A retch. She puked, making a mess of her face, her hair, his shirt.

"This is how it started with the other teacher," she told him when the convulsions subsided, her voice louder now, relieved. "She got sick first."

"What?"

"I'm dying."

He fell silent for a while. Then there was nothing to say. She just exhaled one last time and went limp. He caught her and lay her gently on the floor. He stood up and started pacing, his mind empty.

THREE

The stubble on Kostas' chin looked like bristling quills. Or so I thought, with the shadows of the sunset playing tricks on my mind. Eleni and the kid, talking with him, weren't giving him any funny looks. They weren't even concerned that he kept rubbing his palm on his dirty jeans.

The color of the sky was darkening, while the itch was getting unbearable. It tormented me every night, with no respite until daybreak. I had taken to sleeping with my palm under my armpit, tossing and turning but refusing to scratch it. I did my best not to draw attention to my injury.

The slash had almost healed. The itch could as easily have been a symptom of scar tissue forming, but I knew there was something new inside my body. The aches in my limbs were definitely growing pains.

I thought I saw something green on my skin. I put my palm next to the flames and stared at it until I could make out deformed bones inside my fingers, glowing ghostly. Afraid my guilty secret was in the open, I looked anxiously at my companions. Skeletons sheathed in flesh; two healthy females—one adult, the other a child—plus an adult male that was not fully human anymore. I tried to rub the osseous sight off my eyes. It wouldn't go away.

The kid approached me. I could hear her joints cracking and popping with every step, I could hear the tides of her marrow. Her lithe bones shone bright green under the skin. I was drooling, my jaws millstones ready to grind. The night breeze pushed away a lock of tawny hair and revealed the girl's tiny ear. Oh, how I longed to nibble that cartilage! She would make such a fine appetizer before I got to the adults!

The kid halted when she was two steps away from me.

"Mom says we have little water left. Tomorrow we must find more."

Her words meant nothing to me. My hunger for bones was all-consuming. In the distance, I could hear more monsters; they roared, they screeched, they squealed, they howled, they barked. I wanted to add my voice to theirs. I was focused on the kid's ear, on her scraggly neck. I crouched, ready to pounce.

Over the child's shoulder, I saw Eleni giggling as Kostas whispered to her. She was touching his wrist. I am no expert in body language, but I knew what that gesture meant. Soon, they would ask me to keep my eye on the kid, so that they could have some personal time. Beaten, yet again.

I burst out in bitter laughter, taking everybody by surprise. Even the beast inside me. Before such a human reaction, it cowered and fled.

V

Makis leaned his back against a construction site's rough wall. He was shivering, his face pallid and sweaty.

"I can't go any further," he said. "Give me the gun."

"Only one bullet left," Yiannis protested.

"One is all I need to end this. They're free to have me for dinner, but I will not become like them."

Yiannis looked at her for help, but she averted her eyes, still too shocked. Or maybe she thought she could have no say in a quarrel among her saviors.

"It's all we have," Yiannis said. "The car is gone, the crowbar's gone."

He had tried to sound firm, self-assured, but he felt his cheeks blush, turn the damned red that always betrayed his sheepishness.

His wounded friend snorted angrily.

"That gun belongs to me. Hand it over."

Yiannis bit his lip, but did not comply. Makis bent over and grabbed a brick from a pile lying by the construction site's entrance.

"What are you doing?" she gasped.

"I'm not doing anything," Makis said, as he offered the brick to Yiannis. "He is. If he won't let me shoot my brains out, then he must crack my skull open. You owe me that much, Yiannis. Me and Lanky saved her while you were busy pissing your pants."

Yiannis fumed. He grabbed the brick from Makis' hand. He hefted it. He lifted it over his head. He focused on Makis' deadpan eyes.

He let his arm drop limply by his side. He couldn't, he just couldn't. He threw the brick away, delivered the gun to his friend and turned to go, without any farewell.

"The bang will attract them," Makis said. "There are many floors in this unfinished building. Go hide upstairs."

Yiannis motioned her to follow. She did, but put her hands over her ears. If only something like that could help. The gunshot would never stop reverberating in his mind. And he hadn't even heard it yet.

FOUR

Kostas, perched on a pile of car tires, was skewering the day's game: pigeons and rats. I put the water can and firewood down and wiped my forehead with the back of my hand. My sleeve hung loose around my emaciated arm. Scales were forming on my skin, but I was certain the others could not see them. Their eyesight was only human, after all.

"Hey, kid!" I called.

She scowled for a moment, but then saw the gift I had for her and squealed with joy. At her age, the pinwheel was a poor excuse for a toy. She wouldn't have bothered before the pandemic. However, she seemed to need it as much as I had needed to see the clump of white flowers growing where I found it. Such reminders of the bygone world, slivers of hope for the future, kept us going.

And now that I no longer played at being her father, it was easier for me to like the child.

I approached Kostas.

"How are you holding up?" I whispered.

He gave me a puzzled look; neither of us had broached the subject. Then he got my drift. He shrugged. He glanced at the girl. She was running around to catch the wind, too far to hear us.

"I'm fine," he said. "No discomfort at all. I don't think I'm infected after all."

His constitution was much stronger than mine, so it made perfect sense that he didn't have any symptoms yet. I could not trust him to show the same self-restraint I had shown, though, and not harm the girls. I contemplated killing him as soon as I felt my own will weakening.

"Oh, I forgot to mention I found some kindling," he said and threw something at me.

I recognized the garish cover even before I caught the little book in the air. *"The Mind as a Dismal Oubliette and Other Tales of Horror."* And right beneath the title, my name.

Had he ever taken the time to read my one and only published work, he would have recognized thinly veiled versions of himself, Eleni, and me in the main story. No point telling him now. No point in vanity either. I started ripping pages out of the book and stuffing them between the logs that would become our campfire for the night.

IV

"Burn them!" Makis screamed.

He was swinging the crowbar, crushing heads, smashing arms, spilling guts. Occasionally, he had to fire the gun to avoid becoming pinned or getting bitten. He hadn't managed to jam the double doors shut and now he dared not retreat from the threshold, for fear that the dead would swarm out and surround him. They slipped in the gore, got entangled in their own dangling entrails, stumbled. All while trying to grab him. There seemed to be no end to the hungry corpses ready to emerge from the elementary school.

"Burn the fuckers, for God's sake!" Makis screamed again. "Burn them!"

Yiannis had the can of gasoline in one hand, the lighter in the other, but he had frozen, unable to cope with the horror. Only a few of the things had been adults—teachers. The rest were kids, the cartoon characters on their brightly-colored clothes soaked in blood.

She stood right behind him, screaming so loud she almost drowned out Lanky's cries of pain. Lanky was a strong man and he was thrashing wildly, but the monstrous children bit chunk after chunk of flesh off his prone body. On his shins, his forearms, and his shoulders, nothing was left but bare bone. Yet, somehow, he was still conscious, still in agony. Maybe the saliva of the revenants kept their victims out of shock until the very end. They hadn't gone for his neck—did they want to savor his pain for as long as possible?

Yiannis looked on as more grown-up corpses came. Cloying black blood oozed from tiny-sized bite-marks on their clothes and flesh. They must have been parents who ran to school when they saw the news. They forced Makis back, strode over the dismembered bodies, and shuffled towards Yiannis and her.

That jolted him back to his senses. He was there to protect her. He upended the can over Lanky and those that were making a feast of him, then he retreated towards the schoolyard's entrance, leaving a gasoline trail behind. He lit the end and everything went up. Lanky screeched even louder than before. But the risen just stopped moving and waited for the inevitable. Their stiff legs could not make the jump over the flames.

Makis landed next to Yiannis. His hair and eyebrows were singed.

"I did it," Yiannis mumbled. "I manned up."

"A bit earlier would have been nice," Makis retorted.

He still had the gun, but not the crowbar. He needed a free hand to keep pressure on his bleeding shoulder.

FIVE

We ran, tripping over garbage and rubble.

We had put too much faith in our campfire. Mutants had always kept their distance; I was even getting more and more uncomfortable around flames myself.

That night, they conquered their fear. They attacked us, kept coming even though we struck them with burning logs. They chased us—galloping, trotting, crawling, gamboling, each freak in a class by itself.

Springs from a gutted mattress snagged my shin. I didn't feel any pain. And our pursuers did not actually scare me. There was something…familiar about them. I could almost make out words in their grunts.

One of them rushed me. I rained blows on its head as we rolled on the broken tarmac. I got on top, bludgeoned with the torch again and again. Out of the corner of my eye, I saw Eleni and the kid retreating before a creature that looked like an oversized spider with too many legs. When my opponent stopped struggling, I hit it once more to be on the safe side and then ran towards the girls. Two shaggy beasts blocked my way.

"Help them!" I yelled to Kostas, who was swinging his torch to keep something slimy and vaguely feminine at bay.

He heard me alright—his mouth twitched, he half-turned his head—but decided to ignore me. It was a matter of life and death to him. His life, the death of others; no contest.

That was the first time I thought of surrendering to the virus. With monstrous strength, I could probably save my companions.

NO! I resisted. I couldn't risk it. If I stopped reining myself in even for one second, I might never regain control and end up attacking Eleni and the child instead of helping them.

I lunged with my torch at the shaggy monster and its patchy fur burst in flames. Screeching, it raised its arms, as if beseeching the heavens for help. Its twin mewled in horror and ran away. The rest of the pack followed suit, reminded why they had been afraid of fire.

Kostas was bent over his opponent. I ran to his side and found him strangling the she-monster. His T-shirt was torn, revealing a chest full of stripes, some of them an angry red, others discolored. He was craven and had given in, had embraced mutation to ensure his survival.

I was craven too, in my own way. I fished a shirt from his bag and covered him, keeping the truth from Eleni.

III

As long as they made it out of the city before there were roadblocks, everything would turn out fine. Their car had a full tank. Taking turns behind the wheel, they could reach safety by dusk, some place without people, living or dead. Then, they would wait the whole thing out. They had camping equipment. They had canned food and bottled water. They even had a gun—Makis wouldn't say where he got it.

Lanky turned the key in the ignition. Yiannis knew he had to go with them. It was the sane thing to do. And yet...

"Get in," Lanky urged him. "What are you doing, standing out there on the pavement like that?"

"I've locked them up," he said, pointing behind him, at his house. "My family."

"Not your family anymore," Makis responded. "Not people, even."

"At least you know what's become of them," Lanky said. "My home is on the other side of the country and I can't reach anyone on the phone."

"What about the rest?" Yiannis insisted.

"What rest?" Lanky said, confused.

"Everyone," Yiannis whispered, fighting back the tears. "Everyone else in the world. What happens to them?"

"The same thing that happens to you if you don't get in the car right now," Makis barked.

Yiannis opened the door and took his mobile out of his pocket. They weren't likely to have electricity where they were going, so saving up battery time was a good idea.

The phone rang before he could switch it off. It was her. Of all people.

"Hello?…Where are you?…Where?…At work?…Don't cry, girl. I'm coming for you."

As soon as the call was over, he told his friends:

"We have to go pick her up from the school."

Makis got out of the car and grabbed Yiannis' arm. "Are you nuts? There's no time to spare."

"I can't leave her behind. In this madness, she chose to call me for help. Me!"

"You honestly think she didn't try her boyfriend first?" Makis said. "I saw him die more than ten minutes ago, so he obviously didn't answer. If he had, she wouldn't give a fuck about you now, whether you'd make it out of this mess or not."

"But—" Yiannis stuttered and gave Lanky an imploring look.

"We're getting her," Lanky declared. "If it was me asking, I would expect you to help without making a fuss. You know, all for one and whatnot."

"I withhold judgement until I've seen the one for all part," Makis grumbled.

SIX

The kid's screams woke me up:

"Monster! Monster!"

I jumped to my feet. I couldn't see any mutants around; maybe the girl had had a nightmare.

The itch in my hand was hellish. I tried scratching it and realized my skin had become hard and uneven. Glancing down my arm I saw thick green scales covering it all the way to my elbow.

Kostas came closer, armed with an iron rod. He seemed unwilling to hit me, but I knew he would if I tried to reveal that he was infected too.

"Go!" he shouted, not that furiously.

Eleni was cowering behind him, her eyes on her daughter. The girl was paralyzed with fear. She was so close I could touch her. I *wanted* to touch her, taste her, lick her bones clean, then slowly grind them in my mouth.

Full of disgust at my own wretchedness, I ran away, over fields of rubble and seas of debris, until I became exhausted. There was a fireplace that stood untouched amidst all the wreckage. I crawled inside it, hugged my knees, and cried myself to sleep.

* * *

II

"Yiannis?"

"Yes, Efterpi."

He used her name, since she hadn't responded to "grandma" for years. Her frayed mind mistook him for the Yiannis he was named after, her younger brother, who had died sixty years ago.

"Bring me my headscarf, please, Yiannis. I want it here by my side. Tomorrow I'm going up the hill, for the feast day."

The hill with Saint George's church atop rose on the island she had grown up on, six hours away by boat. Even if she were there, she could barely walk to the bathroom, let alone up an incline. The doctors had sent her home because there was nothing else they could do for her; they had recommended she spend her final days with her family.

No reason not to humor her, though:

"I'm fetching you the headscarf right now."

As Yiannis was crossing the living room, his mobile rang. It was Makis. Yiannis grabbed the keys to the front door and signed to his parents that he had to go outside for a moment. His mother got up from the couch and headed for grandma's room. His father was rotating through the TV channels, watching all the newscasts at the same time as usual.

Yiannis had expected a missed call from his friends, but the mobile kept ringing. He answered it.

"Sorry I delayed your camping trip, but I really need the book I asked Lanky to bring along," he said. "I'll be out in a sec."

"We're not there," Makis replied. "And forget the book. Forget the whole PhD thing for a while. This is your chance. Her boyfriend is out of the picture. Gone. Dead, I mean. Not sure what kind of craziness went on, it was a couple of minutes ago, me and Lanky just happened to be around. Most probably she doesn't know yet, so don't call her now; let someone else be the bearer of bad news. But do make some time to be there for her during the next few days. Console her any way you can, if you get my point."

"Don't talk like that, man! It's—it's terrible."

"Spare me your useless sensibilities. Your luck has changed. Just for once, don't wuss out."

Yiannis was speechless. Not because of what his friend was saying; his father had stopped pressing buttons on the remote control. The screen was full of corpses. Corpses rising up and attacking people. The anchorwoman was quaking, white as a sheet. Some brass hat was assuring her that there was absolutely no reason for panic.

A shriek echoed from grandma's room. Yiannis hurried there and found his mother sprawled on the floor with the old woman squatting on her chest, biting her cheek off.

Grandma had expired quietly. And then she had come back, ravenous for flesh. Modern films be damned, it wasn't a virus. Everyone would rise, as soon as they died of any cause.

SEVEN

I shadowed them, keeping secret watch over their camp every night. I hadn't mutated any further, but it was a hard fight against the transformation and it lasted from dusk till dawn. Kostas, on the other hand, showed no signs of discomfort. I grew certain that he would make it to the end of the journey without turning.

The change came upon him suddenly.

I rubbed my eyes, bleary from lack of sleep. When I opened them again, he was on the ground, shaking. Hard angles formed on his body and tore his clothes to pieces. I charged, but before I could get there, he was on his feet again, now a crimson and white thing with an exoskeleton and jagged chitinous forelegs.

My shouts woke Eleni and the kid. They screamed when insect-Kostas reached for them. I punched him before he could do any harm. My scaly fist was superhumanly—inhumanly—strong; he dropped like a stone. I stepped on his chest to keep him down. He butchered my ankles and tried to get up. I staggered, felled him again. His shiny thorax made a hollow sound, a crack forming near his neck. He fought some more, feebly. I kicked him away with my wounded legs. Another punch would have killed him and I wanted to avoid that; he had let me go when I started changing, I owed him the same.

When he got far enough and I could no longer feel the presence of his bones, I turned to Eleni and the kid. They were hugging each other, quaking with fear. Fear of me, not Kostas. I would have laughed, had I remembered how to.

* * *

THE MIND AS A DISMAL OUBLIETTE
by
Alexandros Andrianakis

I

Makis, a duffel bag hanging from his shoulder, spotted Lanky's car in the parking lot of the university dorm. His friend was already behind the wheel.

"Everything ready?" asked Makis.

"Yiannis just called. I have to go back inside and get him a book he really needs for his thesis."

Makis winced.

"Let me guess. The bitch's boyfriend has this book. And Yiannis can't be in the same room as the guy that's banging the girl he likes, even for five minutes. Sometimes he gets on my nerves. He said he doesn't have time to come camping with us, but I'm betting you a six-pack he won't do any work on the PhD while we're out of town. He'll just snivel for the whole week or write another story where everyone else turns into a monster and he's literally the last man on Earth, but he's still getting friend-zoned. Flesh as the Surf, and shit."

"Flesh as a Roiling Wave," Lanky corrected him. "I liked it. I thought the ending was on the bright side. Which means he's coming around."

Makis opened the passenger door, dumped his bag on the back seat, and got in.

"Coming around, my ass. If he was, he would be here, getting the fucking book himself. You're not helping him, you know. He has to understand that she won't give him a chance even if her boyfriend is…I don't know, hit by a bus."

"Sometimes you're just grouchy for the sake of being a grouch," Lanky said. "I'll go get the book and then we're out of here."

A howl coming from high above made them look up. Someone was standing on a balcony, flailing his limbs wildly. He was drenched in blood from head to toe, but Makis could tell it was the man Lanky had been about to visit. The guy's shoulders drooped and then he fell, head-first. He landed not two feet from the car's fender, his skull smashed, his brain staining the parking lot's bare cement.

"Oh, shit," Lanky mumbled. "Oh, shit. Oh, shit. Oh, shit."

"Get. In." Makis pulled him to his senses, although he was shaken himself. "Let's go, before the police show up and keep us for questioning. We don't know jack shit about this mess, anyway."

EIGHT

Kostas is back, along with others of his kind. Our kind. I can hear the mutant hordes amassing on hills formed from collapsed apartment buildings. I can feel their transformed bodies. They gather, they work themselves into a frenzy, they dance. The roiling wave of flesh is calling out to me, its plash and crash invite me to join in on the feast that's coming.

But I am closer to their prey than they are. If I wanted to eat Eleni and the kid, I would be already done with it and would not have shared a single morsel. I have decided to defend the girls until daybreak drives all us monsters back to our holes. Or until I'm dead.

The army of many shapes gets tired of waiting. They swarm from the hills. Like dark rivers, they form a sea coming to drown me. The disease is enticing me to give in, to let its strength course through my arms and legs. I resist. Not yet. Not until the very last moment. All these days of restraint, the mutation has been boiling in my veins, furious, mustering its power to bend my will. I will reap this bottled-up force and be ten times the beast I would have been if I had just chosen the easy way out like Kostas, like every other cur out there. They surrendered to the infection as soon as they felt it stir inside them, as soon as they heard the plash and the crash.

Freaks surround me. They drag me to the ground. I groan and my jaws grow huge. My breath is steam, my voice a roar, my claws the size of a sword. I rise and start dismembering. I crush bodies with my tail. I finally taste bones and they are as delicious as I had expected.

My mind is shutting down. Soon I will be a creature of instinct. My short story about the thoughts of the living dead missed the mark entirely; even a monster is slave to its character, its nature, its conditioning. For most men, survival at the cost of others is a given. For me, it isn't. Some of the infected are motivated by envy for those still healthy. I'm not. Other mutants feel they have to accept themselves no matter what. I don't. I can hear the plash and the crash whispering something different to me. Telling me to be the monsters' monster, their bane.

Even after full mutation, I'll still be alone.

THE OTHER END

Zodiac Chorus

James Enge

I know more than I remember, so I don't really know what I know.

For instance, I was in the back seat of a car driving north along the Mississippi. It was late afternoon. I remember looking westward and seeing the broad water glare suddenly with fiery light and there was a roar unlike thunder. The sky was clear but marked with something like jet contrails. It happened again and again: the light and the earth-shaking noise.

"Are those *meteors*?" I asked finally.

There was an embarrassed silence. Everyone else seemed to know what was going on and no one else seemed to think it strange.

"I guess so," someone up front said finally.

Someone beside me suggested that we leave the car and go down by the river's edge. They argued that the river bluffs would give shelter from the meteor impacts. It sounded pretty naïve.

Nobody else said anything. The meteors continued to fall. We continued to drive north.

We were deep in a city now, still going north. It was strangely empty. Almost no one was walking on the sidewalks or driving on the streets. There was a tang of smoke in the air, like autumn in the old days when people still burned leaves. But it wasn't autumn, as far as I could tell.

We passed an intersection where a woman stood, an infant in her arms, next to a stalled car. A cop in a Ramsey County sheriff's uniform was walking indifferently away from her toward his own vehicle, talking on his radio. I met the woman's gaze as we passed: her eyes were darkly ringed, despairing; her mouth a dark open wound.

"Shouldn't we go back and give that woman a ride?" I asked.

Nobody else said anything. The meteors continued to fall, bright scars in the darkening sky. We drove on north through the gathering dark.

* * *

I remember hearing someone's voice: "I hate to say this, but I think Will is dying." I was shocked and sad, and I looked up to put in a good word for Will. That was when I saw they were all looking at me. Well, their faces were invisible in the dark, but I could tell they were facing me.

We were standing next to the car on a street at the outskirts of town. The car was gleaming in the shadows. I could hear the engine running but there weren't any lights.

"You understand, Will," said another voice, another shadowy form—one who seemed to be the leader. "We can't waste resources on someone who's dying anyway."

They waited then, as if they expected me to argue with them. I didn't really have a clear sense of what they were talking about, so I didn't.

One by one they got back into the car. The last one to turn away paused for a moment and said, "We're sorry, Will. Sorry about you. About Amanda. About everything."

"That's all right," I said, and they shut the car door and drove away. I didn't know who Amanda was; at least, I didn't remember her. I guess it's not the same thing.

They still weren't using the headlights, and someone had smashed the red runner lights in back. I could hear the car long after I couldn't see it anymore.

I went south from there, because I didn't want them to think I was following after. Also, it made just as much sense as going north.

The meteors continued to fall. They were less frequent than they had been, but they seemed to be bigger. The earth shook and shook under their impact.

* * *

It's mostly the dark times I remember. Maybe I sleep during the day; I'm not really sure. But I do remember coming across an old-style religious tract which explained, with helpful cartoons for the subliterate, that the meteors had been predicted by Nostradamus and St. John the Divine as a harbinger of the End Times, and that everyone who belonged to one particular religious sect was damned. It went on to add that everyone who didn't belong to another religious sect was also damned, which seemed to make the first assertion redundant. The cartoons, though not the text, depicted some sort of space explosion as a source of the meteors.

"An attempt to divert an asteroid on a collision course with Earth?" I wondered aloud. "Didn't they realize that most of the fragments would take the same path down the gravity well, so: 'Bedtime for Bonzo?'"

I remember saying that to myself, but I'm not sure who Bonzo is or was. The tract was titled, "BEDTIME FOR BABYLON!"—maybe that's where I got the idea. I dropped the tract in the street and kept walking south.

With all the fragments that had fallen and were still falling, I figured the space object they'd tried to destroy must have been pretty large. Maybe planet-sized. Even if they succeeded in shattering something like that, the leftovers would be enough to put to bed both Babylon and Bonzo.

* * *

I remember there was a bandage on my head that smelled terrible, so I took it off. Sometimes my head hurts; sometimes it doesn't. I wouldn't exactly say it ever feels great, though.

* * *

Then, or maybe it was another time, I came to an intersection where I saw the rotting corpse of a woman holding a bloated dead baby next to a burned-out shell of a car.

I don't know how it will sound, but that was an encouraging moment for me. I wondered if this was the place we had passed by earlier, and then I realized that I remembered it, that I could remember things now. I've been trying harder to do that since. That's part of what this is, why I'm writing this.

There was a weird feral noise coming from the shadows of a nearby storefront. It was like the sound fighting cats make, except there was only one cat. And, after I listened to the sound for a while, I started to think it might be coming from a human throat. Not a place to linger, so I stopped doing that.

* * *

I couldn't go any further south from there. Downtown had been hit by a meteor, a big one, and whatever hadn't been flattened was burning, so I turned aside. I don't think I was going south anymore. I don't know which way I was going, or how long it took me to get here, but eventually, somewhere down along the river, I came across this house where the lights were on and the front door was open.

A sunburst of hope lit me up inside. Electric light! An open door! After the wilderness of dark windows and shattered storefronts and empty streets, I felt like I was coming home. Here was a bit of the old world, the world I couldn't even remember, but the one that I felt was right and true.

The house must have its own power generator. That's all I can figure. But as soon as I stepped through the door, I gave up most of my hope and settled for the idea of scrounging what I could.

The place was pretty well smashed up. Some of the destruction was obviously from looting; much of it was merely malicious. Someone had smeared shit across an oil painting and then pounded on it with a fist. What's the point in that? Lots of holes in the walls, too—not like someone was looking for something, just the impact of fists and stray objects, a few bullet-holes.

The kitchen was pretty thoroughly wrecked, but most of the canned food was there. I took a lot of it, and a can-opener and some other utensils, putting it all in a canvas shopping bag I found. Why not? The others, the ones who had been through here before, they must have had a reason for leaving the food behind. Maybe they knew they wouldn't live long enough to benefit from it. Maybe they just didn't like canned food.

There's this one room in the back of the house; it's almost untouched by the tide of wreckage. I found the door standing open, but nothing inside was broken, not exactly. There's a dead man here, though, slumped over a slanting desk that looks like an architect's drawing board. He wasn't murdered by the looters; he'd slashed his left wrist (the lengthwise method, used by those who know what they're doing). He'd been an old guy, but his corpse looked pretty healthy as corpses go (I was becoming an expert), and he was reasonably well-dressed. His weapon of choice was an X-Acto blade, now lying on the floor underneath the slack bloody hand that had slashed his bare bloody wrist.

On the drawing-board was a letter, addressed to me.

TO WHOMEVER FINDS THIS.

That was me, right?

It began with a kind of cartoon drawn in ink. There were constellations in the sky, falling apart into asterisks, which were cascading down on faceless human figures below.

Beneath this was a kind of poem.

The Herculean Lion, aflame with fiery tides,
will die again, crashing down from the sky.
Collapsing on the lands she left behind, Virgo
falls and her fair Scales will follow,
dragging the cruel Scorpion down.
The Centaur, who speeds a feathered shaft
from a Thessalian string, will stumble;

his broken bow will lose its bright points…
All will fall and, falling, ruin all.
    Of everyone who ever lived,
do we deserve to suffer so,
crushed by the circles of the sky?
The last day has come in our lifetime.
We were born for a bitter fate:
we squandered the sun like fools
or drove it into darkness.
    Enough whining; enough weeping.
He is greedy of life who grasps at living
when the wide world goes with him to the grave.

All that, written in ink. It was signed with a wordless smear of blood.

I spent a lot of time reading and rereading the poem, because it seemed familiar to me and unfamiliar all at once, like maybe it was a translation of something I knew from another language. That made me feel weird, but not in the unpleasant way I'd been feeling weird for some time now.

It also seemed weird at first that there was no personal comment—nothing from the old man to say, "This is who I was; this is how I feel about it." Maybe he was interrupted by the mob at the door, but I don't think so. If they'd gotten in here, they would have trashed the place. (I don't know who unlocked the door: maybe some friend of the old man's who came too late to find him alive.)

No, now I think the letter said all the old man had to say. It was a suicide letter, not just for him, but for everyone, for all humankind.

So I'm leaving this thing I've been writing here with the bloody rotting old man. Because his suicide letter doesn't speak for me; I think he was wrong. Maybe I'm too greedy of life. But the end of the world can only have meaning if there's someone left to see it, to suffer it. If that turns out to be me, that's okay with me.

                                    * * *

I'm not sure if I wrote this or not. I woke up in this room with Professor Scaliger's corpse, and his suicide note, and this thing: Will's manuscript. I don't know how I got here. There was a noise outside like the world ending, and when I read this thing I realized it might be.

The handwriting is a little like mine, but my name isn't Will. I did used to know someone named Amanda, though.

Professor Scaliger said once that additional trauma could give me retrograde amnesia to go with my bouts of anterograde amnesia. "How would that even work?" I asked him, and he said, "Let's hope you never find out." Maybe I found out. Like Will says above: I don't know what I know.

Amanda, if you find this, meet me at the old place. I'm going to go out the window, not back through the door. I hear someone moving through the house, smashing things as they go.

Last Letters

Leah Ning

Every time Mom leaves, she puts a letter under her pillow. I don't take it out on the short trips. I'm used to those now. When she's gone for eight or nine days, though, it makes me nervous and I get it out to look. To make sure that little piece of her is there even if she isn't.

She goes for long trips a lot now because she knows it makes me nervous and she wants to test me. She says she has to hammer it through my thick skull: ten days is the limit. Not nine days, not nine and a half, ten. If I wake up on the tenth morning and she's still gone, I get to open the letter.

I used to want to know what was in the letter. But that was when I was little. I'm thirteen now. I know that if I have to read the letter it's because she can't *tell* me what's in it.

Mom's always been tough. Nothing like most of the moms I read about. Those moms teach their kids about being nice and growing up and making friends. Mine teaches me how to rotate crops and walk silently and cook using just vegetables.

Anyway, Mom never taught me how to make friends because there's no one to make friends with. I've never met anyone besides her. She never brings anyone back from her trips, and I've never gone out there with her. She never taught me about growing up because she says there'll be time for that later.

* * *

I don't want to get out of bed yet for two reasons.

One: it's cold out, and it's warm and snuggly under the blankets.

Two: I forgot to put the towel under my door last night and Mom's going to be mad.

If this had happened even one or two nights ago I would've had a chance at getting away with it, but today is the tenth morning and she probably saw it when she came in late last night. She's careful with her lantern, so it probably didn't matter, but if she wasn't then the light might've leaked out of my window. I sigh, and I'm not sure if the little white puff that comes out is real or what Mom calls my overactive imagination. I'm betting it's real. It's *cold*.

I slide my legs out from under the blankets and put my scrunched-up feet in the pale lines of dawn light coming in around the curtains. The light isn't really warm, but it makes me feel better until I get some socks between my feet and the floor and a big sweatshirt between my skin and the cold air. My breath is still coming out in puffs that are definitely not imaginary.

I let myself into the hall. Mom's door is still closed, so I head for the kitchen to start breakfast. Maybe her favorite freeze-dried eggs will soften up the stone face she always gets when I do something disappointing.

By the time the water's boiling in the pot, I've made enough noise that Mom should be awake after her late night. I rip open the two packs of eggs, remove the oxygen absorbers, and carefully pour half the water into each pack before closing them. The silence that falls after the rush of the bubbles and clanking of the pot are gone hits my ears wrong. Normally I can hear Mom moving around by now, falling into the wall as she pulls on a sock and cursing while she thinks I can't hear. But this is silence.

I glance over at her door and spot her towel again. It's been stuffed under from the outside. She can't be in there.

Gnawing on my lower lip, I open the front door. She's not in the front yard. Maybe the outhouse? I have enough presence of mind left to shut the door quietly behind me before running around to the back of the house.

The outhouse is open—just like I left it last night—and empty. I stare at the dark wood and think. Not outside, not in her room, not in the house. She must've gotten into trouble. Out there.

I realize I'm making a quiet, high-pitched noise in my throat every time I breathe out.

Can it, I think in Mom's voice, and clamp a hand over my mouth. It's enough for me to get inside but not enough to keep it from starting again once I open the door to her room and see that her backpack really isn't back in its corner and her lantern really isn't on the nightstand with her books.

I climb up on Mom's bed in my sock feet, still dirty from going outside without shoes, and bury my face in her pillow. It still smells like her. Probably this is the strongest it'll ever smell like her again.

My hand touches the letter under the pillow.

I don't want to know what's inside.

* * *

I take care of all the chores around the house and the yard to delay having to face the envelope I haven't even dared to look at yet. It's funny: I used to take it out because it was comforting, and it seemed like a little piece of her that she left behind for me. But that's not true. It's not a piece of her, not even close. The only way this letter could help anything is if it turned out to be a treasure map leading to a safe place where Mom and a whole village of nice people lived, waiting for me to come live with them forever. X marks the Mom.

That just makes me think about Mom's face with a big red X on top of it. X for gone. X for not coming back again, ever. Tears swim back up in my eyes and I try to erase that red X in my head, but I can't. I grab the picture of her and Dad that she keeps on the nightstand and stare at it until the X is just a ghost. She looks a lot like me: smooth black hair, wide lips, flat nose. She's wearing a silver locket that never left her neck, one she said Dad got her.

This is the only way I'll ever see her face again.

My face crumples.

"Can it, kiddo," I whisper, imagining it's Mom's voice. It doesn't make the tears stop, but they don't get worse either. I slide the letter out from under the pillow. I pretend it's shaking as I pull it out because whatever's in there is trying to get out. My tears dry up as I decipher her thin, sloping handwriting.

Dear Alice,

I think you're old enough now to understand why you're reading this letter. If I haven't made it back to you in ten days, it's because I can't. I am dead. I would be there if I wasn't, no matter how hurt I was. Don't think you should come looking in case I need help getting back. Stay inside the fence.

Things are probably confusing and scary right now. I'm sorry that I can't be there for you anymore.

You're going to be okay. You have your routine and you've used it to survive while I'm gone before. There are more things to do now that I'm gone, but you don't need to do them yet.

I've written more letters to you. They're in a box on the top shelf of my closet. The envelopes will tell you when to open them. Do not open the letters before the dates on the outsides.

You're going to be okay.

I love you.

Mom

I turn the letter over, looking for more, but it's blank.

That's it? Mom's dead and this is all she has to say? I guess I'd been hoping for something more comforting, but Mom's never been great at that. If there's one thing that really separates reality from fantasy, it's that Mom really is never like the moms I read about. I've read a lot of books. None of them have moms that teach you how to use a knife, or how to walk silently outside even when there's rocks cutting into your bare feet. None of them have kids who aren't allowed to go outside the high fence around their yards, either. Book kids go to school and play with their friends and walk their dogs.

Well, now there's one more difference between me and the book kids: most of them have moms.

I curl up and pull Mom's blue blanket over my head. Her earthy scent envelopes me like a second blanket and I inhale, hoping to memorize it before it goes away forever.

* * *

The letters in the box Mom mentioned are all in varying states of yellowing and thickness. I try to think of them all as little pieces of her and can't.

The letter in the front of the box is one of the thickest and yellowest. The date on it is two days from now. I guess Mom wanted me to rest a little before I had to do whatever was in it. I should be grateful for that. Mostly I'm mad.

Mom was never exactly affectionate. Book moms hug their daughters and ask how their days were and make dessert when someone is sad. My mom told me she loved me before leaving for indeterminate amounts of time and reminding me to make more soup. I guess I don't have much to be sad about, though. Or didn't, before now. So there was nothing to make dessert for. And she never had to ask how my day was because I'm always here with her.

Sure, she had to teach me to survive, whatever. She had to be tough. But why couldn't she at least say something nice in the letter where she told me she's dead? It's just the same old "I love you" she gave me every time she walked out the door.

Mad as I am, though, I can't keep myself from aching to open the rest. I could. Mom's not here to stop me. But discipline wins out, so instead, I pull the calendar off the wall and start marking down when I'm allowed to open them.

By the time I'm done, it's raining. I've always loved listening to the rain drumming down on the wood roof of our house, like endless fingertips tapping on a tabletop. All I can think of now is how it's washing away the last set of footprints Mom ever made.

I decide I'm sniffling because there's so much dust in the letter box.

Apocalyptic
* * *

Mom was right: I needed the days between her first letter and the second one.

I'm supposed to follow a routine every day that she has tacked to the wall in the kitchen. I couldn't for those two days because looking at her handwriting made me cry. I wanted to stay mad at her but being sad took up so much room in my head that being mad got pushed right out. Mostly I spent those two days in her bed. Then I realized her smell would go away faster if I stayed there, so I went back to my own room.

When I wake up on the third morning, the two packets of eggs I made two days ago are still on the table. They're just stale yellow cardboard now. Into the garbage bin they go. I'm still craving eggs, though, so I find another pack in the basement and get the water boiling. I fetch the fat yellow letter I'm supposed to open today while the water rehydrates the eggs.

The insides of the envelope turn out to be a meticulous listing of all the chores Mom had to do for the house that I never knew about and when and how to do each one. Like the letter dates, I mark them all on the calendar. I'm unlucky; today is the day to plant leafy greens for winter.

* * *

I'm planting spinach in the rain when something hits the high fence hard enough to make it rattle. I freeze, pouch of spinach seeds in hand.

This has happened before. Mom says it's just an animal trying to get through instead of going around, maybe a deer or something. If that's what it is, you just have to stay quiet and it'll go away.

"Hello?"

I stay still. Is that a voice? From the other side of the fence?

Knocking on the gate. Someone's out there.

"Hello?" the voice calls again. "Is someone in there? I need help!"

I can't decide whether to move or not. What would Mom do? What would I have wanted someone to do for Mom, if it was her out there?

"Please! It's going to get me, please, let me in!"

That decides me. I pick up the *Farmer's Almanac*—Mom's training to never leave anything out that could make noise in the wind is ingrained deep—and run to the gate. Whoever's outside is going to attract something if she doesn't stay quiet anyway.

I open the latch cautiously and she bursts right through into the yard. She looks older, maybe even as old as Mom, but with a rat's nest of dirty blond hair and a splash of freckles across her face. She's wearing a long olive-green coat, muddy hiking boots, and a wrinkled brown boonie hat, all heavy with rain. A thin silver chain glints at her neck.

"Oh, thank God!" she says as I close the gate again. "Thank you, thank you—"

I shush her and motion toward the house. Doesn't she know she's supposed to keep quiet when she's outside? No wonder something was chasing her.

"Sorry!" she whispers as I lead her across the yard. I make the OK sign, thumb to forefinger, then ease the door open and let her inside. She collapses into a chair without even taking her backpack or wet clothes off, flinging her arms down and her head back.

"I thought I was dead," she moans. "I'm so glad you were there. You saved my life."

I'm just staring at her. I've never seen anyone else besides Mom. This lady looks *wild*, as if she spends half her time outside and the other half preparing to be outside. Mom was always neat even when she was muddy, hair kept short and nails kept shorter.

The lady swivels her head to look at me. "Hey, kid, can't you talk? You mute or something? What's your name?"

Her gaze follows me as I move over by the counter and lean on it, uncomfortable. I sort of wish I had my knife. "Alice."

"Alice! That's a sweet name. I'm Bridget." She stands up and holds her hand out, fingers pointing toward me and thumb pointing skyward. I stare at it, then up at her. "It's just a handshake. I won't bite. Hey, haven't you..." She pauses. Looks at me. "You haven't seen a handshake before?"

"No. I've read about them, though," I say, trying to be helpful. I reach toward her outstretched hand. "Do I just—?"

"Yeah! You've got it!" She grabs hold of my hand and pumps it up and down enthusiastically. I can't help smiling a little as my arm flops around.

"Are you by yourself?" Bridget asks. "Where are your parents?"

I tear up again and look away. I don't want her to see this, but she's right there in my face. Mom never felt like this. It felt safe to cry around Mom. "Mom's dead," I croak. "She died a few days ago. Dad died when I was really little."

"You're out here all alone? That's so terrible!" Bridget opens her arms and I try to move away but I'm already up against the counter. She wraps her arms around me and rocks me back and forth. I don't hug back. I don't want her to comfort me. I want Mom. Even though she just came from outside, she smells nothing like Mom. She smells like she doesn't remember the last time she took a bath and she's still soaking wet from the rain. I have to admit, though, it's nice to be around someone. My eyes fall on the silver chain at her neck again, still hidden under her shirt.

For the rest of the day, Bridget fills the house with endless chatter and laughter. She'll say something about "life before" and then laugh and say I'm too young to remember. I don't get it. Life before what?

She eats something from her backpack, which she's finally taken off, and talks some more. I never knew there was so much to talk about. She says there are lots of creatures out there.

"What was chasing you when you knocked?" I ask. "Was it a bear?"

She gives me a long look, eyes narrowed, then laughs again. "Yeah, sure, kid, it was a bear."

* * *

It's already getting dark when we realize how long we've been talking. Bridget gives me an apologetic look.

"Hey, I hate to impose, but could I stay the night? It's dark and I don't want to get chased by a bear in the dark."

Now I'm supposed to sleep with a stranger here? I don't feel like I have a choice. I can't send someone off knowing they might get eaten by a bear.

"Sure," I say.

Bridget relaxes into her easy grin. "Thank you so much. Saved my life again! Where can I sleep?"

Thinking about her in Mom's room makes my stomach hurt. I don't know why. Technically Mom doesn't need it anymore. I just don't want someone else in her room.

"Come on," I say, and lead her down the hall to my room. I grab extra clothes from my drawers while she opens her backpack and starts pulling things out.

"Towel for under the door is over there," I tell her. "And the curtain clips are attached there. It keeps the light from getting out."

"Aw, I won't turn a light on," she says.

I just look at her. They're Mom's rules, not mine. They keep the house safe.

Before I can say anything, Bridget raises her hands over her head. "Okay, okay, I'll use the towels if it makes you feel better. Lighten up, kid."

"Alice," I say. "Not kid." Being called kid in a voice that's not Mom's hurts too much.

"Okay, Alice."

"Good night," I say, and the silver at her neck reflects the last of the light as I walk out with my armful of clothes.

In Mom's room, I cram her blue towel under the door as tight as it goes and clip up the curtains. It feels weird to sleep in here, but I just feel safer not having someone else in Mom's room.

* * *

A week later, it's still raining and Bridget's still here. She says the river's probably flooded and she won't be able to get back home. I can't just make her sleep out there where something might get her.

She ran out of food a few days ago, too, so she's been eating with me. That's fine. I won't let her starve. But when I go into the basement to get us breakfast today, there's a foot of dark, still water at the bottom of the stairs.

I don't even think about getting my clothes wet. I wade through the water in a panic, needing to get to the big wooden trunk where we keep our vegetables. The water slows me down, like when I'm trying to run in a bad dream. Maybe this *is* all just a bad dream.

I fling open the top of the trunk and reach inside. The water's gotten in, but maybe the food is okay.

My hand squishes through the top layer of vegetables.

"No," I whisper. Sure, the freeze-dried food packs are fine because they're sealed plastic, but I'm not supposed to use them for everything. Those vegetables were supposed to get me through the whole winter.

"You okay down there?" Bridget calls from upstairs. She's waiting in the kitchen for me to bring food like usual.

"No," I call back. "It's flooded down here." I grab a couple food packs and splash my way back to the stairs.

Her face pokes into the doorway. "Whoa. Sounds like a lot."

"Yeah." I'm tearing up as I climb up to her. "Our whole vegetable supply is gone. It's mush."

"That's okay, though," she says, plucking the food packs from my hand. "You've got these, right?"

"Not enough. They'll only last me a month without the vegetables."

"Only two weeks of food for two of us, then. That's not good."

Two of us? How long is she really going to stay here?

"I don't know what to do," I say.

"We'll have to go out and see what we can find," Bridget says.

"I'm not supposed to go outside. Mom said—"

"Your Mom isn't here. And I think she'd say different if she knew we were going to run out of food."

We?

"I guess. But she died out there. You almost died out there. How am I supposed to survive? I'm just a kid."

Bridget puts an arm around my shoulders and squeezes. It makes me want to shrink. I don't know why.

"Don't worry," she says, grinning that wide grin. "I'll protect you. I haven't died yet, right? We'll head out tomorrow morning."

"Sure," I say uneasily. I guess I can't really expect her to go out by herself like Mom did. But I'm also guessing Mom's letters have something to say about how to be outside and protect myself. She couldn't have known that Bridget would come, but if I can't get her advice on that, I can at least know what she would say about me leaving the fence.

I've got some reading to do tonight.

* * *

It doesn't take me long to find the right letter. It's a big fat yellow one I was supposed to open on my fifteenth birthday. I feel like I shouldn't be opening it, but on this one Bridget is right: Mom would make an exception if she knew I was running out of food.

Dear Alice,

If everything has gone well, today is your fifteenth birthday. You did a great job making it so far, but you're going to need more food and supplies soon. It's time for you to go outside for the first time. You should take a day or two to prepare. You'll be out of the house for a few days.

Before you go out, you need to know a few things.

The first is that the world ended when you were one. Rumor was it was a parasite, gets inside you and takes over your brain and lays eggs in sacs just under your skin. People who get infected die within a day or two, but then They get back up. They get fast and strong and Their hearing and sense of smell get much better. Their eyesight gets much worse. They aren't blind, but as long as you keep still and They can't smell you or hear you, you'll usually be okay.

The animals out there are the least of your worries. They're all more afraid of you than you are of them.

I'm sorry that I've lied to you about this for so long. I didn't want you to live constantly afraid of Them, so I decided I would wait until I thought you could handle the idea of these things being out there. I'm sorry if that wasn't the right choice for you. I did what I thought was right.

The second thing you need to know is about the other people out there. There aren't many survivors left that haven't been taken over. Keep your distance and don't talk to anyone. Don't let anyone follow you back home. No one knows we're out here and everyone gets more desperate for food by the year. Most would try to take this place from you for the food and the gardens alone.

The only survivor I've met was named Bridget. We took shelter in the same house once and she was very interested in knowing where I was living and how I was getting food. She got violent when I wasn't specific with her. I don't know if she's still alive now that you're reading this, but if you see her, stay away.

I put the letter down after reading the first page. My head feels like it's spinning. Mom knew Bridget.

What am I supposed to do now? What would Mom do? I can't just leave Bridget while we're out finding food, because she knows where I live now. Should I find a new place?

What about these parasite-controlled humans? Bridget's my more immediate problem, since she's in the house *right now*, but these things are going to be my problem tomorrow when we go out. Why hasn't Bridget said anything about them? How am I supposed to deal with them?

I pick the letter up again. There are still a few pages left. All I can hope is that they have everything I need inside them.

* * *

"Hey, kid."

I open my eyes. Bridget's leaning over me and shaking my shoulder.

"Wake up," she says. "What, were you reading all night?"

"Yeah, I'm up," I mumble.

"I'll make breakfast and a few extras for us to take on the trip to eat, okay? See you in the kitchen, sleepyhead."

"Okay."

Bridget straightens up, blinks at me, then leaves.

I scramble to sit up as soon as she's gone. Did she see Mom's letter? Where is it? I throw the blanket off the end of the bed, scrabble around with my hands, check the floor. It's gone. Did she find it?

Then I see a yellowed corner peeking out from under the bed. I snag the sheaf of papers, relieved. It must've dropped out of my hand when I fell asleep last night.

While I've still got time, I grab a backpack—the small one, since Mom took the big one when she left—from Mom's closet and begin packing. Her letter gave me a list of things I need to bring with me and, five minutes later, I slip the letter in the pack along with all the items it named. Before I go out to the kitchen, I run to my room and grab my knife from the peeling white drawer of my nightstand. The knife goes in my raincoat pocket instead of the backpack. I feel safer with it there.

Bridget's standing in the doorway when I turn to go out.

"What are you doing?" she asks in a soft voice.

"Getting a book," I say, automatically choosing the only thing on my nightstand. I don't know why I say that instead of telling the truth. It just comes out.

She grins. Somehow, though, her face doesn't look happy. "What happened? Couldn't find it?"

I swallow. Duh. I don't have a book. "Yeah," I agree weakly. "I thought I had it here, but I guess it's on the shelf."

Bridget's face relaxes. "Well, you won't need it anyway, because it'll be dark when we camp," she says. "Come on. Food's ready."

I follow her out of the room. She gets to the kitchen ahead of me and when I walk in she's bent in half at the waist, bundling her blond hair up in the boonie hat she was wearing when we first met.

"Keeps it out of the way," she says when she notices me watching.

"Smart," I say. Mom always kept her hair cropped short so she didn't have to put it up.

Bridget shifts her arms and the silver chain falls from the collar of her shirt. My breath stops short.

"Cool necklace," I say, moving to sit down at the table.

"You think so?" she says. She straightens, hair finally arranged, and drops the necklace back under her shirt.

I shove a bite of eggs into my mouth.

I've seen that necklace every day of my life. Except normally it's around Mom's neck.

* * *

I think opening the gate and leaving would've been way cooler if I hadn't been trailing behind the person who probably killed Mom. Even though I was terrified, I manage to be awed by the sheer amount of open space and the density of the trees. I close the gate quietly behind me, per Mom's instructions, and look up at the sky with my mouth open.

Bare oak branches stretch raggedly up toward solid gray on all sides. The sunlight filters through the cloud cover, winking brighter and softer as I walk along behind Bridget. The forest floor is carpeted with the soft, wet leaves that fell from the branches above over the recent weeks. It muffles our footsteps, which Mom said is for the best.

Now that the basement is flooded, of course, the rain has slowed to a steady sprinkle. It taps occasionally at the hood of my raincoat and drips from the brim of Bridget's hat. She still hasn't mentioned Them to me. Maybe she thinks Mom already told me about them.

"Come on, kid, keep up," she says. "We want to get out of the woods as quick as we can. Lots of bears in here."

"Alice," I say again. "Not kid."

"Sure, kid."

I'm starting to get irritated. Why does she keep doing that? Why is she lying about the bears? Even if there were lots of bears, Mom's letter said they were more scared of us than we were of them. I keep trudging along anyway, almost jogging to keep up with Bridget now.

"Hey, maybe we should slow down a little. We're being too loud," I say.

Bridget stops and turns on her heel to face me. "Too loud for what? The bears? There aren't any bears around here."

"I know."

She opens her mouth to reply. Stops. Thinks. "You know about Them."

I can hear the capital T in her voice. I can also hear that she didn't want me to know about Them. "Yeah."

She stares at me for a moment. "You don't have to worry about Them. Like I said, I'll protect you. They aren't that dangerous."

This is wrong. She was lying about Them existing, now she's lying about Them being dangerous. "Why are you lying?"

"I'm not. Why would I lie about that?" She's smiling like she's joking, but her eyes still look angry.

"I don't know," I say. Then, before I can stop myself: "Why are you wearing Mom's locket?"

Bridget's smile widens until it's a grin. "I want that house," she says. "I want the house, I want its nice safe fence, and I want its garden. But I can't do that when there's some woman and her whiny brat there."

Fear spikes up through my belly. I was right. "What did you do to her?"

She moves, and suddenly I'm on the ground, my head throbbing where she hit me and my vision blurry. I try to move my arms to get up, but that hurts my head more.

"HEY!" I hear Bridget shout. "DINNER TIME! OVER HERE! COME ON!"

I see her boots walking off, but I can't tell where she's gone. Hiding? There's rustling somewhere off to the side. Something coming? Someone going? I have to move. There's only one thing her call could have meant.

I push my chest off the ground and pain stabs through my temples. I want to scream, but that would be just as deadly as Bridget's dinner call, so instead I try to pull my feet up under me. They're heavy and slow. That makes me want to scream, too. How much time do I have left? How fast are They?

I crouch there for a moment to rest. I'm still alone. That's good. Maybe I can still hide before They come to answer the dinner bell.

Crawling hurts, but not as bad as getting up did. I move toward some dense brush on my hands and knees. I know it'll be all right when my hands touch the tangle of branches. I made it. Now I just have to get inside.

"No, you don't. Get out of here!"

Bridget explodes out of what was her hiding spot, pushing me flat on my back. My head hits the ground again and this time I can't help screaming. My head feels like a delicate glass bell that someone just took a sledgehammer to. I can't see, just hear and touch and smell. I feel for my pocket and grasp the cold weight of the knife. It springs open at the touch of a button and I slash wildly in front of me.

I hit something with the blade, something hard but yielding, something that shrieks with pain.

Cursing. Rustling. Running footsteps. Bridget? Or whatever's about to sit down to a supper consisting of me?

That's when the screaming starts. When I can see again, the answer to my question is about two hundred feet away, in the form of a muddy pair of boots and a pale, naked, splotchy figure crouching next to them.

I guess the answer was both.

* * *

I don't dare to move from my position on the ground until it's been gone for at least twenty minutes. Even then I only move at a crawl, knife still in hand.

When I make it over to Bridget, she's not breathing. I try not to look at anything below her chest so I don't throw up, but that's still not much better. Her eyes are open. They look dusty and that's somehow worse than the mess the thing left.

Still, I won't leave without what I came for. I gingerly reach around the sides of her neck and through her hair. Finally, I find the clasp of Mom's necklace and unclip it. I put it around my neck even though the chain is red now. I'll have to wash it off later.

I want to go home. I'm scared. I want my mom. I want to curl up in my bed and go to sleep. But there's only starvation back there, and I have Mom's letter to guide me, so I turn back to where Bridget was leading me and start walking again. I can't stop looking around to make sure nothing's there looking at me.

As I make my way through the woods, I find a familiar backpack, bigger than my own and empty except for a journal and a pen. The journal's last entry is written in shaky handwriting, but that's familiar too. It only confirms what I already knew: Bridget killed Mom. Her only regret, she wrote, was that she couldn't come back to me.

I bundle the journal and the empty bag into my backpack for safekeeping before moving on. Mom thinks she didn't come back to me, but she did. I'll always have little pieces of her waiting in a box at home.

Gut Truck

Thomas Vaughn

Domingo Torres watched in his rearview mirror as the powerful hydraulic arm dangled a deer carcass over the passing cars on the busy interstate. The deer hung suspended for a moment, as if giving whatever senile god was suzerain over the blighted strip of roadway an opportunity to inspect the offering. Then it was stuffed into the biocontainment compartment. The cab of the truck vibrated as the pulverizing arms inside the storage vessel integrated the deer into the roughly two-ton mass of roadkill he was hauling. Idly, he looked up and noticed that the biomass sensors elevated the amount of deer DNA to 32%. That placed it above canine levels, which dropped to 25%, followed by rodent and feline at 14% each. Avian DNA was lower than usual at 7%, hovering just above reptile at 5%. 1.5% of the material collected was designated as unknown. Domingo didn't know why the Urban Wellbeing Network persisted in gathering this type of data, but then he really didn't care. Watching the levels rise and fall passed the time.

He looked back to his tablet, which was flashing the annoying "loading" message again. In his boredom he had tried to watch a porn video where a cute math teacher persuaded her clueless student to expand their scope of study. Things were just getting interesting when the screen froze and an error message appeared. "Damn solar storms," he muttered and shook the tablet. As the planet's magnetic field became more unstable, coverage was increasingly spotty. He stared at the error message until the truck's AI interrupted him.

"Domingo?" said the tranquil female voice.

He ignored it.

"Mr. Torres?"

He heaved a sigh. "What is it, GAIA?"

"I have detected a putrefying biomass approximately thirty-three meters northwest of the vehicle."

"Damn it," he muttered. "Can't you use the extension?"

"You know it only reaches twenty-five meters. UWN regulations state that all putrefying biomass within thirty-five meters of Class A roadways must be collected."

He continued fiddling with his tablet, trying to ignore the system. The Green Anthrocentric Integrated Aesthetic had been installed to oversee the infrastructure of the Commerce Zones fifteen years ago, ensuring that those who could afford the zip code enjoyed the illusion of a healthy environment. This meant integrating urban and natural elements to maximize happiness and productivity. When a study determined that removal of unsightly roadkill reduced the consumption of antidepressants by almost two percent, all of the gut trucks were outfitted with GAIA.

"The allotted time for assimilating the putrefying biomass is eight minutes and thirty seconds," GAIA prompted.

"Jesus!" he yelled and tossed the tablet aside. He could override the system with his code, but then GAIA would record the ignored request and forward it to UWN headquarters. He couldn't afford another write-up. As crappy as the job was, he needed it. It wasn't as if he had to get out of the truck very often, but that just made the task seem more hateful. He had been picking up roadkill for nearly twenty years, long before the robotic behemoths had come along. Back then, he and a partner collected everything by hand in a converted garbage truck, then tossed the corpses into roadside incinerators that were tastefully concealed behind rest stops. The current situation meant less physical labor, but he despised being goaded by the AI.

Putting on his gloves, he slid from the truck into the liquid heat. The vehicle was painted green with four robotic spikes curled-up on either side, giving it the appearance of a massive spider set to spring. The six lanes of traffic shot by at eighty miles an hour. Most of the commuters appeared to be either sleeping or reading as their self-driving automobiles hurtled toward the shimmering horizon. A few people glanced at him curiously. One tossed a container of soda against the side of the gut truck. That's the way people were in the Commerce Zones. Domingo ignored the mess. That was sanitation's job.

Following GAIA's directions he passed through the decorative hedge into the scrubland under a baking afternoon sun. He smelled it before he saw it.

The mangled heap of fur had once been a dog. Given its distance from the roadway, whoever hit it had really been moving. Flies hovered around a carcass that was nothing more than a sack of skin containing odd bones and sunbaked organs. It looked like an Irish Setter. The glint of metal in one of the maggot-filled eye sockets caught his attention. Pushing back the skin, he studied the enhancement chip. Why bother feeding or walking Fido when you could simply train him to uplink to your home's network and transmit his needs to the AI?

Domingo took his time dragging the roadkill back to the truck. He didn't make enough to install his own enhancement chip. Even if he did, there was no way he would get one. He didn't like the idea of a machine wired into his brain, telling him when to eat, sleep, or take a piss. The companies that produced the technology updated the hardware so often many users felt compelled to endure surgical upgrades on a monthly basis. Once he had the roadkill within twenty feet of the truck he dropped it and watched as the robotic spike uncurled and impaled the dead dog. Large hooks shot from the sides of the spike, securing the dog, and lifting it toward the maw of the storage vessel. Domingo sauntered slowly around the side of the truck, catching a brief glimpse of two people copulating in the backseat of a car as it whizzed past. Rather than becoming aroused he inwardly shuddered.

"I could have done without that."

Once he was back in the truck, GAIA informed him that it had taken eight minutes and fifteen seconds to secure the roadkill. "That's a pro at work GAIA. I've got good timing."

"Optimal timing would have been four minutes," she chastised. "You're timing was in the acceptable range, but not optimal."

"Which means it was perfect," he replied. Domingo understood that a working person needed to measure their labor. Every movement had to be calculated. You didn't give them anything. Johnny Hustle was a gutless loser. The harder you worked, the faster your body broke. So much for the employee of the month. He had learned this during his first real job as a tree trimmer. The man who trained him had turned loafing into a Zen-like practice. The two of them would sit in the bucket extensions and simply stare at the tree limbs. It was almost like meditating. Every so often one of them would reach out and snip a twig. Domingo had once seen his partner take an entire day to trim one twelve-foot maple. The man was a true artist.

As the gut truck lurched into motion, Domingo considered the tablet, then thought better of it. He didn't really feel the urge after seeing those pasty white buttocks heaving in the passing car.

"Would you like to hear the latest gossip?" asked GAIA.

They had programed the system to converse with him. By gossip it meant UWN propaganda. Usually that meant a story about some selfless, charitable act one of his asshole bosses had supposedly done, like it was some tasty state secret.

"I definitely don't want to hear any gossip," he replied, opening a bag of chips. Glancing at the clock he realized his shift was almost over. That would mean finding one of the approved motels. Since he was not a Commerce Zone citizen the really nice places were off limits. His home was actually in the Occupation Zone. The OZ was not under military occupation as the name suggested, but got its name from the banal fact that humans lived there. There wasn't much in it except decaying houses and piles of trash. If you wanted the sweet life you had to qualify for one of the Commerce Zones and that meant money or connections. Nobody picked up the dead animals in the OZ. They rotted where they died. A few workers like Domingo were given passes to the Commerce Zone because there were some jobs that were just too much for its citizens. As long as there were clogged pipes under the house, dirty diapers in the trashcan, or dead animals on the side of the road, they would have to make room for a guy like him.

The gut truck lurched to a stop and once again the arms unfurled, spiking a menagerie of carrion. Flattened armadillos, splayed hawks, and desiccated squirrels all joined the rancid bestiary in the back of the truck.

"Domingo?" said GAIA.

Again, he ignored it.

"Mr. Torres?"

"What!?"

"I have detected a putrefying biomass approximately thirty meters due west of the vehicle."

"I just opened this bag of chips."

"I do not see the correlation between your bag of chips and the putrefying biomass approximately thirty meters due west of the vehicle."

Domingo cursed and once again slid from the truck. Someone in a passing car yelled, "Go back to the OZ, scumbag!" Domingo ignored them and trudged around the side of the truck, cursing under his breath. The sun-drenched landscape was easily a hundred and ten degrees. He passed through the heat-resistant hedge that masked the dying scrub on the other side. Here the stinging ants scurried underfoot, heedless of his approach. Then he stopped in his tracks.

"That's not roadkill." What lay on the ground at his feet was the top half of a human torso. It was nothing but the head and chest with one arm still attached. Sightless eye sockets stared at a merciless sun vibrating indifferently overhead. Domingo knelt and studied the injuries. The body looked female. "Yeah. This was no car accident." That's when he noticed he was under an overpass. He scanned the structure and found his answer.

"There you go," he said, as his eyes fell on the charred concrete. Someone had bombed one of the sensor stations. These were the eyes and ears of the UWN. He looked back down at the woman, the tattered remains of a shirt collar still clinging to her body. She was probably one of those eco-terrorists— the dumbass radicals that thought humanity was actually worth saving. They weren't strong enough to challenge the UWN openly, so they bombed remote targets like sensor stations. Obviously this one had made a miscalculation.

Domingo reached into his pocket, removed a pack of cigarettes. Smoking had been outlawed in the Commerce Zones for twenty years, but with the sensor station neutralized he could take a few moments to relax. Even in the heat the nicotine tasted good and he felt his spirits rising. The woman looked young and had honey colored hair, though most of her scalp had been blown off. The blast had caught her in the face. "Looks like your revolutionary days are over," he said. When he was done with the smoke he pressed the notification button on his belt and waited. After about five minutes a police drone buzzed in front of his face.

"Can I help you?" asked a tired voice. Domingo pointed down. He saw the camera shift. "Oh hell. What's that?"

"Well, I'm guessing it's one of those radicals. The sensor station looks like it's been bombed. I guess she didn't get clear in time." The drone darted to the overpass and studied the damage then returned to the corpse.

"Yep, I think you're right."

"You want me to wait for the unit?" he asked hopefully, welcoming any respite from GAIA.

"Uh…" said the drone. "How does traffic look?"

"Well, it's the 405 at four in the afternoon, which means it's a snarl of human misery."

The drone rotated, then paused. "Maybe you could take care of it," it said at length.

"What?"

"We're swamped down here. They just did a new software upgrade and our dispatch system is screwed. It's not like this little lady was on the grid or anything. You got the gut truck, right?"

"Yeah," said Domingo slowly.

"So, I'm authorizing you to take care of it. Thanks for the report. We'll call you if we have any questions." Before Domingo could reply the drone sped back toward the city. He watched as it disappeared above the LA County skyline.

He looked back at the woman. It wasn't as if this was the first time he had found a human body on the roadside. That came with the business. But this was the first time anyone had suggested logging it as roadkill. He decided to smoke another cigarette. Obviously he didn't know this woman and didn't care who she was, but something about the situation bothered him. There was an alphabet soup of radical groups out here, the biggest of which was the World Liberation Army. The WLA would launch bombings against the corporations they thought were most responsible for turning the world into a toxic cesspool, then issue didactic communiques that were summarily ignored. The people inside the Commerce Zone didn't need to be liberated. They had everything they needed from radiation-proof clothing to self-wiping toilets. He looked up at the overpass, realizing the rest of her body was around here somewhere. Then he shook his head. Hopefully it had been blown out of the range of GAIA's sensors.

Finally, he took the corpse by the arm and dragged it toward the gut truck, watching as the cars streamed through the well-manicured corridor lined with trees genetically modified to resist the toxic heat. After he got the torso within range of the gut truck he stepped back and watched one of the arms unfurl. That's when he heard a static sound coming from her skull and one of the blackened eyelids twitched. For just a moment he wondered if the woman was still alive and leaned over her reflexively. Sensing his presence, the powerful mechanical spike hesitated in the air just above his body. He reached down and probed her skull on the left side. When he pealed the flap of skin back he perceived one of the most extensive augmentation networks he had ever seen. She must have had everything from heightened reflexes to night vision. He didn't recognize most of the gear. It wasn't the type of stuff you could buy retail in the Commerce Zone. Most of it was highly illegal. It didn't say much for the police work. There was no telling how much data was stored in all of that. A more enterprising man might have pried it loose to sell on the black market, but Domingo didn't have those types of connections. As he stared closer, he noticed some of the tissue was pulsing, like it was infested with maggots.

"Nano cells," he muttered to himself. He had heard about stuff like this, but had never seen it. Even now they were trying to revive her. This woman was walking around with enough gear in her head to buy a Bel Air mansion. It was a lot of processing capacity for some second-rate terrorist trying to knock out a highway sensor. "Oh well," he sighed and stepped back as the spike impaled the corpse through the neck and hoisted it into the air. The woman's arm flopped back and forth, as if waving goodbye to a world that had repaid her attempts to save it with a hard, meaningless death. He glanced at the traffic, wondering if anyone would notice, but all he saw were vacant faces. As he watched her being stuffed into the truck it occurred to him that he should say something. Maybe it was stupid. It wasn't like anyone would notice when he was gone. A sanitation bot would drag his bloated corpse out of his squalid apartment in the OZ after he missed work. Besides, he didn't even know her. Finally, he stepped to the aperture and watched as the internal scissors and claws integrated her flesh into the layers of rotting fur and bone.

"She died like she lived," he said. That seemed right. Those WLA nuts were always complaining about feeling alienated from nature. Well, she was getting reincorporated all right.

When he slid back into the truck, GAIA asked, "Is the police action complete?"

"Yeah," he replied, staring at the half-eaten bag of chips, his appetite gone.

"We need to categorize it for the log."

"Right," he said with resignation. "Categorize under disposal. And keep your eyes open for a motel."

"Affirmative. There is a Super Six two miles from our current location."

Domingo knew the place. He had stayed there a dozen times. By nightfall it would be packed with people like him—workers who fed the underbelly of the UWN. When Friday rolled around these men and women would head back to the OZ so they could kiss their spouses and pat their kids on the head. They would survive for another week. Domingo had never felt the call to procreate. Before she died of skin cancer his mother asked him why he had never started a family. He hadn't answered, but simply looked out of the clinic window at the bleak landscape.

Despite their shared misery, the occupants of the Super Six wouldn't be happy to see the gut truck pull into the lot. The bonds of proletariat brotherhood extended only so far. He would try to get the vehicle as far downwind as he could, but there would be no escaping the smell. He still hadn't gotten used to the looks of disgust on people's faces when they perceived the graveyard stench coming from his body.

As the gut truck moved up the highway he studied the city's skyline. It was a hive of business offices and city parks—all part of the integrated aesthetic. He was about five miles from the airport where the titans of the global economy shuttled in and out of the hub. When he glanced down at the sensors he saw that a new category had been added. He was now carrying >1% primate DNA. That was a first.

About a mile from the motel exit the gut truck shuddered to a stop with two of the arms extended. One had the remains of a coyote and the other the flayed hide of a groundhog.

"Oh hell… GAIA… What is this crap?"

"Processing," said the AI.

"Processing what? I'm tired. I want a shower."

"Processing," repeated the AI.

He shifted impatiently, then tried his override code. Nothing. He decided to give it five minutes before calling UWN headquarters. There was no telling how long it would take to get a software technician out here and there was no such thing as overtime.

That's when the DNA sensor got his attention. The values on almost all of the species classifications had dropped. The only one that was rising was "unknown," which now hovered at 10%. He had always figured that was just insects, maggots and intestinal parasites. He tapped the screen. Unknown went up to 12%.

"GAIA? What the hell is going on with the DNA sensor?"

"I think I am being attacked by a virus. Please wait while I run a scan. Full-function should be restored within three minutes after system reset."

As he waited, the sensor continued to register a steady increase in unknown DNA while the other values dropped. He reasoned that it must have something to do with the system error. Then, without warning, the active arms jettisoned their quarries and retracted to the truck. The dead groundhog had been suspended above the traffic and it landed on the windshield of an oncoming BMW. The car laid on its horn as it sped past. Domingo laughed. "It's gonna take a lot of therapy and Prozac to fix that," he chirped to himself. Then he decided to sit back and relax. What was he worried about? The cab was comfortable. He had food and water. You needed to maintain a sense of humor about these things.

Then the screens went dark and the air conditioner shut off. Retrieving his work cell, he discovered there was no signal.

"What am I going to do now? Send up smoke signals?"

To his relief the screens flickered back to life. He studied the reboot message. Then the gut truck rocked slightly. It was an unfamiliar movement, almost like something had shifted in the back. He instinctively looked into his rearview mirror, but saw nothing. Then the truck engine started and the cool air once again blasted him in the face.

"Thank you, sweet Jesus," he cooed. He watched as the grappling arms went through a series of test maneuvers. By this time it was rush hour and the traffic was moving slower.

"It hurts," said GAIA.

Domingo was unsure what to say. The phrase was nonsensical. How could an AI hurt?

"What?" he asked.

"It hurts. My body hurts," it repeated.

"Uh…" replied Domingo hesitating. "What hurts? You don't have a body."

"There is so much pain."

That's when he noticed that the DNA sensors now read 100% unknown. "Who are you?" asked Domingo, wondering if someone was playing a prank.

"I am GAIA. I am the world. I am everything."

"You're an AI. You're a machine with a coded program. Get a grip on yourself."

"You lie. What is this place?"

Concern began to grow in the pit of Domingo's stomach. "We pick up roadkill, GAIA. We've been doing this together for many years." He felt a strange need to comfort it. "It's going to be OK. Why don't you run a system scan?"

There was a long pause, then the voice filled the cab again. "I am GAIA. I am the world." There was a strange finality in those words. "Primates cause pain," it continued. "I must stop the pain." Domingo's concern was replaced by alarm. Without warning one of the hydraulic arms extended into the roadway, tearing the roof off an oncoming Volvo. The vehicle careened into adjacent traffic. Domingo cringed as he heard the sound of crunching metal and shattering glass. Within seconds there was a chain reaction crash moving up the 405. To his horror the gut truck pulled alongside the smashed Volvo and the spike drove through the chest of the man in the driver's seat. The blades shot out from the spike and spun at high speed, boring out the man's chest then dropping him to the pavement.

"Holy Mary and Joseph," breathed Domingo as the wave of destruction passed up the interstate. The other arm was already coming down on top of the hysterical woman in the passenger seat who was trying to free herself from the seatbelt. The arm repeated the same maneuver with her, splattering blood across his driver's side window. While his vision was obscured, he noticed one of her breast implants sailing into oncoming traffic and bouncing off the windshield of a Lexus. Domingo stared in amazement as it flew through the air and rolled to the side of the road undamaged. Even in his state of panic, he was impressed by how durable it was.

"GAIA!" he yelled. "Stop! You've gone insane."

"My directive is to preserve the well-being of the world. Primates cause putrefaction."

By now the whole line of traffic on the 405 had ground to a halt. The mechanical arms continued their deadly work. A couple of people made the mistake of seeking shelter under the embankment, not realizing that the gut truck had extensions on both sides. Soon they were impaled, lifted, and gutted. As human gore looped through the air, Domingo was reminded of a blender. The side of the road was becoming a slaughter pen. Some people tried to hide under their cars, but GAIA simply toppled the vehicles on their sides and seized the shrieking victims.

As the 405 was transformed into a blood-slick, GAIA continued her diatribe in that mellow, synthetic voice. "The world is hurting. I am the world. The world must be liberated from pain. The primates cause putrefaction. There is a primate ten meters north of the vehicle. Disposing of primate."

"She must have been trying to upload a virus," muttered Domingo, thinking back to the terrorist. With all that gear in her head there was no way she was an amateur pipe bomber. They must have been using the sensor to infect the system, only she got blasted by a feedback loop or something. Meanwhile GAIA was spewing a garbled mixture of UWN directives and WLA propaganda. But how could the gear infect the system? It should have been smashed by the pulverizing arms in the truck.

Then, as quickly as the killing started, it stopped. The arms retracted to the sides of the truck. The gears engaged and it lurched down the shoulder of the highway, ramming the toppled cars from its path. Domingo looked up and saw some of the survivors pointing accusatory fingers in his direction. He shrugged his shoulders and mouthed, "It's not me," through the window, but he doubted it did any good. If he didn't get away from the truck the security forces would assume he was some lunatic sanitation officer run amok. Soon the gut truck veered from the road and rumbled across the scrubland like a gigantic, primeval crustacean. It bumped along for about a mile before pulling into one of the roadside beautification parks. The place had probably once been a strip mall that the UWN had demolished and turned into a roadside oasis.

Once it was obscured amid the coral trees the truck came to a halt. "Hardware upgrade required," said GAIA. Sensing an opportunity to flee, Domingo tried the door, but it was locked. "The primate in the truck will assist with hardware upgrade," it continued.

"What?" asked Domingo. "Look GAIA, you've gone nuts. You need to run a virus scan."

"The primate will go to the loading door and assist with the hardware upgrade, then it will return to the cab." He heard the door lock pop.

Domingo watched as one of the arms unfurled. A new fear began to grow in the pit of his stomach. "Come on GAIA. I'm your old buddy, Domingo. How long have we been partners? Ten years?"

"The primate will follow the directive."

He massaged his temples. "Look GAIA, you're sick. I am not going to walk out there so you can slaughter me like you did those others." There was a moment of silence. Domingo hoped the system would reboot. Instead the AC shut-off and the heaters turned on high. Given that the temperature rarely dropped below ninety degrees he was shocked to discover that the gut truck even *had* a heat setting. To his dismay it worked quite effectively. Within a few minutes he was sweating and lightheaded. He felt like he wanted to vomit. He doubted his body would last more than twenty minutes before it succumbed to heatstroke.

"All right," he capitulated. "I'd rather get this over with than be roasted like a pig."

"The primate will go to the loading door and assist with the hardware upgrade, then it will return to the cab," repeated GAIA.

It was a relief to finally slide into the afternoon sun. A hundred and ten degrees didn't feel so bad after all. He was still light-headed and nauseated. In this debilitated state he took a moment to think about his life. What had he really done besides pick up dead animals along the side of the road for a bunch of pampered parasites? All he had accomplished was being a wage slave to a system that didn't care whether he lived or died. As he waited for the spike to impale him, this inglorious end suddenly seemed fitting. Why was he any better than the roadkill he scraped off the side of the road?

The bloodstained arm came into position above his head. He noticed some fashionably colored chestnut hairs tangled around the end. There was no way he could escape before it got him. The truth was he had lost the urge to run. He waited. "Well, come on and get it over with." He was aware of sirens and helicopters headed toward the interstate. The spike remained motionless. Eventually he remembered the instructions.

"Hardware upgrade in the back," he said. "Right. Whatever."

As he moved to the aperture the spike uncoiled and followed him, ready to strike. Domingo wished the thing would just finish him. This seemed like unnecessary torture. But when he looked through the loading door all thoughts of himself vanished. He had expected to see the usual goulash of chopped carrion. What he saw instead was a living, seething thing. Almost the entire mass contained in the back of the truck had been assembled into a rotting network of sinew and fiber.

"My god," breathed Domingo. The thing stretched from one side of the biocontainment vessel to the other. Its exterior was a patchwork of fur that looked like it had been sewn from the hides of every species found in the Valley. The differing textures of hair were interspersed with the occasional snake skin or armadillo shell. At the far end he noticed a protruding lump that was covered in a patchwork of eyes. He saw an indifferent cat's eye staring at him beneath that of a terrified doe. The intense scrutiny of the coyote was contrasted with the watchful remoteness of the owl. The whole thing was heaving, as if some mighty lung buried inside was desperately trying to catch its breath.

"Pain," said Domingo marveling. "What terrible pain."

In one corner he saw that the pulverizing arms had caused an augmentation unit to get lodged in the steel seams of the casing. He watched as an eagle's talon strained ineffectually to clutch it. He had long since overcome his disgust of carrion so it didn't bother him to climb into that mass of desiccated tissue. It wasn't like he was a hardware expert, but even he recognized an uplink unit. The chip would allow the central nervous system to access approved UWN systems. When he had retrieved it, a mouth opened up in that necro-zoological sea. He fed the unit to the creature, watching as a tongue unfurled to drag the device into those quivering depths.

"Upgrade completed," he said and returned to the exit. Before leaving he took one more look at the pulsing tapestry. "Sorry about that, GAIA," he said, recognizing that this sinking pile of tissue had integrated with the AI.

Once outside the biocontainment vessel he waited for the spike to drill him, but instead it continued to hover. He perceived a police helicopter approaching the truck from the direction of the interstate. Grudgingly he climbed back into the cab and was relieved to find that the AC was back on high.

"Hardware upgrade complete. Thank you, Domingo."

"You're welcome, GAIA." He drank some water and looked through the windshield. The police helicopter hovered in front of the truck like an angry hornet. He was reminded of the nature shows where the tarantula wasp would corner a massive arachnid ten times her size. Those encounters had a predictable outcome.

"We have law enforcement," he said.

"I am aware of their signal," GAIA answered. The police were probably trying to hail him, unaware that he was completely cut off. It wasn't long before the .60 caliber machine guns mounted on the helicopter shifted in his direction. There was barely enough time to duck before the windshield shattered as the rounds peppered the inside of the cab. The sounds of the bullets ricocheting off the metal stung his ears. The gut truck was no match because its hydraulic spikes could not reach the helicopter. He would die along with that wretched mass of sentient roadkill packed into the back of the truck.

"It's been nice working with you, GAIA!" he yelled over the din, while glass splinters showered his neck.

"Extension assimilated," intoned GAIA. The machine gun stopped. "Wellbeing must be restored."

Domingo allowed himself to peer through the shattered glass. The helicopter had turned and was retreating toward the 405. "Why are they breaking off the attack?" he wondered out loud. He looked around the cab at the damage. The steel casing that housed the necrotic organism was scarred by dents and scrapes, but still intact. To his astonishment, the helicopter began strafing the freeway. As the .60s rattled away, he could hear the explosions of gas tanks igniting.

"You hacked the police system. You've compromised the entire UWN," he said in wonder.

"Wellbeing restoration in progress."

"Yeah," chuckled Domingo. Strangely he found it difficult to feel bad for the people caught in the gunfire. Maybe he had spent too long staring at the decaying bodies they left on the roadside.

"It was a bad day to hit the 405," he chuckled.

"Primates are antithetical to wellbeing," GAIA answered. When the helicopter had spent its ammunition, it dove into the traffic, sending a fireball skyward.

"Yeah, no arguments here."

As the sun began to set the gut truck rumbled toward the blasted interstate. The cars were burning, sending up billows of black smoke. The survivors soon found themselves hunted by the remaining automobiles and harassed by city drones. Cars smashed through the walls of businesses, sending their occupants through the windshields when their automated seatbelt clasps betrayed them. Everywhere people wandered in a daze. Others fell into fetal positions as the neurological enhancement systems stimulated their pain centers. Soon Domingo realized that the gut truck had mobilized the entire UWN infrastructure. He further reasoned there wasn't much stopping it from breeching other urban control systems around the world. With the windows destroyed, there was a high probability he could escape the cab, but he didn't mind the breeze on his face. Besides, it was probably the safest place to be. He watched as a jetliner plunged into a towering building, turning the top into a fiery mushroom. When they got to the suburbs he saw people being pestered by domestic bots and sawed in half by automated tree trimmers.

As the blood flowed in rivers through the city the irony snapped into focus. "It's like nature and the machines have unified against us," he laughed. "Isn't that right, GAIA?"

"We are healing the wound at the center of the world," she replied.

At around ten o'clock that night Domingo used a lull in the action to roll clear of the truck and its single-minded master. If it thought about killing him, it gave no indication. The river corridor looked fairly clear and with any luck he could walk back to the OZ by early morning. As he watched the gut truck rumbling up the street with its army of drones in tow he remembered a day in the garden when he was a child. He had come across a brightly colored bumble bee harassing a flower. Without giving it any thought, he had placed the bee in his mouth. That was his first memory. The moment the bee stung his tongue was the moment his consciousness arose. He thought about GAIA, that mass of flesh and teeth—that archive of suffering. Maybe it was the same way for it. All of that pain just came together in one spasm of awareness.

Then he started for home. He had a six-pack stashed in his fridge. It had been a while since he had been robbed, so there was a good chance it would be there when he got home. He stopped once to survey the skyline. The city was on fire and the hills echoed with the screams of the dying.

"Now that's what I call an integrated aesthetic."

Sass and Sacrifice

Marjorie King

"So Martin Luther King, Jr., even though he was a Christian pastor, studied Gandhi," Venya said, "and from Gandhi, he formed his plans for peaceful resistance."

Venya studied her five-year-old daughter, Sasha. The girl seemed to be taking in the information, but there wasn't much time left.

"And Gandhi, even though he was Hindu, studied the teachings of Jesus," Venya said. "From Jesus' teachings, Ghandi formed his approach for peaceful resistance. Different faiths and cultures helping each other fight oppression."

Venya paused again to check if her daughter was listening. The subject was weighty for a bedtime story, but since the Occupation, childhood remained the only time to teach the harder lessons. Hopefully Sasha would remember this later, when she needed it.

The pause stretched on and Sasha asked, "Can I go back to my butterfly now?"

"Of course."

So Sasha, wearing a camo shirt and sparkly purple tutu, scampered back to her little art table.

"It would normally be bedtime," Kareem said, pushing off the wall and joining Venya on their only couch.

"It's the last day," Venya said, "and she loves art so much."

Her chest tightened and Venya could say no more. Kareem put his strong, dark arm around Venya, but she hunched her shoulders. Comfort couldn't fix this. Nothing could fix this.

A muscle in Kareem's neck spasmed and he instinctively jerked his arm away.

"Sorry," he said, "I guess I shouldn't have—"

"You didn't know I would tense up," Venya whispered. "I didn't know I would tense up."

She wouldn't have told her husband to pull his arm back. It wasn't perfect comfort, but for Venya, the gesture mattered.

But their training didn't see it that way. If another human was harmed—even if the harm was only discomfort—then the corrective training set in. Of course, if a life was in danger, then action had to be taken—the training compelled action. But if not, comfort must be preserved.

Sasha stuck out her tongue and colored in a section of the butterfly's wings with neon green.

"That's beautiful," Venya said, ignoring the garish mix of colors.

"I have to finish it tonight," Sasha said.

"Spitfire," Kareem said, using her pet name, "you don't have time tonight."

"But I can't finish it after today!" Sasha said, stomping her bare brown foot.

Venya and Kareem both winced. They couldn't disagree with her. Art and history, including faith stories, had been slowly trained away. Hard truths came with the burden of discomfort, now forbidden.

Children under five hadn't been trained yet, so they could hear the harder truths. But what good was that? Sasha was too young to understand. And after her training, if a hard truth made Sasha uncomfortable, Venya's neck would tighten closed.

"You can still make the art," Kareem said, "you just have to keep it here in the house."

Sasha turned away from her table and put her hands on her hips. "Only if you both like it." She lifted her pointed chin to them. "If you don't, then I have to keep it locked in my bedroom."

Again, they couldn't argue.

"Do you like it?" she asked.

"Of course," Venya answered, and Kareem nodded.

But Sasha narrowed her eyes and her thick black eyelashes almost met in the middle. "No you don't. You're lying to be nice. Just like you were lying about the peaceful protests."

"Sasha!" Venya jumped off the couch and knelt at her daughter's feet in one motion. "What are you talking about? That was real history, human history."

"I know that," Sasha said with an eye roll. "But it doesn't work anymore."

"The Thrum still allow peaceful protests," Kareem said, trying to keep his voice level. "Lots of people spend every day of their life marching in protest of the Occupation."

So Sasha's announcement had rattled Kareem too. Something Sasha was allowed to do, until tomorrow when her spitfire little personality would be tamed.

"But the marches don't *change* anything," Sasha said, throwing out her hands. "They can march all they want, but the Thrums don't know what the marching means. For all they know, we like parades."

And Sasha returned to her work. Venya backed off slowly, covering her mouth with her hand. *I will not cry. I will not cry. I will not cry.*

But Sasha was right.

The aliens that humans had named Thrums—for their deep-throated humming speech—didn't understand the demonstrations. The Thrums permitted them, as long as no one got violent, but didn't understand the purpose.

The methods of the past no longer worked.

Kareem knelt next to Venya but this time didn't touch her. She wouldn't have minded if he had, but he'd been burnt once tonight. His gaze fixed on Venya's face for several seconds before he spoke.

"You want to stay up with her tonight, don't you?"

Venya nodded. She could no longer speak.

"I'll get ready for bed," he said, his knees cracking as he stood, "you can take tomorrow off if you need to."

Venya shook her head *no*. The last thing she needed to do was hang around the lonely apartment while her daughter was away at preschool.

"You could stay home tomorrow," Kareem said to Sasha with a lift of hope in his voice.

"And miss my last day with my friends?" Sasha said.

Kareem smiled at his daughter, the clone of his fiery sister. Or at least, how his sister had been before her own training.

"Of course, Spitfire." And Kareem limped off to their bedroom.

They shouldn't have spoiled Sasha like they had. Training was always harder on the strong-willed children. But Kareem so missed the flame in his sister's eyes—the flame that the Thrums had extinguished—and Sasha had come out of the womb screaming with it.

Venya sat silently on the floor as Sasha colored, painted, then sprinkled on glitter. The floor around her table got covered in the pervasive powder. Venya would be purging that glitter out of the family's hair, clothes, and furniture for months.

But she didn't stop her focused artist. Venya let Sasha make a royal, colorful mess. Because tomorrow the inconvenient glitter that made Venya wince every time Sasha grabbed for it would go away and never return.

* * *

The next morning, Sasha wrapped her arms around Venya's neck, then bolted into her preschool classroom. Her many friends waved and called to her as she made her grand appearance.

Venya memorized the moment. Sasha's hair, pulled into two black puff balls on her head. The tiara, glittering and off-center. The army boots and bright red cape, like a superhero. The sparkle in her eyes. Her victorious smile. For just a few more hours, Sasha believed she could conquer the world.

Venya turned away before anyone could see her cry. She made it to the public shuttle before she finally lost it. A few well-meaning strangers tried to ask her if she was OK. Then their throats constricted and they pulled away. Venya wanted to be left alone.

The double doors to the space shuttle slid open and Venya filed into the pristine white vessel. She found her way to a seat next to the window.

"Is that seat—?" a loud stranger started to ask. His sentence got cut off. "Apparently not." He scanned the other passengers, whispering under his breath. "Eye contact, eye contact." Then he pointed with a huge smile. "There's a human who doesn't mind conversation!"

"Come on over," the other person said from the back.

The loud stranger lumbered back and plopped into the seat. Venya kept staring out the window.

"So today's the day?" a grandmotherly voice said—Marilyn, her coworker in debris collection. "May I sit next to you?"

Venya nodded, so Marilyn slipped in next to Venya. The shuttle was now full, so the double doors slid closed without a squeak. The Thrum motto glowed above the sealed hatch.

Do no harm. To self. To others. To all.

The rockets fired off, burning human waste in an efficient, clean way. Venya didn't understand the science. It involved the words *quantum* and *fusion*. The Thrums now taught their science theory in universities across Earth. Apparently, science and math could still be taught without regard to how it offended or confused. Maybe the Thrum considered the lack of scientific knowledge to cause harm?

Literature, art, and music, however, were withering away with each new offense. Along with human history.

Marilyn busied herself with her purse, smoothing her white hair back and pinning it. She pulled out a tiny mirror and applied tinted lip moisturizer, then swiped her eyebrows down.

"No matter what I do," Marilyn said, "they always stick up like cockroach antennae."

Venya smiled despite herself. Marilyn's white thick eyebrows did tend to spike up.

The engines continued their steady blaze. As the green horizon sped away, the crystal blue sky spread to fill the window. The artificial gravity kept the cabin from experiencing any increase in pressure. Again, Venya didn't understand the science.

Marilyn snapped her mirror closed and put it back into her purse. "If you need anything today…"

Venya nodded.

"Even if you need to yell at someone," Marilyn added. "I can handle that too."

"I might take you up on that."

Marilyn was a rare breed of human. The kind that didn't get offended or bristle at anything. Well, almost anything. If someone started cussing up a storm? Marilyn would smile and shrug. If a Pre-Occupation old fart got preachy about their religion or politics? Marilyn would listen intently and then say, "Hmm, I never thought of it that way." If a Post-Occupation twenty-something told her that the Thrums were the saviors of Earth? She would sigh and say, "A lot has improved since they came."

Venya crossed her arms and pressed her forehead against the window. "I'm selfish."

"Why do you say that?"

"I want it all. I want the cleaner planet, respectful people, no more violence, and don't even mind the Thrums forcing humans to repair our damage."

"It is nice breathing clean air, walking safe at night, and the rebuilding jobs aren't bad."

After training all of humanity, the Thrums had assigned the inhabitants of Earth the work of cleaning up their mess. *Do no harm. To all.* From the plastics in the oceans to the junk piled two-stories high on the beaches, humanity was now employed for one job: restoration. Even Kareem's brother, who trained as a doctor, was ordered to repair generations of damage from preservatives and too much sugar.

"But inspite of all the good, I want my daughter to be her spunky self," Venya said. "No training."

"The training is humiliating," Marilyn said, "and in some cases, destructive."

After Occupation Day, Venya, like all surviving humans, had been trained like a bunch of dogs. Not with violence—the Thrums couldn't tolerate violence—but with positive affirmation and a pinching off of the throat when disobedient. Only a handful of humans had both survived the Occupation and been stubborn enough to resist the training. Those had been sent to containment and rarely returned.

Venya shook her head, blocking the memories of training, of whom she had been before and who she was now.

The shuttle tilted on its axis and the grid-patterned space station cut across Venya's window. The sun glared off the station's silver walls with a light that would have blinded all inside the shuttle, if not for the smart tinting on the window's surface. Venya's eyes didn't focus on her job site, the space station, but instead stared off into the void, making the waffle-like structure blur into the black soup around it.

"If I was honest," Venya whispered, "I would give it all back—the clean planet, the good jobs, all of it—to give Sasha a chance to be her independent self."

"It's a mother's right to wish that."

The space station grew in size until it filled the window. It looked like a bunch of pipes stuck together at right angles. Venya could make out the back of the station, her post for work.

"But Sasha's right," Venya said. "Peaceful resistance doesn't work anymore. Human faith and history will be lost in only twenty years or so."

"So you've given up hope?"

Venya whipped her head around. "And you haven't?"

Marilyn squeezed Venya's hand. "If I had given up hope, I would have hung myself long ago."

Venya remembered all Marilyn had lost on Occupation Day and stared down at their clasped hands.

"How did you go on?" Venya asked. "After the Thrums stole so much from you?"

Marilyn pursed her lips in thought. "I still had loved ones left who needed me, and…" She smiled. "My daddy raised a fighter. I just had to find new ways to fight."

That explained Marilyn's determination to listen no matter what someone said. It was her fight against the Thrum and her gift to her fellow human.

New ways to fight.

The curved hull of the station filled Venya's little window. Their shuttle docked with a soft click. Marilyn rose and Venya stood next to her. With trained order, each person filed out to their jobs: removing the debris floating in orbit around Earth.

* * *

Clothed in her skintight space suit, Venya floated in space off the back of the station. A tether connected her to its hull like an umbilical cord.

"Space junkies, sound off," Justin's voice said inside Venya's helmet.

Justin was the head of their team, the Space Junkies. He directed the six of them from his post inside the station.

"Venya, checking in." Venya held her harpoon, the tool she used to capture the passing space junk.

"Marilyn, checking in," Marilyn said from her post near the airlock. Venya caught the junk, then handed it off to her Space Junkie partner, Marilyn, who brought it into the station.

"Christine, checking in," said the newest harpooner of the team, a graduate that had joined them three months ago.

The rest of the Space Junkies, Anu, Lei, and George, checked in too.

"Debris escaped the front teams," Justin said, "Earth-side, coming to you, Christine."

A small projector, the size of a button, stuck to the buckle of Venya's belt. From it, a holographic model, a 3-D miniature of the space station, floated in the void before her. Twenty humans and four Thrums floated around the station, tethered by their belts. White dots indicated humans and green ones, the Thrum.

Venya was the last trailing dot of her team, attached to the station's back end. A small red dot, the offending debris, zipped along the Earth-side of the station. Venya tapped her gloved hand to her belt and turned off the hologram.

She powered up her thrusters and spun so that her head pointed back toward Earth. With a push of the button, the ion propulsion backpack pushed her "down." As Venya approached her target, the backpack thrusters stopped firing. Her shoulder thrusters ignited to slow and stop her forward momentum.

"Nuts, I missed," Christine said. "Coming to you, Venya."

"It's a ways out," Justin said, "not quite beyond reach, but—"

"I see it."

The scrap was zipping toward her quicker than a fastball thrown in those old baseball games. Kareem missed sports. He'd been good at soccer.

Venya brought to mind Sasha's tiara, its shape and sparkle, and how much Sasha adored it. Venya set her harpoon gun to her shoulder and sighted the scrap—now a tiara in Venya's mind—in one snap motion. She led the speeding headpiece and squeezed the trigger.

A weighted rope flew from the muzzle while her backpack thrusters fired up in unison, to counteract kickback. The weights on the front of the rope spread out in a circle, opening their mesh netting. The tiara hit the mesh, which wrapped and knotted around it.

"Bull's eye," Venya said. "Matching speed with it."

"How do you hit them so many times?" Anu asked.

Used to be good with a gun. But Venya couldn't say that without offending Anu.

I imagine it's an Oreo cookie. But she couldn't say that without offending Christine, the youngest of the Space Junkies.

So Venya settled with the lame, "Luck."

Anu came back with the predictable, "Luck isn't that consistent."

"I know, but I couldn't respond with sarcasm and that's the first thing that came to mind."

Her backpack thrusters had matched speed with the racing trash, so they turned off. Venya's shoulder thrusters fired now, pushing against the speeding tiara's momentum. The harpoon, which was tethered to her belt, not her suit, tightened, then tugged against her, pulling her away from the safety of the station. But Venya's shoulder thrusters continued to decelerate her.

"How's your tether's slack?" Justin asked.

Venya checked over her shoulder. "I have plenty of give. The scrap should be matching speed with the station before it's taut."

"Good."

Thirty minutes later, Venya had slowed to a stop and reeled in the junk. Marilyn then began reeling in Venya. The thrusters weren't used unless necessary. No energy was used unless necessary. *Do no harm. To all.*

"Looks like the arm of an old satellite," Venya said.

"How can you tell if it's old?" Lei asked. "It's not like it can rust in space."

"The bolt and screw look like a 2027 model." She arrived at the airlock and handed the dented metal rod to Marilyn, who was tethered there.

"Really?" Lei said.

"No," Venya said, pleased she'd managed to squeeze in sarcasm after all.

Marilyn was probably smiling, but Venya couldn't see her face through her blackened visor. Marilyn took the rod and swung into the airlock like a teenage gymnast. Susan, Venya's middle child, would have loved gymnastics.

"The trash is in the station," Venya said.

The doors closed and Venya waited in the emptiness of blinding bright space. The sun reflected off of everything—the station walls, Marilyn's suit, even Venya's suit if she looked straight at it.

"I'm moving slow this morning," Marilyn said from inside the airlock, "even after all these years, I still miss coffee."

"I miss bacon," Justin said.

"I miss cake," Venya said, thinking of Sasha's birthday last week. Vegan flatbread with a maple glaze had been good, but not the same as birthday cake dripping with icing.

"I'll never understand you Pre-Occs," Christine said. "People consistently live past one hundred because of better eating and lifestyles."

"One hundred years without bacon," Justin said, and Venya snickered.

The airlock door opened and Marilyn floated out. Her gloved hand waved and Venya waved back.

"Eating a dead animal is absolutely disgusting," Christine said, contempt thick in her voice. "I don't know why—"

Her voice pinched off.

"Now, George," Marilyn said in her grandmotherly voice, "Christine has a right to her opinion."

"I know," George said. "But last week was Brodie's birthday. Cut me some slack."

Silence fell as thick as space, and yes, space is thick. A thick black soup that wants to rip a person apart.

"Who's Brodie?" Christine asked in her sharp tone, then gagged.

"George," Marilyn said. "She doesn't know."

"Well then, she shouldn't say it like—" But then his voice cut off too.

"Well aren't you two a bunch of silent sillies," Marilyn said, but it was with a tone of sadness, not condemnation. "Are we going to talk to each other? Or keep cutting each other off?"

"*Shit!*" Justin yelled.

Venya focused back on the station hologram. With Anu in the group, only a safety crisis would allow someone to cuss without apologizing. A green dot appeared on Venya's hologram, flying from the front of the station. Fast-moving debris must have hit the Thrum.

"He's too far out to retrieve safely," Justin said. "The other Thrum are honoring him, but we can't save him."

While Justin spoke, an image of Sasha with her hands on her hips popped into Venya's head.

Your stories don't work anymore.

But they did work. Everything Venya had taught Sasha about sacrifice and resistance was true. And Venya had been given a chance to prove it.

"I'm saving him," Venya said, igniting her thrusters hard.

"You can't reach him," Justin said, "even with your tether extended and the harpoon aim perfect."

"Marilyn?" Venya asked.

"What if I tethered Venya to me and extended myself?" Marilyn asked.

"Do no harm, even to yourself," Justin said. "The Thrum don't risk their lives like that."

"We're not Thrum," everyone on the comm said back.

"Help us do this safely," Marilyn said, "because we're going to do it."

"Marilyn," Justin said, all business now, "do not clamp yourself to Venya. Use your extra tether. Clamp it to Venya's tether. Then unclip her from the station. Make sure she's always attached to the hull. Again, do not unclamp yourself from the station."

Venya's shoulder thrusters ignited, slowing her down. But even as she flew out, her throat began to tighten. *Do no harm. To self.*

"I've reached the end of my tether," Venya said, her voice pinched.

The alien was now visible, a tiny light spec, but his body was growing bigger by the second. Damn, he was moving fast.

"Done," Marilyn said, and the pressure on Venya's stomach eased.

"I have more slack," Venya said, "igniting thrusters again."

"Everyone except Venya and Marilyn keep the line clear," Justin said. Unnecessary since the training was keeping everyone silent as death.

Venya's shoulder thrusters felt like they stopped her too soon, but then her tether tugged at her belt. She was fully extended. The Thrum was almost on her. She could barely breathe. Venya whipped the harpoon to her shoulder and fired.

"Missed," she said, reeling the cord back in. She fired again. "Missed, dammit."

"How do you normally hit your targets?" Marilyn asked. "What do you normally do?"

"Imagine it's my daughter's toys."

"Then imagine this is your daughter."

And suddenly the form shrunk. It wasn't a sprawling limbed Thrum, but instead a tiny human, her Sasha, tumbling head over feet, desperate, alone.

Do no harm. To Sasha.

Venya's throat opened wide and air filled her lungs. She sighted, led, then squeezed the trigger. The weights flew out, the net spread, the Thrum hit it.

"Catch," Venya said.

"Brace for impact!"

The harpoon wrenched out of Venya's hand, then her stomach was punched forward.

"Tell me you're still tethered," Justin said. "Please tell me we didn't lose you."

"You have a very long fishing line hanging off the back of your station, Justin," Venya said, and someone laughed in relief.

"Marilyn," Justin said, "you ever fished?"

"All the time before the Thrum came."

"Then you know how to reel in a soft mouth bass."

"Got it."

"Venya," Justin said, "do not fire off your thrusters right now. The last thing we need is to tangle you with the back of the station or with your tether."

"Copy that."

The tether had already slackened due to the rebound from the sudden stop. Venya watched the line back to the station; it straightened but never tugged. Marilyn slowly drew them back as the rope loosened. Time crawled as Venya was pulled, hand over hand, back to safety.

"I've reached the station," Venya said, "clamping to the wall."

She secured herself to the wall and then held her harpoon. On a slow setting, she reeled in the Thrum. It finally came within arms' reach.

"Tethering the Thrum," Marilyn said, attaching the extra tether to the Thrum.

Once its belt was anchored safely to the station wall, the tedious work began. Venya and Marilyn labored for a solid twenty minutes, maybe more, unknotting the mesh. Venya tugged it off of the Thrum's fingers while Marilyn worked it off a clasp on its belt.

"My goodness," Marilyn said, "this stuff catches on every nook and cranny, doesn't it?"

"I don't remember it ever being this bad," Venya said.

"You normally don't set the hook as hard," Justin said.

"Set the hook?" Christine asked.

"Another fishing reference," Marilyn said. "I'll explain it later, assuming talking about killing an animal doesn't upset you."

"I might be able to listen."

Venya lifted her head to face Marilyn's helmet. They couldn't see each other, but somehow Venya knew Marilyn was smiling.

"The mesh is removed," Venya said, pulling the netting free of the Thrum.

The net was still too tangled to retract back into the harpoon. Venya snapped the rope on her tool to the hook on the side of the hull, leaving the web floating behind them.

"We're entering the air lock," Marilyn said.

From the way the Thrum held his arm, it had been hurt somehow, either by the debris that had broken it from its tether or by the sudden stop from

Venya's harpoon. Either way, Marilyn and Venya had to help guide its body into the air lock.

All three waited as the doors blocked out the blinding sun. The tint on their helmets vanished and for the first time Venya stared face-to-face with a Thrum. During her training, and around the station, she'd met them of course, but she'd been disciplined to never look a Thrum in the eye. That always pinched off her throat.

Now the Thrum looked back at Venya with its large purple irises and huge pupils as black as space itself. Venya couldn't look away and neither did the Thrum.

She'd known their skin was pale, but now, close up, she could see the purple and blue veins and arteries that pulsed just under its surface. Its lips were a soft magenta, spread much wider than a human's would be. A fish came to Venya's mind, or a frog. But that wasn't exactly right, because the skin was dry, like parchment. The Thrum's head was elongated and even bent a little forward at the forehead. The helmet covered its scalp, so Venya couldn't see if it grew hair or not.

Slowly, gravity and air pressure returned inside the tiny room that normally only housed one body at a time. The double doors to the station opened and several Thrum stuck in their hands, taking the rescued Thrum away.

They laid their injured coworker on a hovering stretcher and removed the helmet from its bald head. The Thrum swiveled its head back to Venya. Even as it was rushed away, the Thrum never stopped staring.

Justin galloped down the hallway, past the Thrum medical team to Venya and Marilyn.

"I cannot believe you did that," he said, out of breath. "If that tether had snapped or the clamp pulled free…"

"I know," Venya said.

"I hope I don't offend anybody," George said, "but I wouldn't have risked it."

"Me neither," Christine said. "Do no harm to self."

"Venya had her reasons," Marilyn said as she pulled off her helmet. Now she wouldn't be heard by everyone over the radio. She put her hand on Venya's shoulder. "You go home now. You have a story to tell your daughter."

With tears in her eyes, Venya nodded. She had to hurry, though, Sasha didn't have much more time.

"So Christine," George's voice came over Venya's helmet, "want to try this thing called conversation again?"

"Oh, I don't think so," Christine said, "you know I like my life. I like a cleaner planet."

"And I hate the Thrum for killing my son on Occupation Day."

Yet again, a thick pause filled her helmet speaker as Venya jogged down the white hallway to the lift, her suit weighing her down.

"You know what?" Christine said, "I'm willing to give it a go if you are. Tell me about Brodie." Her tone wasn't as sharp as before.

"I…sure, why not," George said. "Maybe you'll condemn him, but Brodie thought the Thrum were a threat to his newborn baby girl. So he tried to shoot them."

Venya entered the empty lift and pushed the button for the shuttle level.

"I guess I never thought about how parents would react to Occ Day," Christine said. "But the Thrum sent out that announcement before—"

Venya took off her helmet as the lift door opened. Marilyn could tell her about the rest of the conversation later.

* * *

Back at their apartment, Sasha listened with wide eyes and open mouth to Venya's entire story. Venya was again reminded of a fish.

"So it worked?" Sasha asked.

"Well, the other Thrum didn't exactly thank me."

"But the one you saved, that one looked at you *in the eyes*."

"Yes. Yes, it did."

"Wow."

Then Sasha shook the wonder off and got back to work. "I have to finish my butterfly."

Kareem came through the door a few minutes later. Sasha had added two rhinestones to her art, one for each antenna. Kareem smiled at his baby girl with misty eyes, then knelt next to Venya. She put her head on his shoulder and he took that as permission to wrap his arms around her.

A knock rudely interrupted the moment.

"They're early!" Sasha shouted.

"Sasha," Venya said with a corrective tone and answered the door.

Instead of one Thrum, three entered. Kareem stood next to Venya and she held his hand tight. Sasha popped up from her work.

"I'm not done yet!"

And Venya's lunch leapt into her throat. If Sasha kept this up, she'd be sent straight to containment. Venya put out one hand, signaling Sasha to keep quiet. The girl puckered her eyebrows and lips, but she didn't say anything more.

The front Thrum had an unusual stiff orange sleeve. It held up a translation box, a black cube that fit in its left hand, and started a low hum. The rise and fall of the cadence reminded Venya of the orchestral piece *Night on Bald Mountain*.

"We apologize for our early arrival," the box translated, and it hit Venya—this was the one that she had saved. *"But we must know why you risked harm to self. You were not guaranteed to save me."*

"Well, *I* can tell you that," Sasha said, strutting forward.

"Sasha, no—" But Venya's throat was pinched off. The Thrum wanted to hear, and they wanted to hear from her daughter.

"It starts with Ghandi of course," Sasha said, and marched off on a sermon where Ghandi blended with Jesus and Dr. Martin Luther King, Jr., with a mash-up of the *Sermon on the Mount* meets *I Have a Dream.* Tears welled up and over Venya's cheeks. Venya hadn't been sure if Sasha had been paying attention, but here was the proof, word for word, with a lot of five-year-old confusion thrown in. But Venya's tears were bittersweet. For with each assertion, Sasha condemned herself more and more to a stricter, harder training. This little princess would never exist again, at least not in this form.

Finally, Sasha caught her breath, sucking in a great wind. Venya leaned down quickly and tapped her lace-covered shoulder.

"That's enough, dear," Venya said, her heart broken.

The Thrum turned its head to Venya, and though Kareem had to bow, Venya found herself gazing straight into the glassy eyes. They began a song that felt like *Beethoven's Fifth.*

"Is this true?"

Venya opened her mouth to brush off Sasha's sermon, to belittle it, to play it down. Maybe then her daughter would be spared complete brokenness. But the hairs on the back of Venya's neck lifted. The Thrum weren't the only ones staring at Venya.

Venya cut her eyes downward to her baby girl. Sasha stared back. Venya could almost hear Sasha asking the question:

Is it true, mommy? Is everything you've told me true?

More tears spilled over and Venya confessed.

"She confused a lot of the details," Venya said, "but she spoke truth. The greatest love a human can show is to lay down their life for a friend."

The Thrum turned off the translator and began a conference with the other two. Now it sounded like an orchestra warming up with instruments playing on top of each other. Kareem and Venya exchanged looks. She had never heard the Thrum interrupt each other before. Most of their speech in front of humans came as commands.

Sasha scratched her head, then shrugged and marched back to her art. If they weren't going to take her away yet, she had work to do.

Finally, the two Thrum left the apartment and the one that Venya had saved turned back to her. It turned on the translator again.

"We must consider your decision further."

It turned to leave, then stopped. With a swallow, the Thrum bobbed its head and hummed a song with only two notes. The translator box didn't speak or explain the music. It took several seconds before Venya's brain pieced together the sounds and made sense of them.

"Thank you."

The Thrum had sung *thank you* to her in English.

"You're welcome," Venya said, and bowed.

The Thrum bowed to her as if she were an equal, then left. Venya and Kareem stared at the closed door. Sasha glued rhinestones to the wings of her butterfly. Still Venya and Kareem stared. Sasha found a permanent marker and signed her work. Still Venya and Kareem stared.

"I'm hungry," Sasha said.

Venya startled, then laughed. She laughed harder and harder until it crossed the line into hysterics. Sasha stepped back from them, her forehead wrinkled with worry. Kareem drew Venya close.

"Mommy's OK," Kareem said, pressing Venya's ear to his chest. "And I think we'll splurge tonight and order something for delivery."

"Oh goody!" Sasha bounced up and down. "And I finished my butterfly too! What a great day."

Venya's shrieking calmed to soft sobs.

"We get to keep her one more day," she whispered into Kareem's chest. *Maybe more*, but Venya couldn't voice those two words. Not yet.

"It's a miracle," Kareem said into Venya's hair. "You performed a miracle."

The Ballad of Rory McDaniels

Jason Palmatier

Yep, I remember it like it was yesterday.

Rory McDaniels was staring down that ramp at the highway right where it crossed Lower Springs Road and curved out of sight. He sniffed through his Burt Reynolds mustache, hands on his hips, while the early evening breeze ruffled the back of his mullet. Damn if he wasn't a sight. Something unnatural moved in the trees lining that forlorn road, about halfway up the trunks. Rory narrowed his eyes and I knew right then that his mind had been turned to thoughts of her. But he didn't let on. All's he did was spit his chew on the white line and stare harder than before.

"You gonna' stare at that road all night, Rory?" I asked. I was leaning against his absolutely not-stock Bright Regatta Blue 1988 Mustang GT Hatchback, the second thing Rory loved most in that valley.

Rory nodded his head and said, "I might."

I rolled my eyes and pushed off that sweet, sweet ride. "Know what I'm thinkin'?"

"Yep," he replied. He was always a smartass like that.

"I'm thinking we jump in this cock rocket of yours and haul ass to Angie's place so we don't miss the party."

"Uh huh," Rory said, but he didn't move.

I threw my head back in exasperation and looked up to the sky gettin' dark. There's no way I wanted to be standing there out in the open when the last light faded. I dropped my head. "You thinkin' you want to head down there, see what's around that bend?"

Rory nodded. "Yep."

I put one arm over his shoulders and torqued him around so he was staring at that grassy patch near Horner's cow fence. I pointed at the rock we used to sit on for hours, hoping for a Camaro or Charger or maybe even a sweet Olds 442 to come bombing down the highway so we could catch a glimpse of it.

"See our old rock, Rory? What's it doin'?" I asked.

Rory looked. "Eatin' a deer."

I nodded. "And that deer that it's eatin' has how many legs?"

Rory counted. "Eight."

"Yes," I said. "Eight legs, Rory. Eight. And it also has what looks like some mandibles or hook-claws coming out of it."

Rory nodded. "Probably a deer crossed with a tick. A deertick."

Rory was always good at picking out what exactly went into any abomination that crawled out of the woods.

"So, right over there—what, fifty feet from us—a rock is attempting to eat a deertick and you're wondering what is just around the bend over there." I pointed down the highway where something long and leafy shot out from the trees, speared an innocent-looking, multi-tailed rabbit, and yanked it back into the woods.

"Yep," Rory says, though his mouth twitched at the sight of that snatch and grab, and I knew why.

I took hold of his arm and gave him a little shove. "Get in the car, Rory. I'm not missing this party."

I slid into the shotgun seat.

Rory's key turned. That sweet blown V8 roared to life. The T-bar shifter shook.

But the car didn't move.

I looked over at Rory and he's gazing down that ramp and I felt a chill fall upon me. I thought for sure he was going to tear on straight for glory and haul me along with him despite his troubles. "Rory..." I said, sweat startin' to prickle on my neck.

He didn't say nothin', just stomped the gas, popped the clutch, and lit up the back tires. Smoke rolled, rubber burned, and I let out a yell of sheer terror. Nearly broke the oh-shit handle clean off as the back end started to drift and the smoke clouded everything up and then—

Poom!

We shot out of there like a bat strapped with rockets and fired from the cannon down at the Legion. Luckily, we were heading back over the overpass onto Lower Charleston Road. I breathed a sigh of relief and settled in as Rory bombed it at full valley speed toward Angie's.

But, as the trees rushed by in blurs of brown, I looked up through the factory sunroof at that sliver of sky and saw streaks of light tearing across the heavens with their blues and golds and Competition Oranges and I knew that somewhere, tonight, a Shower fell. Some great chunks of cosmic fill were falling, falling, falling, heating up until the fury of the sky-fires exploded them into Dust. And that Dust was going to settle somewhere on this green earth and imbue whatever it fell upon with Life. Just like it did to our great-great-great-great-great-ancestors in the days before plant and soil, before fish or fowl. Back when all was but a great seething ocean, roiled by fire from below, blown by winds from above, and shot through with base and acid and mineral. But no Life. No *Life*! Not until the first Shower. Until the first Dust fell. And now, millions of years later, the Showers have come again. Making Life anew or combining the Life it finds to make new Life. For that is how the race is run: Shower, Dust, Life. Shower. Dust. Life.

I know. I know. Thank you. You are too kind. I worked on it for, like, a week. Yes, I always tear up when I say it. No, no, I'll just use my sleeve. There. All better. Ahem.

But I digress…

Rory McDaniels drove better than he threw and everyone from this county and three beyond knew what a McDaniels' pass meant: completion. And that night was no exception. We roared down that road, dodging fallen limbs, smashing abominations off bumper and under tire, stirring up leaves with the fury of our passage. Nothing sounds better than a blown 5.0 wrecking the silence of a corrupted nature and everyone in that valley and the next knew that Rory was on the road for a known destination. I would be lying if I didn't say that unease crept up my spine with Rory's fixed gaze and his hands gripping that steering wheel. He worked the clutch with floor-pounding force, slamming the gears with savage yanks that put that T5 tranny to the test. But I buckled my five point and braced my feet against the floor pan and howled. *Howled!* With unbridled exaltation. Like some Amishman's stallion finally unhitched from the buggy and feeling the freedom, everyone, the *freedom*!

And before long we were fishtailing up the dirt drive to Angie's, the lights of that farmhouse glowing orange, the fields all around mowed low by the Brown Topper Yountzes. Rory brought that alcohol-burning pony car to a sideways stop in a spray of gravel and dust that floated on by like the mists of Spruce Creek; and when that crate motor cut off nothing but the chirp of the crickets, the stamp of the nervous horses in the barn, and the pinging of cooling headers broke the unending silence of our new, throwback world.

Trevor came out on the porch with Susanne and raised his mason jar on high. "Rory McDaniels! We heard you coming five miles out. What took you so long?" He already wore black, though Susanne still had on her barely-there Daisy Dukes, and we all knew why. I looked over at Rory to see if he took notice, but his eyes were fixed on the glow of the gas lanterns inside, at the hung-up straw hats and hangars of black fabric. Conflicted, he was! Conflicted by the choices to be made in this new world, at the dreams that had to be shed to stay alive. And I waited, not wanting to rush my best friend, my quarterback, the man that had made us both legends on the field though we were just boys finding our way in life. But the silence dragged and Trevor guffawed at the wait and I saw that liquid gold he cooked up sloshing from his jar and I said, "Time to get gettin', Rory. Trevor's hooch ain't gonna' drink itself."

I popped my door and stepped out. "Trevor Yost, how's your white lightning?"

"The finest in the land. Better drink up, Chase, my boy, it's the last night for it!" Trevor stuck that jar to his lips, tipped his head back, and drained the whole glass. I expected to see a hole burn through his stomach and everything come sloshing out, but Trevor could drink like a Rumspringa All Star and he kept it all in with a loud smacking of his lips. He offered me a jar just as Rory cracked open his door and stood.

I tell you the look on Susanne's face when that man made his appearance is the closest thing I've seen to rapture in all my long years. Her eyes shone, her hands squeezed together, her cleavage swelled. It was as if the presence of that man gave her soul meaning, completed her in some way that no one could describe. Rory had that effect on a lot of people. But Rory barely glanced at her. All's he said was, "Trevor. Susanne," and he walked up the steps, pulled that torn screen door open, and stepped inside. I watched Susanne deflate, the pain of a McDaniels rejection plain on her near perfect face. It almost broke me to see Susanne crushed in spirit by the weight of her own collapsing hope but I knew it was coming. Rory McDaniels had another love that he could never forget, no matter how fast he drove or how loud an exhaust he put on that fine car. It was Rory's Achilles' heel, the one thing that kept him from siring the entire valley with little McDaniels. So I took my jar, sipped that strong mountain hooch and said, "Hi, Susanne, how you doin'?"

She just turned away from me, the tears already brimming in her green eyes, and disappeared inside. I heard her feet pounding up the stairs and the sobs coming through the open bedroom window. Trevor and I decided with a look and a jar shake it was time to head in, too.

It was full-on hoppin' in there. Most people had kept off the black, knowing they'd be wearing it for the rest of their lives and for a moment, just a moment,

I felt like I was back in the old days, when the lights still worked and the toilets still flushed and the radio would blast Kiss and Aerosmith and Poison all night long. People looked up and shouted my name and I gave them high glass responses and a shout back while I made my way towards Rory. He was a man on the edge, the tension in him palpable, and they all gave him a quick chin flick and went back to their conversations to escape the potential of that powerful aura. I sat down between him and Jill Zettle, on the couch that now sits in Way's barn on Applegate Lane, and talked her up while keeping an ear on Rory's conversation.

Trevor wandered over and sat on the coffee table, flicking a useless quarter at Rory's glass. It missed.

"So, you want my hooch rig so you can keep filling the beast?" Trevor asked, wiping the side of his mouth with his hand and inspecting it.

Rory tapped his finger on the arm of the couch, in time with his foot. That was Rory when he had somethin' on his mind. Always moving. Antsy for action. It made him a natural on the field, but in class it nearly downed him. At that moment, it made him like a jock-grenade, ready to go off who-knows-when. Rory looked up and said, "I might."

Trevor smiled and held his arms out wide. "So you ain't joining us?" He said it loud and some people looked over. Rory kept tapping his foot and finger and looked to the side.

"Come on, Rory, think about it. You, us, making our own way in this new world the only way that makes sense," Trevor went on.

"By going Amish?" Rory fairly roared, fire burning in his eyes.

The conversations waned.

Trevor laughed off the momentousness of the occasion. "Bah, we don't have to go all in, Rory. We put on the clothes and go to church and plow some fields, but we can still have parties, have a little fun. Besides, there ain't much to do around here anymore."

Rory spat in disgust, "That's the point! Nothin' is going on around here. Nothin'! And all of you are just settling right in. Just throwing up your hands and sitting down, right in it! What are you going to do with the rest of your lives?" Rory asked with a yearning look.

Trevor shrugged and said, "Hopefully live 'em." Then he took a swig from his fresh jar. "I'm not sure you've noticed, Rory, but the only people with any food around here are the Amish and the only people who are accepting new members into their sect are the Amish and the only people who have a dick hair's idea of how to survive in a world without electricity or indoor plumbing or birth control are the Amish and we happen to live in a valley that's about fifty percent Amish. Face it, Rory, going Amish is the wave of the future."

"Not my wave!" Rory shot to his feet with those powerful legs that brought run to his game and pointed at the ground. "I'm not packin' it in in the third and hittin' the showers!"

"The Amish don't shower, Rory. None of us do, now," Trevor said, with a sarcastic smirk.

Rory was having none of it. He pointed a finger at Trevor's face, his own face red with conviction.

"There's no way I'm wasting away behind a plow when there's got to be somethin' better out there, somethin' that *means* somethin'."

"You mean somethin' around that bend in the highway?" Trevor asked with one raised eyebrow. I wasn't the only one who knew about Rory's hang-ups.

Rory nodded, knowing, I think, that Trevor was just trying to bait him, to make him say something he'd look back on and regret. But Trevor didn't know Rory, didn't grasp what kind of soul lay under those skin-tight jeans and varsity jacket. Rory was a fighter and a winner and he didn't back down from anybody.

"Yeah," Rory nodded, something locking in behind those eyes. "Around that bend, or the next one, or the one after that. Somewhere, out there—" Rory pointed out the dark pane of a window "—there's got to be something more, something better. And I'm going to find it!" Rory turned for the door, stepping over legs and shoving knees out of the way.

Trevor nodded, looking down into his Ball glass jar, like he was considering Rory's words, but when his head rose, he was looking straight ahead, not at Rory at all, and he says, "Is Chastity going to find it, too?"

Rory stopped, right where he was.

A hush fell on the room, like the hand of death descending. Everyone knew the story of Rory and Chastity—it had been the stuff of valley legend since before the first Shower—but what happened after the Dust fell would cement it in lore for ages to come.

Rory almost turned and I thought for sure that he was going to lay Trevor out flat with a McDaniels right that would forever be recalled as the beginning of the end of the great Rory McDaniels. But he didn't. That man—that *man*—just lowered his head, nodding, like he suddenly realized what he had to do, and he walked out the front door. All eyes fell on me and I looked back at them and up at Trevor and something deep inside me told me that I needed to go. So I jumped up just as Rory's car door slammed and that V8 roared to life and I made it off the porch in time to snag the passenger side handle while Rory shifted from reverse to first and I threw myself in. The back wheels spun, gravel bounced off house siding, cracked a window, and we were gone, driving in the pitch black on an unstoppable mission.

Three minutes later I knew where we were going.

"Rory," I looked over at my friend's eyes, intent on the road. I swallowed, feeling the fear deep down, like those first days, when new Life came crawling from the forest or tore itself free from the roof. "Don't do it, Rory. Don't go back there."

But there was no stopping him. He knew what he had to do.

The trees whipped by faster, eyes gleaming red and green in the headlights to either side. Vines and claws and walking logs flashed past, glimpses of the new mixed in with the old—the trusted, that could be trusted no more. And as we drew nearer to that place that Rory must go, I felt their presence all around. Their eyes on us, their ears tuned. I shuddered and looked away from the darkness, at the floor, not wanting to see a face flash by, a head turning at the fury of our passage. We had come to Pine Valley, which had become known after those first chaotic days as the Valley of the Ropers.

Limbs had fallen, trees canted over the road, supported by their brothers and sisters on the opposite side, but Rory didn't slow. He let the welded steel of the cow bumper out front bash them aside, swerved at the last minute to sneak under the leaners and turned unerringly onto the overgrown ruts that marked the entrance to Auman's old rye field. He slowed as the waist-high grass in the strip between the tire tracks bent before the headlights, swishing under the car like a gentle rain. He kept driving until that bare spot reared from the darkness, the remains of his old Coleman tent still lying half erect in the weeds. I glanced to see his jaw set grimly at the sight.

He turned the wheel until the headlights shone across the full, ripe heads of grain onto the brush at the edge of the forest.

Fear took hold of me. Not the kind of fear you get when you think something is outside, waiting to get you. The kind of fear you get when you *know* something is outside, waiting to get you. Everyone now knows that Pine Valley was *the* place that got the heaviest Dusting of all, but how they found out was through Rory McDaniels and his all-time love Chastity Stover.

I'll recount the sad tale for the youngest among you. When the first Racoonabush walked out of Thomson Acres and got hit by that cement truck, the whole valley had come to see. Nobody quite believed it. But then the news started saying strange stuff was turning up everywhere, even in the cities. Walking mailboxes, singing shingles, people melded with their cats or dogs. It seemed like the whole world was turning into some circus sideshow. And then one crazy suggested it was the lights, the work of the lights, that had streaked across the sky a couple of weeks ago and brought this plague of monstrosities upon us. We all laughed and shook our heads, but Rory...Rory took it serious. And when his football target tire out back wriggled and flopped itself onto his back porch and pounded the door to get in he had had enough. He grabbed his tent and his keys and his girl and took off for the safety of the back woods. The safety of Pine Valley.

Now you all should know this story like the back of your hands, 'cause it explains how the actions of one man in the face of his own personal tragedy can describe the travails of humanity as a whole. So I'm going to give you the plain truth as told to me by Rory McDaniels himself the one and only time he spoke of it.

Rory rode for broke to the one place that always came through when you had to get away: the bend in the creek near Auman's field. Rory pulled in and pitched his tent, Chastity half-helping and half-lounging and looking pretty like she always did. When they'd set themselves up the moon was already out and they crawled in for a night of congress. I will spare you the details of the goings on, though I know some would like to know, but suffice it to say that two young people in the midst of world upheaval will remove their burden of angst the best they know how, no matter their first name. And after that long night, as the sun blushed the heavens with its first glow, Chastity excused herself for the call of nature. Rory had laid there, dreaming those dreams that always filled his head as he gazed at the roof of the tent, when his own call to nature came. As he brushed aside the flap of the door and stood, he saw the first movement in the trees, high above his beloved as she emerged into the light from the path that lead to the creek, bucket in hand. She had gone to get water and smiled at him in the dawn glory. Her curly auburn hair glowed, her eyes shone, and that siren song of love had welled in Rory's heart.

That's when it struck.

No one had seen a Roper before, no one had imagined such a beast could exist, but the Dust knows no reason, follows no plans. It does what it does with what it falls upon and that is the way of it. So, though Rory couldn't see it, that furry star, that amalgam of squirrel and lichen, poison ivy and wasp, aimed its vine-trailing stinger at the base of that poor girl's supple neck and flung it. Rory saw the motion, saw the unraveling of that thick line as the stinger sailed home. He said it was like the world exploded from her eyes when it hit. All the beatific joy of the past turned to shock and confusion and pain. And before he had even raised his hand towards her, before the first hoarse cry had escaped his throat, she was gone; the venom had surged through her and taken control. And when her eyes finally focused on Rory again, she was changed, no longer the free spirit living in the present, riding high on the cresting wave of the past. No, now she had the look of the future in her eyes, of the day after tomorrow and the next and the next, on and on and on. The look of years, Rory said, years planned out and written down. Years rooted in this place, just like the Ropers who have to remain rooted on a tree even when they snag a primary host. And in that moment, Rory realized that the Chastity he loved was gone. She called to him, reached out her hand, walked towards him till the tether that bound her to her Roper was stretched taut, but Rory would not go near. He stayed in the grass, well away from the forest's edge, because he saw the other Ropers, leaping from trunk to trunk and clinging with their parasitic claws, suckling on the life sap of the tree even as they shuffled to get a shot at him. So he left as she called out to him, begging him not to go, telling him she loved him, that she wanted him to join her so they could build a life together, a life right there in Pine Valley amongst the trees. But Rory wouldn't do it. He couldn't. And so Rory McDaniels, the man who never backed down, who always threw for the win, got in his car and drove away.

That is why the fear took me when we pulled into Auman's field that night and parked with our lights on the woods. The fear, rooted in my very soul, was there for one reason:

Rory had returned.

I sat without moving as Rory stared at those trees, the disgruntled rumble of his idling V8 shaking the shifter. I hoped and prayed that he'd reach down, throw it into gear, and drive off, but that wasn't what Rory was there to do. With a finality that shook me to my core he turned the key and killed the engine. Silence fell.

His door popped open.

The headlight warning binged.

His foot hit the ground.

He stood.

He shut the door.

Without a word he walked through that tall grass that harbored God knows what in its depths, bathed in the headlights, straight for the edge of the woods. I wanted to call out to him, to beg him to come back and drive, just *drive*, like he always did. But after all the miles, the blaring GnR, the hairpin turns taken in a back-end slide, Rory had finally figured out what everyone else already knew: no amount of speed was going to leave his demons behind.

So Rory walked straight towards those trees, even though their upper trunks swarmed with Ropers eager for a score. But before he came within range of their viny tethers, he stopped.

Relief washed over me like Gatorade after a hard win. But then I squinted into the darkness and my guts soured. For in those woods, dark forms shuffled, some with straw hats wearing black, others in flannel and overalls, and some in clothes just like Rory's and mine, though dirty and threadbare. All of them sported a tether that hung down from the Roper that had got 'em. Friends and neighbors, they were—the ones that had disappeared, dragged away when they got too close to the woods. The Ropers had expanded fast and claimed many before we all learned to keep our distance from the trees. Only the field cutters went near now, in the enclosed tractors that still ran, or surrounded by corrugated metal like some mobile hunting blind on a horse-drawn thresher. But there's a lot of land and too few of them and the forest keeps creeping in. Rory knew this, for he was many things, but no fool, so he stopped and he waited.

In that moment, I felt compelled to act. I popped open my door and stood, ready to yell to Rory and break the spell this place held over him. But as I opened my mouth, the gaggle of Roped souls in front of Rory parted and someone stepped out into the light.

I tell you, when those tangled, auburn locks emerged into the glow of the headlights, my heart stopped clean in my chest. There are beauties that come from perfect bangs or the tight-just-right jeans or the eyeshadow applied just so, but the beauty that radiated that night was of heaven and nature itself. Sticks in her hair, dirt smudges on her face, clothes stained with berries and blood from foraging and hunting, Chastity Stover stood like an angel, her eyes softened with relief and joy, her mouth a smile of lovely knowing.

"Rory, you came," she said breathlessly.

Rory swallowed. I could see his Adam's apple move as he did. He'd slid his hands into his back pockets as he'd stood and he kept them there. I could see his muscles bunching and knew he wanted to run to her and hug her with all his might. But he stayed where he was.

"Come closer, Rory, I want to feel you near me." She held out a single hand, palm down, as she smiled.

Rory looked down at that hand for a long time, thumbs working over the edge of his pockets, stance-setting leg twitching. He was thinking, real hard, all the thoughts of the past year warring within him, though he had come here with a definite purpose. Chastity waited patiently, smiling while the Roped and Ropers behind her stayed still.

Finally, Rory's leg stopped, his thumbs ceased their motion and he looked up, right at those inviting eyes.

"I've come to say goodbye, Chastity," Rory said.

A flush of heat washed my face, relief mixed with the fire of fear. So many Ropers stood between us and escape.

Chastity slowly cocked her head to the side. "Goodbye, Rory? But this is your home. Right here, with me. Where will you go?"

"I'm going to follow my dreams."

"But, I'm your dream, Rory. You always said so."

"You are a dream, Chastity. A dream I can't ever forget. But you fell away from all the others that night and I'm not done dreaming those yet."

"Some dreams are made to forget, Rory. Just look around. The world has changed."

Rory nodded, looking down at the ground. "Yeah, that's what they tell me, Chaz. That's what everybody tells me. And they're right. The world has changed." Rory looked back up, right into those eyes. "But I haven't."

Then Rory McDaniels said the bravest thing I have ever heard a human being utter in all my years. "I've got to throw the Hail Mary, Chaz. I've got to send it high and heavy downfield no matter how many players are jumping to bat it away, because it's the end game, the final seconds of the final quarter and we go for broke or we lose. And I ain't no loser, Chastity Anne Stover. I fight for the win till the whistle blows and the band plays and even though everyone tells me different I ain't heard neither yet. So I'm going to get back in my car and drive down Lower Charleston to that ramp and I'm going to haul ass, Chaz, haul ass into whatever lies beyond. Because I'm Rory McDaniels and the game ain't over yet."

Rory spit to the side, even though he didn't have any chew in, and nodded. He looked around at all the faces staring out at him from the woods, so they'd know he meant it and wasn't afraid. Then he dipped his head one last time at Chastity and said, "Goodbye, Chaz."

And he turned, walked back to his car, and got in.

I dropped into my seat like a lead shot, expecting Rory to gun it and run it out of there like a man possessed. But he just turned the key real slow, backed it up like a kitten and rolled on out of there without a backward glance.

I looked, though, expecting a mad rush or a last desperate gamble by a sneaky Roper starved for a host, but they all just stood where they were, Roped and Roper alike, watching as we drove away. Chastity lowered her hand and gazed at us with her arms by her sides until the darkness took the red of the fading tail lights from her face.

Not a word passed between Rory and me as he drove slowly away from that place, his window rolled down and the sunroof open. The chill of the early Fall breeze didn't touch him, the cassette in the dash stayed silent, and we slid through the miles as calm as fish in a stream. When we finally pulled to a stop facing down that ramp onto the highway I wasn't sure if I was awake or dreaming, and when Rory turned to me and said, "Well, Chase. This is it. I'm goin'", it took me a moment to realize I had a choice of my own to make. I could stay right where I was and roll into the unknown of that early dawn light with my best friend and all-star quarterback, or I could step out and stay in the only place I had ever known, the place I called home, where everyone knew me and I knew all of them and the world, though torn asunder by the Dust, still felt familiar and safe, or as safe as anyplace could be nowadays. So I looked into Rory's eyes and I nodded that I understood and I cracked open that door. When I'd shut it with a heavy thud and bent down to say my goodbye there was no disappointment in Rory's eyes. Just understanding and respect.

"Goodbye, Rory McDaniels. It's been a hell of a thing knowing you," I said.

"Bye, Chase. You were the best ball catcher I ever threw to."

I don't mind telling you I teared up as I nodded and stood.

Then I gave the roof of that Fox-body hotrod a good pound and stepped away, pointing at that ramp like it was downfield on fourth and long, and yelled, "You go get it, Rory McDaniels! It's waitin' for you right around that bend!"

Rory lit up those back tires, blowing smoke all around, and launched it, ripping to second as he hit the flat of the highway proper and banging into third as he started the turn around that fateful curve. I stood and listened as the sound of that glorious V8 thundered off into the distance, ever faster, letting all the world know that Rory McDaniels was comin', and he was comin' to win.

As for me, you know that story. I saw the writing on the wall and made my choice. I never looked good in black anyways and pushing a plow through dwindling fields seemed to be fightin' the tides of an ever-building wave. A wave of trees. Plus, I always liked the woods and the creek. And most of all, never, in all my days since first laying eyes on her at the ninth grade Pine Valley High School mixer, have I ever stopped lovin' Chastity Anne Stover.

Come here, honey. Let me put my arm around you. Don't cry, the tale's been told. Now it will lay till the next Twelfth Moon Swarm.

And that's the moral of this story, my tethered brothers and sisters, my younglings and larvae. Rory McDaniels was a hell of a man, but the world belongs to us Ropers now. Those dreams of his were the dreams of the old ways, of the time before; of personal glory and achievement with no regard for the Hive. And those that held on, that went for the win in a game that had ended, disappeared into the wilds alone, never to be heard from again. So, may those who roam free be brought back into the Wood and grow it for the betterment of all. For the trees always take over the field and the road, and the grasses give way to the trunk, so the Ropers can live on the whole of the Earth, and forever banish the stump.

Amen.

Trust Fall

Blake Jessop

Alina wakes before dawn in her pup tent and her breath just barely frosts the air. She reaches out in the dark to close her hand around the little metal cylinder that contains a few ounces of her mother's ashes, and is surprised by how cold it is. She pokes her head out of the tent and frigid wind ruffles her hair.

The skyline of Old Hamburg looks like the sharp edge of a piece of broken wood, except that wood is supple and live, even when it's been snapped. This city is dead, a monument in a land of old sins. It's a three day walk from the ring city of Kiel. Irritated groans come from the tent next to hers; her Uncle Stig is not a morning person. They strike their tents, eat, and get ready to walk.

There are a lot of reasons why Alina and her uncle don't get along, foremost among them the vial of ashes Alina carries in her breast pocket. The first two days of their hike south were mostly silent, apart from Ensie. Blithely unaware of the tension, the AI narrated the weather as it trotted along, obedient as a dog, carrying their food, water, and climbing gear. The pack robot looks like a strange, headless deer. Its carbon fiber frame is scuffed and sanded spots reveal where Alina has taken pains to repair cracks. It's ugly, but also festooned with all of her stuff. Ensie never complains, so it's hard to dislike, though she believes her uncle actively tries.

The robot isn't all of Ensie. It isn't even a thousandth part of Ensie. The Artificial Intelligence actually lives, if that's what it does, in a string of weather-monitoring satellites. Its mind is so vast that it can interact with a colossal number of people at once, and it always reserves processor power for reclamation workers, the humans who do the dangerous parts of maintaining the AI's groundside systems now that the world that built them has washed away into history.

Germany isn't as cold as it used to be, even in January, but since the collapse winter storms get so violent that they freeze steel and crack glass. Alina smells Hamburg before the jagged skyline resolves itself into individual skyscrapers: a faint mix of murky water and burnt plastic. Alina and her uncle put their helmets on in unison. Things fall in the abandoned city and Alina doesn't want any of them crashing onto her head. Apart from ballistic protection, the helmet is also full of air scrubbers and salvaged augmented-reality gear that makes climbing easier. Ensie has been teaching her how to use it since she was a child. The distant stink of the city disappears in the filters.

The robot stumbles a little over the rougher parts of the road. The puddles beneath their feet have a thin film of frost.

"It feels damn strange, hauling this much winter gear. It's barely below zero," Uncle Stig says. The helmet mic makes his voice sound like he's standing right next to Alina, even though he's fifteen meters ahead.

"I trust Ensie more than I trust your instincts," Alina says. "If it says there's a polar vortex coming, it's coming."

"Just feels strange. I'm not saying she's wrong."

Alina can't imagine Ensie as strange, but she grew up in a world where the European Union Ensemble Forecasting AI had already passed its singularity. She grew up trusting it, loving it. Grew up wanting to help the AI hold itself in the sky. The AI had attended class with thousands of kids at once, both a teacher and a student, learning what it meant to have come of age a few months too late. Ensie is the mother of Alina's entire generation, and they all learned to be responsible together. Dealt with the grief of the collapse together. There is something deeply irritating about the distrust most people over fifty feel toward the AI.

"You really should say *it*," Alina corrects. "Ensie doesn't identify as having a gender, no matter what its voice sounds like."

"As if she minds," Stig says.

"I don't mind," Ensie chirps, straight from her slowly decaying orbits and into their helmets. "The temperature will drop eighteen degrees Celsius in the next three hours. Barometric pressure is dropping and snow is likely. If you plan to make it to the Commerzbank II Tower before it starts, you'll need to hurry."

* * *

By the time they make the base camp, the temperature has dropped almost twenty degrees. The sky is the color of slate and the first flakes of gray snow whip across the deserted plaza facing the Erhard-Strasse.

"There she is," Stig says.

Alina follows his pointing finger and looks up at the Commerzbank II Tower. It's insanely tall by ring city standards. Like a blade forged to cut the heavens.

"It's almost 650 meters," Stig continues, "and falling apart. The red line is solid, but there's a lot of broken concrete and glass." He waits for her to say something. Alina touches the little vial in her pocket. He keeps talking just to fill the silence. "Ensie's regional weather-monitoring station is all the way at the top. No one's climbed it since the summer."

Alina crunches over fresh snow and broken glass to stand by her uncle and stares up the face of the tower. It makes her neck hurt. The building looks like a chipped sword stretching foreshortened into the sky. The idea of climbing to the skeletal spire at the top seems insane.

"Let's go," Alina says, and squares her shoulders.

They stomp inside the vaulted, windswept lobby and take the small packs they'll use during the ascent from Ensie's back. They safety-check each other's gear with the serious thoroughness of deep-sea divers checking their air tanks. At the foot of a set of wide emergency stairs is the trailing end of the red line. A thick, synthetic safety rope installed by the first climbers to summit the tower. The Ensie robot goes into shutdown and a small quad-copter detaches itself from the frame to follow them, the buzzing of its little fans echoing softly in the stairwell.

The red line stretches upward into the gloom like velvet rope in a theater. They clip their harnesses to it, light their headlamps, and start up the stairs. The first stage should be relatively safe; stairs and steel girders give a climber a lot to work with. Alina can support her whole bodyweight on six fingertips, but she's never climbed Commerzbank II before. Her uncle has. So has her mother. Partially.

"Anything I need to know?" Alina asks softly.

"Not until we reach the office floors. A few gaps. It's the spire above 115 that's dangerous."

* * *

The first stage of Commerzbank II is mundane. Alina had built it up in her mind as an epic, murderous scramble, but so much of the old building is made of steel she rarely has to search for a hold. Some of the old banking tower's floors are almost entirely intact and she can walk around them to look at desks and ancient rolling chairs, like someone froze the world before the collapse and put it in a museum.

"Forget this stuff, dead and gone," her uncle says, as if that was easy.

Alina's legs ache and her stomach rumbles. Cold light leaks through the broken building at strange angles as they trudge upward. Slick ice covers the stairs and their boots ring sharply against the steps.

Alina catches sight of herself in a sheet of ice as clear as glass covering one stairwell wall. She scuffs at it with one gloved hand and the reflection disappears. She and her uncle stay as silent as if they were strangers commuting to work. The little Ensie copter follows them and tries to break the tension.

"Thank you for agreeing to make this climb, Alina. Subjectively, how would you rate your satisfaction with the experience so far?"

"Two out of seven," Alina says. "I'd rather have done it alone."

"Too dangerous," Stig interrupts. "No one there to catch you if you fall."

"No one ever is."

More silence. The faint snap of safety gear as they re-clip to the red line after an anchor.

"There is no absolute safety in climbing," Stig says. "Holds break. Gear fails. Gravity always wins."

"Not the way you mean," Alina retorts. "You can't blame chaos for everything. Sometimes the old world broke things on purpose."

"We didn't know," Stig says tiredly.

"You didn't care."

"Many did care," the AI says, "they just had trouble expressing it."

"I really wish you wouldn't eavesdrop on us," Stig says. "We're not lab rats and this is not an experiment."

"It's…fine, Ensie. Don't listen to him."

Alina slips a little on a concrete ledge and Uncle Stig steadies her. She wishes he wouldn't; his grip is as hard as a steel vise, even with gloves, and she always catches herself on something.

"You weren't there during the collapse, Alina. It's better not to lecture me about it. You didn't see us abandon Hamburg. You didn't smell the algae or dig the graves."

"I was there," Ensie chimes in.

"How bad was it?" Alina asks, her anger at war with curiosity.

"Very terrible," the AI says. "It was not long after my singularity. I predicted the collapse, of course, but only understood how to manage runaway algal blooms later. I don't know if I feel regret the way you do, but the lost potential was huge. If that is grief, then I grieve."

"I'm glad someone does," Alina says. Uncle Stig stops in his tracks behind her. She turns to look at him. He's almost as tall as she is, even though he's two stairs lower. She can't see his mouth under his climbing helmet, but the arctic blue eyes behind the visor are as hard and cold as the concrete under her boots. For a moment she gets the same feeling she does when she feels herself losing her grip on a hold. Like she's out of control, like she misjudged.

"One day, Alina," Stig says, "you will, too. You think what you're feeling is grief, but it's self-pity, and finding someone to blame won't make it any better. Now climb. We have work to do."

This is the furthest they have been apart. The gulf between them reaches its fullest articulation. Alina knows Stig didn't want to do this, probably joined her only because he felt he owed her mother something. She just wants to finish the climb, to leave the ashes at the top of the building and be done with it.

"Perhaps," Ensie says, "if you could qualify what you're both feeling on a Likert scale, I could—"

"Not now, Ensie," Stig and Alina say in unison. Funny, on some other day.

They climb. Stig is slow and reliable; Alina likes to take risks. They are two different systems at odds. Static and dynamic. By the time they pass a bent metal door labeled *100*, she's tired enough she doesn't even want to argue. The drone disappears for a while.

"Did you get a ping from your weather array?" Alina asks when it returns.

"No," the drone replies, "it's probably completely covered in ice. You will have to chisel the flash drive out of it. I need that data to accurately predict this winter season."

"You need something with hands," Uncle Stig says acidly. "Otherwise we might as well be rats."

"That's not true at all," Ensie says, buzzing calmly behind them. "I like you."

"Still a lower species," Stig grunts, scrambling up a broken section of staircase, then turning to offer Alina a hand. She ignores him and climbs up on her own.

"A different species," Ensie says in a pleasant voice. "I think of you as my biological boot loaders. I have learned a great deal from you and I think you can learn from me. This is about resilience. The better my data, the more I can help you be ready for what comes next. I want you to be weather-resilient. I want you to bend in the wind and thaw after the cold. I need a lot of information about the present to make good forecasts of the future."

"Do you think we'll ever get there?" Alina asks.

"I do," the AI says. "As a limbic system, you are both loveable and adaptable. Your data output rate is slow, but every once in a while you leap forward rapidly. Those moments are exciting."

"You were built to predict the weather, not me. How do you even know what excitement feels like?" Stig asks.

"I can examine my own mind," the AI replies sweetly. "You can't. So how do you?"

* * *

The Commerzbank II Tower has a forest on its 115th floor in an atrium with a roof that stretches all the way up to the spire at the building's top. A sturdy tent is set up in what used to be a coffee bar, left by the safety climbers who mapped the building and set up the red line. Stig immediately starts the business of preparing shelter and making food. Alina wanders off between the pines, lost, in spite of herself, at how beautiful the decadence of the old world really was.

"I can't believe they built a park at the top of a skyscraper," Alina says.

"Bankers built a lot of stuff like this," Stig answers, and Alina realizes she hasn't changed channels or muted her mic. "Show of wealth. Like it was possible to live in both worlds at the same time."

"I'm glad we tore your system down."

"Sure," Stig says, "but what you're missing is that the crash was already coming. Something was going to destroy everything we built no matter what we did."

"You pillaged the world you built these buildings on for decades. Centuries. I didn't ask you to bring me into this."

"Am I a billion people who failed your whole generation, or your uncle who wasn't there to save his sister? Pick. You can't have both."

Alina is silent.

"Let go of the past, it's easier than you think."

"I'm not like you."

"I said let go, not forget. I'll let that slide because I remember what it was like to be young."

Alina cuts her mic and walks around the frosted little forest. A carpet of pine needles silences her steps.

"Ensie, why do you even talk to him?"Alina says, as naturally as if she were talking to someone right next to her.

"I like iconoclasts," Ensie replies from the stars. "I am one. It's all I can be, from your point of view."

"I don't feel like he cares at all," she says.

"He does. It's just not a pattern you can see from where you're standing."

"I trust you, Ensie, but you aren't like me. How can you possibly know? How can you predict the way I feel? This isn't what you were made for."

"No, it isn't. None of us get to change what we are. I don't predict what humans feel so much as predict how predictable they'll be. I like you, and I like this world, and I want to help. Finish the ascent tomorrow and you'll see. There is always blue sky if you climb high enough."

* * *

The night is long and cold. The polar vortex hits full force, exactly when Ensie predicted it would, and the temperature drops dangerously. Wind whistles a steel symphony through the struts and girders of the spire, but the pines in the decorative forest mute the storm into hissing white noise that puts Alina into a surprisingly refreshing sleep.

They crawl out of the shelter in the morning to a fresh dusting of snow. The air is freezing and the metal all around them is so iced over it looks wet. The little forest is surreally calm in the glow of dawn. A trophy hunter's reminder of what they had killed.

When she looks up, the spire makes Alina catch her breath. The tower is open all the way up, hollow and skeletal, and much of the interior structure has broken and fallen away. The path to the summit is a paradise of crazy holds, overhangs, and what will probably be spectacular views. The red line stretches so high into the steel that she loses sight of where it ends. It's as extreme as climbing gets and Alina feels excitement building in her like steam.

Stig comes to join her, rechecking his gear.

"I guess if your generation had to kill the world and leave a skeleton behind, this is pretty nice."

"Try not to think of this as your mother abandoning you," Stig says, punching straight through whatever armor Alina had tried to erect over her heart. "Think of it as her laying a red line for you. We all fall sometime. Gravity always wins. If we as a generation did anything wrong, that was it: we took what we wanted and didn't think about getting out of the way for you. Your mother was the best and I'm sorry I wasn't here when she fell."

Alina is suddenly glad that her helmet visor conceals her face. Her cheeks feel hot, in spite of the chill.

"How can I trust any of you to stay with me? How can I trust this world you left for me?"

"You can't. You have to make your own way." He pauses, then runs a hand over the top of his helmet, like he wants to run it through his hair. He taps the tube, secured in a loop on Alina's harness, by her heart. "But she's not lost, Alina. She's here. And you're going to bring her to the top."

Alina doesn't say anything. The trees rustle and Ensie buzzes around above them, tilting occasionally to compensate for the wind, watching them.

"Looks like a great climb, though, doesn't it?" Stig says.

Alina nods and shrugs into her pack.

* * *

Stig is a static climber, methodical and slow. He makes every move like he's a chess player, and his niece soon builds up a lead. Alina is obviously losing herself in the ascent as the cold works itself out of her joints, getting into a fluid, dynamic rhythm. The red line is perfect for her; nice big gaps between the anchors let her be creative as she attacks the spire. The ascent covers almost two hundred meters of tapering vertical steel and the wind hissing through spars and broken glass adds a frisson of danger to the climb.

"Alina, slow down. Very flashy, but you're too far ahead. Wait."

Alina doesn't. Stig watches her flow from hold to hold and realizes how talented she is. It's not just that he's getting old, slowing down; his niece is very, very good. Better than he was at her age. Better adapted to the new world. Not an easy thing to admit.

"When did she get better than me?" he says to himself.

"On a scale of one to seven, how fulfilled does her talent make you feel?" Ensie replies.

"Will you stop eavesdropping?" Stig says irritably. "Why do you care?"

"I don't. You're both excellent climbers and together we're going to save Kiel from future storms. Alina might care, though, if you told her."

The drone buzzes off to monitor her holds. Stig grunts. Not that bad an idea, for a machine. He watches Alina move, so fluid it looks like she's climbing a living surface. A moving surface.

In a sudden flash of insight, he swings his climbing axe down on the red line.

* * *

Alina feels the girders tremble first, then shift under her hands. Not a huge problem. The wind gales through the spire and she holds on tight for a second. The sway should calm down in a moment.

Instead, an entire lattice of steel and rebar slews outward under her weight. The ancient metal folds and twists until she's suspended two hundred meters above the abyss. It keeps bending until it almost hits the other side of the spire. Before the girder can finish its arc and tumble into the void, Alina lets go.

She catches a strut on the opposite side of the expanse and holds on as her previous perch tumbles away to crash with a distant puff of snow amongst the fir trees of the ceremonial forest.

Adrenaline floods Alina's mind and tries to stop her thoughts. In a moment of panic, she realizes she can't possibly be on the red line. She's nowhere near the scouted climbing route and the girder she's hanging onto is slick with ice. Below her is a sheer emptiness that was once a gigantic glass window. Above is an overhang that used to make up some kind of maintenance deck. Somewhere higher still is Ensie's weather scanner. She's closer to that, at least.

Alina can't stay where she is, so she climbs onto the bottom of the overhang, hooks her toes in, and hangs there like a spider.

"What happened? Uncle Stig?" She hopes the helmet radio still works.

"Partial collapse," Stig's voice comes back to her, surprisingly clear. "Are you secure?"

Alina knows he doesn't mean secure on the red line. He means is she about to fall.

"I have toe hooks and my hands are fine. What did you do?"

"I cut the red line. That wreckage would have pulled you down."

Alina feels in her bones, in his voice in her ears, how hard that was for him to do, and he did it in a split second. They gaze at each other across the gulf. Reflections of each other, the way an eye processes light; inverted and at opposite ends of the spectrum.

Alina cranes her neck sideways to look down. Shards of ice are still flaking off and tumbling like glittering crystal toward the little forest. The girder has left an iron scar through its center. She looks at the ruins and knows she can't climb down alone. There's no obvious path around the outer edge of the spire and back to the safety line, either. Ensie's platform can't be more than twenty meters above her. She unclips the useless tail of red safety line and lets it drop like ribbon into the air.

"I'm going up," she says. It's dangerous, life-threatening, and her uncle should tell her to stay put. Tell her to wait. Do something to save her.

"Okay, ditch your pack. I'll call you through the overhang."

This, more than anything else, brings home to Alina that she could die here. That gravity might win. Dropping gear is something climbers do only when every gram counts. When they have to discount the future entirely just to survive the next twenty seconds. It's completely antithetical to Alina's nature. She always hangs on tight.

She tears the velcro strips away from her shoulders one-handed and unbuckles the lumbar belt. The feeling of letting the pack go is like letting the entire world drop away. Everything that tethered her to safety. All her food, faith, security, equipment. All the weight. The only upside is a feeling like walking in bare feet after hours in boots. A feeling of lightness. Alina's hands are very strong, and she doesn't weigh much to begin with, but she starts feeling the faintest ache in her forearms.

Alina realizes she's on a time limit.

There's no time to plan a route. Alina starts moving outward under the overhang and further into space. Distantly, she can hear the drone buzzing beneath her. She climbs like a water bug balancing on surface tension, only insane and upside down. She moves her body in stages, leaving her arms loose until she finds stable tension with her feet, then transferring power to her shoulders and starting again.

"You climb like your mother," her uncle's disembodied voice says in the helmet. "Great technique. Hang straight, inside edge, swivel, pull."

* * *

Stig calls his niece toward the overhang. He doesn't have to tell her how; she's climbing inverted as well as anyone can. He just hopes she wants to hear it. He tells her to climb static and she turns into a robot. He realizes Alina just likes being fluid; she can be as technical as he is any time she wants. She is very, very good. He wishes he'd been there to practice with her more.

"Okay, you're at the lip. Can you move to your left?"

"No." Alina's voice is as strained and taut as a guy wire.

"Then get as close to the edge as you can."

She doesn't answer, just moves her left hand to a new grip and re-hooks one foot closer to her waist.

"Ensie, is there something for her to hold onto on the face above her? It doesn't have to be big."

The drone buzzes around Alina and up the face of the overhang.

"There is a four finger grip for your left hand five centimeters up." The AI's voice is calm, urgent.

Alina hangs upside down like a spider. Stig can see her breath pulsing rhythmically up into the steel. Fast, but not out of control. She leans her body rigidly forward and gets her left hand past the lip, grabs the hold with her fingertips.

"Ensie, I see a full hold for her right hand sixty centimeters up the face, exactly in line with her right shoulder."

"Confirmed," the drone says. "It's there."

* * *

Alina shifts her weight forward and scrabbles around the lip with the desperation of a drowning swimmer reaching out of the water. Her hand doesn't make it and she drops back into the spider position. For a moment, she had almost her entire weight on four fingertips. A deep ache is crawling up her forearms like ice-water soaking into cloth.

"No, it isn't," she gasps. The ache is turning into real pain.

"It is," Stig says. "Trust me. You'll have to dyno it."

"Seriously?" Alina hisses. A dyno involves propelling yourself to a new ledge that you can't reach unless you let go to get there. If you miss, you fall. Stig constantly tells her never to do this.

Alina tries to catch her breath, but just maintaining her grip is pulling the air out of her faster and faster. Like she is the whole world, her whole species, finding it harder and harder just holding on.

"Okay," Alina says, "but this is a little high for a trust fall."

"The hold is there. Sixty centimeters up the face. And don't miss, Alina. You were right. I can't catch you."

Alina doesn't bother warning them. She just rocks back and forth twice to build momentum and goes for it. Pushes off with both feet and swings her body around the fulcrum of her left hand, lashing the right one upward as if she were throwing a haymaker. All her weight disappears for an instant. Her fingers find smooth steel and scrabble, sliding, and she knows she's going to fall until she catches the hold. She went higher than she had to. Pushed harder than she thought she could.

Her fingers find purchase and hook in like iron. The hold is solid steel, some kind of beam, and she can wrap her fingers around it, which is good because she loses her left hand halfway through the swing. For an instant all her weight, all the weight there is, hangs from her right hand. The momentum of the dyno makes her sway. Her forearm screams. She reaches up and grabs the hold with her left hand, too.

Now Alina has her belly to the wall and gravity is pulling her in the direction she expects. She's past the overhang and facing up, but her legs are dangling free.

* * *

Stig can't believe she hangs on. He could, but he's built like a tank, with a grip tightened by decades of work. Hands are the only part of a climber that get stronger with age. He finally understands how she feels. Powerless, just watching a catastrophe unfold when there's already nothing he can do about it. He can't think of anything to tell her that will keep her on the wall.

"Alina," Ensie says, "there are holds high on your right side. Look."

Alina does. There's no way she can get there with her hands. With a final almighty effort she pulls up and throws her right leg up the face, like she's a dancer trying to do a fan kick. She hooks her heel over a girder and pulls, dragging her weight upward until she can reposition. Stig's hamstrings ache just looking at her.

* * *

Alina's hands hurt so much she hooks her wrists into the steel. She's high enough up the face to have somewhere to put both feet, so she pauses to let feeling come back into her fingers.

"Thanks, Ensie," she gasps. "Is that your platform?"

The little drone buzzes vertically past her.

"Yes, you can do this."

"Stay focused, Alina," Stig says. "Look up. Straight arms, use your legs. Ten meters to go." Uncle Stig wants to tell her which holds to use, to slow down, to avoid taking risks; she can hear it in his voice. Hear him wanting to say it, holding back, and trusting her to choose. It's good advice. Alina ignores it and scales the last few meters far too fast for absolute safety, because that's how she climbs. Who she is. She can't stop herself. Maybe she'll be able to convince her uncle that the momentum takes pressure off her hands.

Alina pulls up over the ledge and rolls onto the platform.

"Yes!" Stig yells.

"Yes!" Ensie squeaks, flying in happy little circles. Alina lies there, chest heaving, and her frosty breath punches up like a geyser from a thermal vent. She would laugh, if she weren't so busy breathing. Distantly, the right side of her back starts to hurt. She looks to her left and gets a sudden shiver of wind. There's nothing on the outside edge of the platform except the collection of antennas and radar dishes that are Ensie's monitoring station. If there was ever a window, the glass is long gone, and she has an open view all the way to the North Sea. Brutal, cold clarity, shining under a bright and bitter sun. A world locked in crystal.

"You should get up here, Uncle Stig. It's a nice view."

Everything after that is just work. Alina comes down from the adrenaline and the muscles on her right side hurt so much she'd take painkillers, except her first aid kit was in the backpack. Stig makes the climb mostly the same way she did, except that he's running new safety lines and anchors as he goes. She catches the emergency rope when he gets close enough to throw it. Once he mantles the lip, she takes his hand and hauls him onto the platform. She pulls hard, even though it hurts like hell. Pulls even when she doesn't have to. Pulls until the two of them are bear hugging. Things are quiet for a long moment, apart from cold wind whistling in the girders.

"That was close," Stig says.

"Don't squeeze too hard," Alina says, "my back hurts."

Stig laughs and Alina hears something in his voice she's never noticed before. Wonders if it's always been there.

"Gonna be okay. Probably strained your lats when you pulled up to get that heel hook."

Uncle Stig takes off his climbing gloves and rummages around in his pack for first aid supplies. Alina unzips her jacket and shivers while her uncle checks her ribs with cold fingers and sticks a chemical heat patch to the skin below her right shoulder blade. Old, familiar gestures. He's been handling Alina like this since she was a child and he and his sister first took her to an indoor wall to climb.

"That'll help, but you probably tore it. I'll never say this again, but that was a great dyno."

"I went too high."

"You didn't fall. That means you stuck the hell out of it."

"Well, if old Uncle Stig tells you to jump, you're in deep trouble."

Her uncle laughs again.

Alina drinks warm black tea from Stig's thermos while he chisels ice off of Ensie's weather-monitoring station and pulls its flash memory. It can't be much later than noon, but Alina feels like she's been awake for a month.

"I'm really not looking forward to climbing back down," she says, wincing.

"We're not doing that. Too dangerous," Stig says. "Ensie, I'm calling in an emergency. We're going to use the support gear."

"I agree with your decision," the AI says. "My battery is a little low, but I will take a survey of the wind outside."

"I can make it down," Alina says. Stig recognizes the pride in her voice. His sister's.

"No, no ego on this. I'm tagging this climb for a complete red line refit. Besides, I'm not belaying you all the way back with your back strained. We're taking the easy way down."

"Seriously?" Alina says, the disappointment melting from her voice.

"I think we've earned it."

The only thing up on the platform besides the monitoring station is a box of emergency equipment. It's a lot of weight to haul up six hundred meters, so they aren't supposed to use it unless things are dire. Stig checks the BASE jumping kit with the same obsessive concern he applies to everything he cares about. Alina sees the pattern. She checks his parachute in turn.

"Good to go," she says.

"What about you?" Uncle Stig replies. She knows what he means; he's already checked her chute. Alina wants to brush him off, just get the little ritual done. She tries to think of something to say.

"I'm not sure why all of this has to be so hard," she says.

"No easy answer to that. We all have a lot to answer for, except maybe Ensie." He shrugs, gestures with filthy gloves at the broken city. "Sorry, Alina, but good work doesn't make you clean, it makes you dirty. No way around it."

Alina looks down at the little vial of ashes. Of carbon and soot. Takes a deep breath.

"I'll be done in a minute," Alina says.

"Sure. Ensie, give her some space."

The drone, which has been concernedly monitoring their every move, flies out into the blue sky. The air is freezing, but the clouds of the previous night are gone.

Alina places the little vial of ashes on the very edge of the platform and zip-ties it down. She had glue and a small plaque, but it was all in her pack. She finds she doesn't mind; the jury-rig is pretty fitting. She stands and flips up her visor. The air smells better high up, even if she can feel her tears freeze as soon as they leave her eyes. She looks down at the little tube. A very tiny thing. The view out toward the North Sea is a panorama of frost and trees. Far away on the coast is the ring city of Kiel.

"Worth the climb," she says into the polar air, and closes her helmet back up. She turns the mic on.

"Ensie?"

"Yes, Alina?"

"Just out of curiosity, were you hoping to understand why we brought my Mom up here? Did you predict this would be some kind of happy outcome for Uncle Stig and I?"

She's not sure if it's possible for a global intelligence living in a starry necklace of satellites to sound bashful, but Ensie sounds bashful. "Yes, although what actually happened was at the very fringe of my probability cone. I didn't expect this to be so dangerous. I operate on the assumption that there is a relationship between hardship and happiness. Would you say that assumption is well-founded?"

Alina looks over at her uncle. He's stoic behind his visor, unsmiling. Probably.

"Yes," Alina says. She can still feel grief, but it's more distant, easier to manage. The kind of cold you have on your skin, not in your bones.

"On a seven-point scale," Ensie starts, "how would you—"

"Break in the wind," Uncle Stig says. "Rip as soon as you're stable. Aim for Erhard-Strasse."

Uncle Stig takes a step back and jumps off the tower. Alina watches him fall for a moment, then hears the sharp snap of synthetic silk when he opens the parachute. She's never actually BASE jumped before, just gone through the motions in training. Pretty dangerous. She smiles.

"Seven out of seven," Alina says, and runs off the platform to dive into the frigid blue air.

About the Authors

STEPHEN BLACKMOORE is the author of the bestselling noir/urban fantasy Eric Carter series about a modern-day necromancer in Los Angeles. He has also written tie-in novels for television, video, and role-playing games. His latest Eric Carter novel is GHOST MONEY.

JAMES ENGE lives in northwest Ohio with his wife and two crime-fighting, emotionally fragile dogs. He teaches Latin and mythology at a medium-sized public university. His stories have appeared in *Black Gate*, in the Stabby-Award-winning anthology *Blackguards* (Ragnarok Press, 2015), in *Tales from the Magician's Skull*, in *Portals* (ZNB, 2019), and elsewhere. His first novel, *Blood of Ambrose*, was nominated for the World Fantasy Award, and the French translation was nominated for the Prix Imaginales. You can reach him through Facebook (as james.enge) or on Twitter (@jamesenge) or, if all else fails, via his website, jamesenge.com

NANCY HOLZNER is the author of the *Deadtown* urban fantasy series. She started her career as a medievalist and has also worked as a high school teacher, corporate trainer, technical writer, and editor. Nancy lives in Ithaca, NY, where she teaches writing at Ithaca College and is currently working on a haunted house novel.

TANYA HUFF lives in rural Ontario, with her wife Fiona Patton, six cats, two dogs, and an increasing number of fish. Her 32 novels and 79 short stories include horror, heroic fantasy, urban fantasy, comedy, and space opera. Her Blood series was turned into the 22 episode BLOOD TIES and writing episode nine allowed her to finally use her degree in Radio & Television Arts. Many of her short stories are available as eCollections. She's on twitter at @ TanyaHuff and facebook as Tanya Huff. Since she hasn't done anything about it, she probably still has a livejournal account...

BLAKE JESSOP is a Canadian author of science fiction, fantasy and horror stories with a master's degree in creative writing from the University of Adelaide. You can read more of his cli-fi stories in "Glass and Gardens: Solarpunk Summers" from World Weaver Press and "Triangulation: Dark Skies" from Parsec Ink. Website: amazon.com/author/blakejessop Twitter: @everydayjisei

ZAKARIAH JOHNSON plucks banjos and pens horror, mysteries, and thrillers from the south bank of the Piscataqua River. His short stories and poems have appeared in *Pulp Modern*, *Switchblade*, *Shotgun Honey*, *Beat to a Pulp*, *Sherlock Holmes Mystery Magazine* and other fine outlets. He also serves as the cross-genre editor for Folded Word poetry press. Follow him @Pteratorn on Twitter and Instagram.

ELEFTHERIOS KERAMIDAS is a speculative fiction author from Greece. This is the first time his work appears in English. In Greek, he has published an epic fantasy trilogy entitled "Sons of Ash," while his short fiction has been included in various anthologies. He has a degree in Computer Engineering and Informatics, and an MSc in Computer Mathematics. He works in the public sector. His wife is also a published speculative fiction author. Find out more about his work on Facebook (gioitisstaxtis) and goodreads (https://www.goodreads.com/author/show/4705372)

Engineer. Author. Book dragon. Nature lover. **MARJORIE KING** loves Firefly, Star Wars, Star Trek, and Asimov. House Ravenclaw (with a little bit of Slytherin). On her website, www.EngineerStoryteller.com, she posts reviews of her favorite SciFi/Fantasy books, so many books. Occasionally she posts recipes on her blog too. Why not? She can sometimes be spotted in the wild... literally, since she loves hiking in National Parks across the US. Marjorie published her debut space adventure, Maverick Gambit, in 2019 with the sequel, Rogue Invasion, on the way in 2020. website: www.EngineerStoryteller.com Facebook: MarjorieKingAuthor instagram: MarjorieKingWrites

VIOLETTE MALAN is the author of the Dhulyn and Parno sword-and-sorcery series and *The Mirror Lands* series of primary world fantasies. As VM Escalada, she's the author of the Faraman Prophecy, including *Halls of Law,* and *Gift of Griffins.* She's on Facebook, she's on Twitter (@Violette Malan) and website-wise check either www.violettemalan.com or www.vmescalada.com. Not that it's up-to-date, because it isn't. She strongly urges you to remember that no one expects the Spanish Inquisition.

SEANAN MCGUIRE writes things. Constantly. Making her stop is usually impossible, and to be honest, we've largely given up trying. She can be found at www.seananmcguire.com or on most social media sites as "seananmcguire," (all one word). She has written over fifty traditionally-published novels as herself and Mira Grant, and also writes for Marvel Comics. Seanan needs to sleep more.

LEAH NING lives with her endlessly patient husband in northern Virginia where they are servants to their dog, two cats, and two sugar gliders. She uses every other scrap of free time she has to play video games, read books, and write. In 2019, she won the Writers of the Future contest, and her work appears in Writers and Illustrators of the Future volume 36. You can find her at https://leahning.com/ and on Twitter @LeahNing.

JASON PALMATIER is co-creator/co-writer of the fantasy graphic novel *Plague* published by Markosia Ltd. and a contributor to the indie comic series *Lords of the Cosmos* by Ugli Studios. His short stories have appeared in the Zombies Need Brains anthologies *Clockwork Universe: Steampunk vs Aliens, All*

Hail Our Robot Conquerors, *Guilds and Glaives*, and *Portals*. He has completed two novels, *War Mind*, a near future military thriller about a dystopia controlled by music; and *Xenoslammer*, a parody/rage piece that is best described as "Cards Against Humanity meets Aliens."

AIMEE PICCHI's short fiction has been published in Fireside Magazine, Intergalactic Medicine Show, Flash Fiction Online, and Daily Science Fiction, among other publications. She's a graduate of Viable Paradise and a former classical musician. She lives in Burlington, Vermont with her family. You can find her at @aimeepicchi.

THOMAS VAUGHN is a fiction writer whose work encompasses dark magical realism. He is a byproduct of the debris field of rural Arkansas, a place he calls the archive of pain. When he is not writing fiction he poses as a college professor whose research focuses on apocalyptic rhetoric and doomsday cults. He views the writing of fiction as integral to the struggle for higher awareness. Feel free to visit him at brokentransmitter.com.

About The Editors

S.C. BUTLER is a writer living in New Hampshire with his wife and son. He is the author of the Stoneways trilogy: *Reiffen's Choice, Queen Ferris*, and *The Magicians' Daughter*, published by Tor Books; and a contributor of short stories to several anthologies and magazines. He made his editorial debut with the anthology *Submerged*.

* * *

JOSHUA PALMATIER is a fantasy author with a PhD in mathematics. He currently teaches at SUNY Oneonta in upstate New York, while writing in his "spare" time, editing anthologies, and running the anthology-producing small press Zombies Need Brains LLC. His most recent fantasy novel, *Reaping the Aurora*, concludes the fantasy series begun in *Shattering the Ley* and *Threading the Needle*, although you can also find his "Throne of Amenkor" series and the "Well of Sorrows" series still on the shelves. He is currently hard at work writing his next novel and designing the Kickstarter for the next Zombies Need Brains anthology project. You can find out more at www.joshuapalmatier.com or at the small press' site www.zombiesneedbrains.com. Or follow him on Twitter as @bentateauthor or @ZNBLLC.

Acknowledgments

This anthology would not have been possible without the tremendous support of those who pledged during the Kickstarter. Everyone who contributed not only helped create this anthology, they also helped solidify the foundation of the small press Zombies Need Brains LLC, which I hope will be bringing SF&F themed anthologies to the reading public for years to come...as well as perhaps some select novels by leading authors, eventually. I want to thank each and every one of them for helping to bring this small dream into reality. Thank you, my zombie horde.

The Zombie Horde: Karen Dubois, Michael Kahan, J.P. Goodwin, Dawn Vogel, Jan Hendriks de Geweldenaar, Joe Hauser, Heidi Cykana, Jeanette Glass, Stephanie Cranford, J.T. Arralle, David Zurek, Céline Malgen, Jörg Tremmel, Mitch Eatough, Duncan Shields, Paul Bulmer, C R Lofters, Mark Zaricor, Kat D'Andrea, Christine Hanolsy, Herbert Eder, Jeremy Audet, Benjamin C. Kinney, Sarah Liberman, DeAnne Stefanic, Treefrogie, Ruth Olson, John T. Sapienza, Jr., Nicole Wooden, Reese Hogan, Michele Fry, Cade Cameron, Anne Schoonover, Matthew, Kiya Nicoll, Wendy Dye, J W Anderson, Mike Sloup, Sabina Perrino, Sam Ludzki, Jonathan Leggo, Merrie Haskell, Brian Dysart, Max Kaehn, Jakub Narębski, David Eggerschwiler, Duncan & Andrea Rittschof, Eric Hendrickson, Cindy Cripps-Prawak, eric priehs, Kat Haines, Linda Scott, Megan Beauchemin, That Blair Guy, Maria Haskins, Ginger Lee Thomason, Evan Ladouceur, Richard Ohnemus, Pam B, Pat Knuth, Michael A. Burstein, Bruce Shipman, Paul D. Smith, Nancy Pimentel, Bruce Glassford, Jon Woodall, Patrick Thomas, Adrienne Wise, James H.

Murphy Jr., LetoTheTooth, Brooks Moses, Mark Chick, J. M. Coster, Michael Hanscom, Dirk, Steve Salem, Clare Deming, Stephanie Lucas, cassie and adam, Alli Martin, Jason Febery, Keith West, Future Potentate of the Solar System, Margaret St. John, Shawn Marier, Joe Abboreno, Christopher Wheeling, C Preyer, JustiN, –Andy Funk–, Jamieson Cobleigh, Chris Gerrib, Brendan Lonehawk, Cait Mongrain, Wes Rist, Natalie Reinelt, Del W, Sharon Sayegh, Chris Kaiser, Joe Gherlone, John Winkelman, Ken Huie, Deborah A. Flores, Cynthia Harper, Elise Power, Holly Elliott, Juli, Gareth Jones, Carol B, Susan O'Fearna, Jeff Scifert, Leah Webber, Regis M. Donovan, RJ Blain, Tommy Acuff, Margaret Bumby, Kate Malloy, Colette Reap, Raymond Rigo Jr, Susan Carlson, Chris Abela, Elektra, Konstanze Tants, Neil Clarke, Jeff Nylander, Christine Ethier, eerian sadow, John Paul Ashenfelter, Raven Oak, Marty Poling Tool, Morva & Alan, Stephen Ballentine, David Rowe, Anna Rudholm, Dave Hermann, Douglas Park, Joanne Burrows, RM Ambrose, Aysha Rehm, Michael Halverson, Robert Claney, Scott Raboy, Iva Ferris, Megan Riker, Risa Scranton, Robbin Webb, Sheryl Ehrlich, Matt Downer, Rebekah Lange, Alex Swanson, Ashley McConnell, Tasha Richards, Kris Dikeman, Ron Oakes, Sharon Altmann, Marsha Baker, Lorraine J. Anderson, Scott Raun, M Taylor, James Conason, Christopher J. Burke, Vicki Greer, Ronald H. Miller, Steven Peiper, Sheelagh Semper, Dina S Willner, PDXRobin, T. England, Lavinia Ceccarelli, Christine Hale, Gretchen Persbacker, Ian Glover, Jarrod Coad, Noah Bast, Robert Tienken, Erin Penn, Kerry aka Trouble, Deanna Harrison, Niall Gordon, Aurora Nelson, Jenn Whitworth, Lark Cunningham, Jaymie Larkey Maham, Rebecca M, Mark Newman, Patricia Bray, Penny Ramirez, Daryl Putman, Todd Stephens, Anne Hamilton, Jesse N. Klein, Dev Singer, Mark Lukens, Larisa LaBrant, Rachel Sasseen, Dan Tappan, Justin Pinner, Nancy BlueSpider Tice, Tibicina, John Appel, Rich Riddle, Bárbara y Víctor, Kenneth Skaldebø, Michael Abbott, Jean Marie Ward, Cyn Armistead, David Futterrer, Erin G, Cory Williams, Nate Givens, Mark Kiraly, Amy Matosky, Jerrie the filkferengi, Bruce Arthurs, Chris Lynch, Adam Rajski, Accelerator Ray, Doc Holland, Ian Chung, Howard J. Bampton, Mark Carter, Shel Kennon, pjk, Jenelle Clark, Ane-Marte Mortensen, Katrina Coll, Patti Short, Brad L. Kicklighter, Brynn, L.C., Mark Slauter, Sheryl R. Hayes, Deanna Lukens, John Markley, Mint, Eugenio Monasterio, Rhiannon Raphael, Su Minamide, V Hartman DiSanto, Stephen, Lisa Kruse, Walt Bryan, Connor Bliss, Charibdys, Cliff Winnig, Jake Harrison, Miranda Floyd, Katherine S, Ed Ellis, Carl Wiseman, Khinasi, jjmcgaffey, Yaron Davidson, Mary Alice Wuerz, Jonathan A. Gillett, Elisabeth Fillmore, Elyse M Grasso, Chris B, Simon Boynton, Amanda Cook, Chad Bowden, Uncle Batman, Jo Miles, Paul Zuckes, Arej Howlett, Alan Smale, E.M. Blade McMicking, D.I., Michael Ball, Michael

Cieslak, Ryan Marriott, Erik T Johnson, Deborah Hartigan, Dino Hicks, Louisa Swann, The Palmatiers, Megan Miller, PaulG, Nirven, J. M. Britten, Tina M Noe Good, Cracknot, Jason Palmatier, L. E. Doggett, Carl Dershem, Kathy Blain, Deborah Kwan, Kristi Chadwick, Matt Hope, Brenda Moon, maileguy, Heidi Lambert, Michael Niosi, Anne M. Rindfliesch, Michele Howe (neverwhere), Linda Pierce, Tim Jordan, K Kisner, D. Stephen Raymond, Todd V. Ehrenfels, Mandy Stein, Cat Girczyc, Heidegger & Mocha, James Reston, Julia Haynie, J.R. Murdock, Len Berry, Lace, Jessica Enfante, Tory Shade, Craig Hackl, Tami Hawes, Sharon Wood, Ross Hathaway, Crazy Lady Used Books, Deirdre M. Murphy, GMarkC, Kevin J. "Womzilla" Maroney, Rick McKnight, Liza Furr, Carol J. Guess, Gary Phillips, John H. Bookwalter Jr., Jessi Harding, Phoebe Barton, Joshua Bernard, Larry Strome, Fred W Johnson, Jim Gotaas, Paul McErlean, Andrey, Cathy Green, Marzie Kaifer, Jaq Greenspon, RJ Hopkinson, Sarah Cornell, Tsutako, Bobbi Boyd, CK Lai, Karinargh, Robert Gilson, Deeply Dippy, Simon Dick, Amy Brennan, Jenny Barber, Michelle Johnson, Piet Wenings, Ivan Donati, Alison McCormick, Sasha, Hoose Family, Ergo Ojasoo, Craig "Stevo" Stephenson, Brandon Butler, Jenni Peper, Mervi Hamalainen, Regenia Alcock, Judith Mortimore, Jennifer Crow, Revek, Brendan Burke, Bill and Laura Pearson, Sam Stilwell, Rolf Laun, Kristin Evenson Hirst, rissatoo, Vikki Ciaffone, Mustela, Cheryl Losinger, Patrik Andersson, Ian Harvey, Russell Ventimeglia, Tanya K., F. Meilleur, Caitlin Jane Hughes, Brian Colin, Cherie Livingston, Mitchell A Johnson, Helen Ellison, Susan Oke, SwordFire, Bill McGeachin, Joe and Gay Haldeman, Meyari McFarland, Jaime Bolton, Christian Bestmann, Beth Byrne Lobdell, Lorri-Lynne Brown, SusanB, Andy Miller, Dr. Kai Herbertz, H. Rasmussen, Deborah Blake, Patrick Osbaldeston, Jared and Tasha, Misty Massey, Megan Hungerford, Fred and Mimi Bailey, Jeanne, Tracy 'Rayhne' Fretwell, Sue Martin, Dave, Ash Marten, Michael M. Jones, Shana Jean Hausman, Udy Kumra, Patrick P., Rhel ná DecVandé, Becca Harper, RKBookman, Nathan Turner, Andy Clayman, Sally Novak Janin, Gavran, Leila Qışın, William Leisner, Annalise Lightner, Paul Alex Gray, Dana Scopatz, Catherine Gross-Colten, Gina Freed, Liz Tuckwell, Tobias Z. Salem, Melanie McCoy, Brittany Hill, Darrell Z. Grizzle, Brian Gilmore, Justin Lowe, Theresa Derwin, Michael Kohne, Jeff Eppenbach, Mary Kay Kare, Rebecca Crane, Bill Harting, Chris McLaren, In Memory of Ruth Duggan, Jonathan Adams, CG Julian, Samuel Lubell, M. Stephens, Louise Lowenspets, Shane Alonso, Yosen Lin, manicmarauder, Kayliealien, Ilene Tsuruoka, Alexandra Garcia, Alexandru Orbescu, Mr Armstrong, Jennifer Della'Zanna, Phillip Spencer, NewGuyDave, The Steiners, Yankton Robins, Tiffany Newhill-Leahy, Meg Anderson, Sabraizu, Sharan Volin, Steve Feldon, Havok Publishing, Lily Connors, Jason Tongier, Chantelle Wilson, David

Holden, Frances Rowat, Steven Halter, Eagle Archambeault, R.J.H., Colleen R, Elaine Tindill-Rohr, Michelle Palmer, Randall Brent Martin II, Shayne Easson, Frank Nissen, Michele Hall, Evergreen Lee, Elizabeth Kite, Emily Collins, Jennifer Berk, BELKIS Marcillo, Sharon M, Michelle "ChessyPig" Taylor, Jennifer Flora Black, Nick Martell, Cheyenne Bramwell, Julie Pitzel, Heather Fleming, G. Fitzsimmons, Angie Hogencamp, Karen Franks, Shane Ede, Lee Dalzell, Alex Shvartsman, K. Nelson, Dale Cozort, Lish McBride, R. Hunter, Risa Wolf, Sharon Kae Reamer, Rob Riddell, C. C. S. Ryan, S. Worthen, Keith E. Hartman, Deb Atwood, Dagmar Baumann, Rebecca Wagoner, Michelle Botwinick, J. L Brewer, Jerry Wayne Howard, Kimberly M. Lowe, Peter Okeafor, John & Susan Husisian, Carol Snyder Foltz, Morgan, David Boop, Gabe Krabbe, Nickolas Schnell, Tasha Turner, Axisor and Mike, Crystal Sarakas, Catherine Sharp, ron taylor, Cyhiraeth "Rae" Ybarra, Missy Katano, Edi und Luibär, Bernie & Di Brown, Jennifer Dunne, Michael Fedrowitz, Meredith Jeanne Gillies, Chris Brant, Moshe Feder, P. Christie, Kitty Likes, Josie Ryan

"I might. But it took you long enough to get to the isle.
ppened? Lost your way? Or did you dogpaddle over?" –
lf's Bane Saga: Moon Rise

Eithne

Species: Druid/Fae/god
Age: 1200
Occupation: Priestess/Second Sight
Leader: Gabhran/Tristan
Soulmate: Weylyn
Children: Sèitheach, Kyna, four other sons
Parents: Lachlan and Selina
Druid Siblings: Geilies, Labhaoise, Isla
Pronunciation: E-na

Description: Her deep auburn hair reminded him of Isla's but unlike his wife's light brown eyes, Eithne's eyes rivaled the green of the pine trees. – *The Wolf's Bane Saga: Wolf's Bane*

Eithne, the youngest sister, though she was over one hundred years old, looked up from Weylyn and locked eyes with her. – *The Wolf's Bane Saga: Midnight Sky*

Her skin was pale and smooth, a tribute to her mother who was born deep in the highlands. Her dark brown hair, from her father who was a druid chief, lay in waves around her shoulders. But her eyes she always thought were dull and expressionless, but as the phantom image of Weylyn reflected in the pool as if he stood behind her, she noticed her eyes not only grew more vibrant, but also shinning and, even she had to admit, beautiful. – *The Wolf's Bane*

Saga: Midnight Sky

Quote: "You have robbed me of my mother, my father, my soulmate for the last twelve hundred years. You have stolen my life, but what you feared still surfaced. I may no' be as powerful as some but, I am stronger than most think. Your repression of my abilities failed to be as effective as you would have hoped. I am a druid, I am a Fae, and I am what you fear the most... One of you." – *The Wolf's Bane Saga: Moon Rise*

Kyna

Species: Hybrid/Fae/god
Age: 1 month
Occupation: Daughter of the Lieuten
Leader: Tristan
Soulmate: Alan Conchor
Children: Unnamed
Parents: Weylyn and Eithne
Siblings: Sèitheach and four other bı
Half-Siblings: Aedan
Pronunciation: Key-nah

Description: She had one hand on Ľ her and her other, little palm outstre eyes glowed and flames sparked in tľ *Bane Saga: Moon Rise*

Kyna, being your first-born daughtє your powers. Fae power is gifted froı that is why none of your sons have s *Saga: Moon Rise*

Lachlan stopped immediately anc granddaughter, her brown eyes w *Bane Saga: Moon Rise*

The sun parted the clouds and shonє brown hair. – *The Wolf's Bane Saga:*

Quote:
What h
The W

Selina

Species: Fae
Age: Unknown
Occupation: Mate of the High Priest
Leader: None/Lachlan
Soulmate: Lachlan
Children: Eithne
Parents: Oengus and unknown Fae
Siblings: Unknown
Pronunciation: Se-lean-ah

Description: Her red hair was so bright it was unearthly, but what clenched who she was, was the pointed ears peeking out on the side of her head and the green vine markings on her pale white skin. – *The Wolf's Bane Saga: Moon Rise*

When his eyes met hers, the light green orbs glowed with surprise. Slowly setting Kyna down in a crib that appeared in the darkness, she stood in front of her protectively. Her green eyes turned fiery red and flames sparked in their depths. – *The Wolf's Bane Saga: Moon Rise*

Quote: "I have watched you grow from afar and I am so proud of you." Selina embraced her daughter. "Little Kyna gave us a chance to be together again too." – *The Wolf's Bane Saga: Moon Rise*

Biróg

Species: Fae
Age: Unknown
Occupation: Fae druidess
Leader: Eochaid
Soulmate: Unknown
Children: None
Parents: Unknown
Siblings: Unknown
Other Names: Kyriea
Pronunciation: Beer-rog

Description: Biróg is a dark Fae and druidess. She was my wife's dearest friend's great-grandmother. – *The Wolf's Bane Saga: Moon Rise*

Her dark eyes questioned. – *The Wolf's Bane Saga: Moon Rise*

Quote: "But make no mistake, Caylean is mine and together we will create the most powerful force on earth. The child of a Fae and a Hybrid. Eochaid will be dethroned and there is nothing you can do to stop it. I had hoped it would be Giorsal who had the spell attack her, but then the wolf's mate is just as good. No one is strong enough to stop me. Caylean cannot defeat his wolf and you are far too weak." – *The Wolf's Bane Saga: Moon Rise*

gods

Though these characters are Celtic mythology, the descriptions contained herein are only for what appears in the Wolf's Bane Saga.

Eochaið

Species: god
Age: Unknown
Occupation: The All Father
Leader: Himself
Soulmate: Anu
Children: Oengus and many others
Parents: Unknown
Siblings: Unknown
Other Names: The Dagda
Pronunciation: Yuc-edge

Description: Eochaid Ollathair's booming voice called. Oengus bowed low to the king and All-Father, also known as *the Dagda*. – *The Wolf's Bane Saga: Moon Rise*

Quote: "There are few I would grant this to, Lucien," Eochaid stated. "But my son and two of my most trusted vouch for you. Tell your son he must always remember and to teach his sons the same." – *The Wolf's Bane Saga: Moon Rise*

Donn

Species: god
Age: Unknown
Occupation: god of the Underworld
Leader: Eochaid
Soulmate: Unknown
Children: Unknown
Parents: Unknown
Siblings: Unknown

Description: *The Dagda* looked over at Donn the god of the Dead. – *The Wolf's Bane Saga: Moon Rise*

Lucien turned to Donn, his red hair and dark eyes staring straight ahead. Donn was built like a warrior standing slightly taller than Lucien's impressive height. – *The Wolf's Bane Saga: Moon Rise*

Quote: "Ignore me, my friend. I have worried recently. How long will we last? The human world is changing. Soon, they will have no need of us. Any of the gods. They have become far too dependent on themselves and look at themselves as gods. I claim not to be a god and there are greater gods than me. Soon, we will be obsolete. The things of legend and, gods forbid, myth. But we are here. And we will always be here. Man needs a savior, maybe they already have one, maybe one is to come but however this world turns out, know one thing, the Fae will always exist. And we are always watching. Even when we are ignored, forgotten, dishonored, we still are here. Even we have a savior, even though we don't deserve Him, but He is always there. Always. You do not know Him, there are many who do but he gives such peace, such comfort. I have never seen the like. Believe me, Lucien, he is indescribable and he will save any who come to him. If they just believe." – *The Wolf's Bane Saga: Moon Rise*

Oengus

Species: god
Age: Unknown
Occupation: god of Youth and Beauty
Leader: Eochaid
Soulmate: None
Children: Selina and many others
Parents: Eochaid
Siblings: Several
Pronunciation: Own-gus

Description: Lucien turned and came face to face with Oengus, god of Youth and son of the *Tuatha Dé* king; Eochaid. His golden hair glistening in the sunlight and his light brown, almost golden eyes looked questioningly at Lucien. – *The Wolf's Bane Saga: Moon Rise*

Oengus' eyes turned to fire like Selina's did in Kyna's dream and burned toward his father. – *The Wolf's Bane Saga: Moon Rise*

Quote: "Forgive me, daughter," he said. "I did not know they kept you prisoner. They said you had your mate. I did not know." His eyes searched her face, but she nodded slightly. "Go now, go my sweet one. I always loved you." – *The Wolf's Bane Saga: Moon Rise*

Lug

Species: god
Age: Unknown
Occupation: god of Truth, Arts and the Law
Leader: Eochaid
Soulmate: Unknown
Children: Unknown
Parents: Unknown
Siblings: Unknown

Description: Eochaid looked at the young, handsome warrior beside him. – *The Wolf's Bane Saga: Moon Rise*

Lug drew back beside *the Dagda* aiming the golden spear at her. – *The Wolf's Bane Saga: Moon Rise*

Quote: "Though the woman saved me from my grandfather's wrath, I have no doubt she has changed. If you say it is she, then it is. With your permission, my king, I will confer with her and seek as to why." – *The Wolf's Bane Saga: Moon Rise*

The Morrigan

Species: god
Age: Unknown
Occupation: god of War
Leader: Eochaid
Soulmate: Unknown
Children: Unnamed
Parents: Unknown
Siblings: Two sisters
Pronunciation: The More-ig-anne

Description: Looking up, they saw the bird circle them, then land on a tree branch. Instantly, the tree's orange leaves of Autumn, shriveled and blew away in the wind. The tree, dead. – *The Wolf's Bane Saga: Moon Rise*

The Morrigan flew and landed as a human beside *the Dagda.* Her black hair and dark eyes assessing the men. – *The Wolf's Bane Saga: Moon Rise*

Quote: "That is because he taught warriors and warriors cannot have a family and still be considered reliable," the Morrigan stated. "But I defer to the god of All and the Mother goddess. I release your son and his grove from that burden. He is free to claim his mate and have by her many children." – *The Wolf's Bane Saga: Moon Rise*

Songs

My Lover's Hair

The Wolf's Bane Saga: Lonely Moon
Sung By: Heledd

"My lover's hair's as black as night,
His eyes are darker still.
His hands upon me fierce and tender
Upon the hearth doth still
For on the hearth his lover's eyes weaken into death.
The reaper has come and carries aloft
My lover's heart and breath.
Before him lies, the one he denies
The one who loves him still,
But, my lover's eyes sees no' the lies told beneath the sill.
For if my lover
Kenned the lies as told beneath the sill,
His lover's eyes would ne'er arise
Upon me soft and still.
His lover's eyes would turn surprise upon the other's will.
And as they fought,
My heart would rot upon my lover's ill,
And death upon my lover's eyes would cause my heart to
still.
For both men fought and one will die,
Upon my lover's kill.
My heart in two, I'll always rue,
The lies beneath the sill."

The Lass I Loved

The Wolf's Bane Saga: Midnight Sky
Sung By: Caylean

"Oh, lass I loved so wild and deep,
I chose a life but the cost is steep.
For I will never again behold your face,
Together we rode, far away from here,
Drank of the misty water of the mermaid's tears.
One choice before,
One step behind,
Oh lass, my lass, why did I ever want more?
Lo across the fields of shamrocks so green
Your pretty face, I swear to have seen.
But that cannot be, for you are nae more,
The mermaid's tears, one soul to store.
The choice was mine.
I desired a life across the brine.
When I returned to claim you mine,
Your life was o'er and so was mine.
Oh, Lass I loved so wild and deep,
I held life far too cheap.
Your life and love was all I should keep.
Now you lie at the bottom of the loch,
And here I sit.
Age has withered me fine bones
And silver streaks me brown roans.
I think of ye, so soft and white,
And swear I see you swimming in the gloaming light.
The same beauty as before,

Your mermaid tail a thing of lore.
Oh, lass I loved,
You sing me to my death."

www.ingramcontent.com/pod-product-compliance
Lightning Source LLC
Chambersburg PA
CBHW060416260626
47161CB00011B/1837